Burn Me

Burn Me

Shelley Watters

COPYRIGHT

Paperback ISBN-13: 979-8-9929818-2-7
Hardback ISBN-13: 979-8-9929818-3-4

Cover design by: Image generated by Shelley Watters using Canva
Printed in the United States of America

Trigger Warnings

Graphic depictions of sexual acts
Sexual assault
Stalking
Car accidents
Attempted rape
Blood
Gore
Murder
Serial Killer

Contents

1

Chapter One

The mournful wail of bagpipes drifted on the warm breeze over the sea of firefighters. Each deep thump of the bass drum mimicked the pained pounding of Greyson's heart. He swallowed at the lump lodged in his throat.

"Forward, march!"

Like a zombie, he lurched forward, matching the strides of the firefighters around him. He snuck a glance at Eric, who marched silently beside him. His service cap may have shaded his eyes, but there was no hiding the despair in his brother's face. Losing a partner in the line of duty will do that to a firefighter.

The picture of the flag-draped casket on the back of E-288 burned into his brain. The only thing worse was the sight of Dave's devastated wife and kids. One barely old enough to walk, now fatherless due to an arsonist. And the bastard was still on the loose.

The bag pipes wailed on as Greyson's blood boiled, melting the ice that solidified in his veins when he picked up Dave's helmet. He'd find that bastard and bring him to justice. For Dave. For his family. For the faceless victims he burned alive. The sound of their pained cries mingling with Dave's scream as the roof collapsed on them would haunt his dreams forever.

They marched on, following the procession of bagpipes and drums past a motionless ocean of somber firefighters. As they approached the church, his crew came into view. Captain Jake nodded at him as he passed. Kevin, as usual, stared straight ahead. But it was the way Kat's gaze held his before flitting to Eric that made his stomach clench. But Eric didn't move, didn't acknowledge his girlfriend's presence or even glance her direction. A single tear trailed down her soft cheek as she lowered her eyes.

Quiet whispers and shuffling of hundreds of feet punctuated the heavy silence as the procession crammed into the church. Greyson's gaze shifted to Dave's wife, who sat juggling their eighteen-month-old daughter in her arms while their four-year-old son clutched her other arm. Confusion was clear on the little boy's tear-streaked face.

Greyson's throat burned, but he couldn't tear his gaze from the boy. Dave loved his family more than anything else in the world. He'd even considered giving up the job for them. But, like his father before him, firefighting was in his blood. It wasn't just a job, it was an essential part of his life, like eating or breathing.

One by one, Dave's friends and family took the podium, reminiscing about a poignant or funny time with him. When it was finally Greyson's turn, his feet dragged as he paced toward the podium beside the casket. He cleared his throat before leaning toward the microphone.

"Dave Rice was my best friend. A devoted husband and father, he embodied everything that I hoped someday to be." Greyson's gaze traveled over the sea of black and navy blue filling the church. Like a beacon of light, Kat's face stood out in the crowd, a few pews back from his brother. He cleared his throat again. "He was an incredible firefighter and he always did his job with a smile on his face. He was one of the happiest people I've ever met. The world is a darker place without him."

With that, he returned to his seat. Eric stepped to the podium. With his eyes still locked on Dave's casket, Greyson wondered if he even realized there were other people in the room.

Eric cleared his throat and wrenched his service cap in his hands. He finally tore his gaze from the coffin and locked eyes with Greyson. He leaned towards the microphone and spoke, his voice ragged with emotion. "I'm sorry I couldn't save you, brother."

A chill tingled over Greyson's skin. They were the first words his brother had spoken since the night Dave died. Eric returned to his seat while the chaplain scrambled to return to the podium.

The rest of the service was a blur of faces and voices. Before Greyson knew it, they were back outside and on their way to a bar a few blocks down from the church. They piled into a booth in a corner of the bustling pub, which was already stuffed to the hilt with dress-uniformed firefighters from the funeral procession. It reeked of sweat and alcohol.

He slid into the booth across from Eric. A few moments later, Kat scooted into the booth beside Eric. She leaned over and placed a gentle kiss on Eric's cheek, her soft voice barely registering over the noise in the bar. "You okay?"

Eric turned towards her, finally acknowledging her presence. He nodded briskly before turning his attention to the cocktail waitress. "Tequila."

The busty brunette nodded. "Single or double?"

"Bring the bottle."

Kat put a hand on Eric's arm, which he yanked away like she'd burned him. She frowned and glared at him. But whatever she was about to say, she bit it back.

The waitress shrugged and got the orders for the rest of the group before disappearing into the writhing throng of navy blue.

Greyson clenched his jaw and glared at Eric. It was understandable to be upset that his partner had died in the line of duty, but that was no reason to be an asshole to his girlfriend.

A few moments later the waitress returned with a tray laden with alcoholic beverages. She slid the bottle in front of Eric with a shot glass and winked. "If anyone asks, I didn't give this to you."

Kat shook her head and sipped her iced tea thoughtfully. It wasn't like her to keep quiet when something was irking her. He'd worked the same shift with her for over a year, so he knew her personality. And this was *so* not like her.

Greyson held up his Sam Adams. "To Dave, wherever flames may rage." His skin tingled when the toast was repeated throughout the bar. Eric mumbled along before downing another swig of tequila.

They sat in silence, drowning their emotions in a never-ending supply of alcohol. Before long, Eric wrapped one arm around his less than half-full bottle of tequila and his head hit the table with a thump.

Kat nudged Eric with her elbow. "I should get him out of here," she said to no one in particular. He grunted and swatted at her before snuggling his bottle closer. Kat snorted. "At least he likes to snuggle with *something*."

Greyson frowned. It was meant as a joke, but he knew the truth behind it. Eric was one hell of a firefighter, but his first love was being a fireman. His girlfriends, and therefore romance, came a distant second.

He studied Kat's features in the dim light. When she first signed on to his shift at station three, her eyes practically glowed with life and possibility. Six months later on one of the toughest rigs in the Chandler metro area, and the light hadn't faded. That was the day Eric told him that he was asking Kat out. But in the past few months, day by day, that fire in her eyes dimmed a little.

He didn't deserve her. She needed a man who would make her feel beautiful. A man who could break through her tough exterior, to show her what it really meant to be a strong, powerful woman. A man who could put her needs above all else. And that man was *not* his brother.

Kat raised her gaze to meet his. A glimmer of hope flickered in the smoky depths of her eyes. He flinched and dropped his gaze to study his empty beer bottle. She was his brother's girl, which meant hands off. Regardless of how much he was physically attracted to her, there was a huge flashing stop sign over her head.

He slid from his seat and moved to her side of the booth. "Here, I'll help you get him to your truck."

Kat lifted her gaze to his and he was captivated by her. "Thanks, Greyson." His name on her lips was like honey on the air.

He grunted something unintelligible and ran a hand roughly through his hair. *Stupid. She's your brother's girl, you idiot!*

She slid out of the booth and his breath caught in his throat when her breasts brushed his arm as she squeezed by him. Eric flopped ungracefully onto the bench she vacated. Greyson cleared his throat and hefted Eric to standing and threw one arm over his shoulder. "Come on, lover boy."

Eric grunted but allowed himself to be half-carried, half-dragged from the bar. They were feet from the door when a guy bumped into them.

"Sorry, man!" the inebriated firefighter apologized. He leaned in and squinted his blood-shot eyes at Eric. "Hey, you're the guy that killed your partner, right?"

The previously almost-unconscious Eric was suddenly very much alert and lunging for the drunken man.

Greyson scrambled to hold him back. He spun Eric around and shook his shoulders. "He's drunk! Let it go, man!"

The uninhibited rage was almost tangible in Eric's face. He turned and lunged at the drunkard, his fist smashing into the man's nose, blood spewing from behind his fist. The noise in the bar exploded and suddenly there were bodies everywhere. It took two guys to hold the bleeding drunk back, and Kat scrambled to grab Eric's other arm.

"Shit!" Greyson growled and muscled Eric back. "What the fuck, Eric?"

"You heard what he said!" Eric wrestled against his steel grip, but he wasn't letting go. Kat held her ground admirably on Eric's other side.

Greyson nodded. "You're drunk. Go, sleep it off!"

"Fine," Eric muttered. "Get the fuck off me." He shrugged out of their grasp and shoved his way through the crowd out the door.

"Eric!" Kat called and ran after him.

Greyson was hot on their heels. Eric had an explosive temper, but he'd never seen him at this level of instability, even stone-cold drunk.

He could hear Kat's frantic voice as he raced for the parking lot on the side of the building. "You can't drive like this. Please, let me take you home."

His feet skidded on the concrete sidewalk as he turned the corner. "Get the fuck off me, Kat!" Eric shouted and shrugged her off. She stumbled over the parking block and landed hard on her back.

"Eric!" Greyson bellowed and flew across the parking lot. Before he knew what he was doing, he had Eric shoved up against the door of his Civic. "What the hell are you doing? She's your *girlfriend*, bro!" He shot a quick glance at Kat, who was standing and brushing herself off, rubbing her back gingerly.

"Yeah, and *you* should remember that, *bro*," Eric seethed.

The air left Greyson's chest. Up until that moment, he was positive he'd kept his attraction to Kat a secret. But, even though he tried to hide it, Eric had seen it.

"Well fucking act like it. You just shoved your girlfriend across the parking lot, you asshole." He wanted nothing more at that moment than to let his fist connect with his brother's face. "You don't deserve her. You never have."

"I didn't shove her!" Eric grunted, but his eyes shot to Kat for a second before returning to glare at him. "Must sting like acid, watching me with her, huh, Greyson? Knowing you can't have her."

The feel of Kat's hand on his shoulder somehow managed to instantly calm him.

"You're drunk, Eric. You don't know what you're talking about." He released his hold on Eric's neck and turned to Kat. "Are you okay?"

Kat nodded. "Thanks. I can handle this."

Greyson studied her face for a moment, noticing the smear of dirt on her cheek as evidence of Eric's carelessness with her. He didn't fucking deserve her.

She stepped around him and leveled her glare on Eric. "Keys?" she demanded and held her hand out.

Eric dug into his pocket and handed over the keys. Greyson's throat tightened when his brother closed the distance between them and cupped her face in his hands, his thumb tracing the smudge of dirt on her face. "Are you okay? I'm so sorry, babe. I didn't mean to hurt you." She nodded. He placed a soft kiss on her lips and her eyes slid closed.

Greyson swallowed hard as he watched the scene before him. But like a train wreck, he couldn't turn away. When they pulled apart, Eric shot a triumphant look at him. "Later, brother." With that, he got into the passenger seat and closed the door.

Greyson frowned at Kat as she crossed in front of him to go to the driver's side. "You sure you'll be okay?"

Kat smiled reassuringly. "He's drunk and he's in pain. I can handle him. Don't worry about me, Greyson." She got into the car and closed the door.

He watched helplessly as she pulled the dirty white Civic out of the parking lot and the glowing tail lights disappeared into the darkness.

2

Chapter Two

Smoke billowed into the air like the aftermath of an atom bomb blast. White-hot flames licked up the side of the terracotta stucco of the old mansion, leaving scorched trails in their wake. Wailing sirens in the distance and the furious hiss of water shooting from the hoses barely registered over the roar of the fire as it devoured the building.

Behind yellow crime scene tape, bystanders strained to see the blue-sheet shrouded body. Shock and horror rippled through the group when they heard how she died: burned alive, tied spread eagle to her four-poster bed. The flicker of the red and blue emergency lights reflected off their dazed expressions as they stared at the flames.

Kat cleared her throat and shifted her weight onto her heels in the small bucket suspended high above the structure. The heat from the rising smoke singed Kat's face as she aimed the monitor to shoot the high pressure stream of water onto the roof.

"You okay up there, Kat?" Greyson's deep voice rasped from her radio. Even though he was her boyfriend's brother, his smooth voice never failed to send tingles through her body. *Head in the game, Kat.*

Unable to take her hands off the controls, she exaggerated a head nod. She'd been on the top of the ladder for probably fifteen minutes, trying to battle the flames into submission. She pulled back the lever to fully open the nozzle. The water arced thirty feet into the air and plummeted into the flaming bowels of the mansion. Furious hissing and a massive cloud of white smoke erupted from the structure.

Kat smiled. She'd hit the hot-spot dead on.

But before she could celebrate her small victory, the wind shifted and the massive mushroom cloud engulfed her.

"Kat!" Greyson hollered into the radio.

The bucket beneath her feet vanished in the blanket of smoke. It was almost as if she was suspended inside a cloud. But this cloud choked her with super-heated toxic smoke.

Her emergency siren wailed on her shoulder. *Stay low and go*, her brain screamed. But that only worked when you were in a building, not when you were suspended on a ladder above one. Her heartbeat pounded in her ears. The white smoke turned black again, indicating the blaze had re-ignited.

Her eyes burned from the fumes and tears streamed down her face. She fumbled with her mask for a moment in the blinding smoke before stuffing it against her face. Her lungs protested as she sucked in that first quenching breath of clean air. It felt like she'd swallowed sand. She forced herself to slowly breathe in the oxygen through the mask.

The smoke continued to billow around her. Now that she was able to breathe, she reached out to search for her controls when the ladder lurched beneath her feet.

Greyson had taken over the controls from down below and was lowering her back to the truck. Anger rushed through her, making her flame hotter than the inferno blazing below. *Damn it. I'm ok! Let me do this!*

"Kat!" Greyson's hoarse voice shouted from the radio on her shoulder.

The haze cleared a bit and she could make out the shape of Ladder 281 as she descended towards it.

"Damn it, Greyson!" She coughed into her radio. "Get me back up there. I'm fine!" She glared down at him. Always her knight in shining armor, whether she wanted to be rescued or not.

"No way. Firefighters bigger than you have fallen due to smoke inhalation. I'm not losing anyone on my watch," he said into his radio, his smoky eyes locked with hers.

"If this is because I'm a wo—"

"Don't go there, Kat. Just don't," he growled and raised a dark eyebrow.

Her aching lungs seized a moment before the ladder finished its descent and she doubled over as she tried to cough up the scorching black ash that irritated her lungs.

Kevin waited at the base of the ladder in full gear ready to take her place. *Damn him.*

"Stay there. I'll come get you," Kevin shouted and scaled the ladder.

"I'm...fine!" she managed between coughing spells.

"Like hell you are. Geez, Kat." Kevin rolled his chocolate eyes. His chiseled face and chestnut hair was streaked with soot from working the front line. He was at her feet in a matter of seconds. "Take it easy," he said and guided her down the ladder.

"Thanks," she muttered. She tried so hard to show no weakness. As the only girl on the crew, she had to prove she was just as worthy as any of the guys. But as Greyson had said, smoke inhalation got the best of the best, gender non-discriminating.

Kevin threw her arm over his shoulder and helped her to the bottom, where he handed her off to Greyson. Jake stepped up to take over the controls while Greyson helped her to the paramedics to get checked out.

"This is stupid, I'm fine, really," Kat grumbled, but accepted his support as they climbed off the truck and headed for the ambulance.

"Shut up and sit down." For such harsh words, his touch was extremely gentle as he lowered her to sit on the bumper. He reached behind her to grab a face mask off the oxygen tank inside the ambulance and held it to her face. He shrugged his bunker jacket off his wide shoulders before he went to work on removing hers.

His gaze caught hers, worry lines etched into his broad forehead, his oh-so-kissable lips stretched tight in a frown. Kat flinched at the direction of her thoughts.

"Seriously, I'm fine," she tried in vain to stifle the heavy wheeze as she inhaled the pure oxygen.

She watched as his large, tanned hands deftly unhook her jacket one metal loop at a time. Her eyes traveled up his arms to where heavily muscled biceps strained at the thin cotton of his Chandler Fire Department t-shirt. His brows knitted in concern over his deep brown eyes. She'd never noticed the golden flecks that swirled in their chocolate depths before.

His hands came back up to unzip her jacket. The rip of the metal tines as they released rang in her ears. The air was cool on her overheated skin when the protective jacket fell open. Her t-shirt was plastered with sweat to her chest and her breasts strained at the thin fabric, her nipples tightening at the cool air that suddenly caressed them through the material.

Greyson's hands hesitated for a moment before he shoved the jacket from her shoulders. She rolled her neck as the heavy weight fell away. He finally raised his gaze to hers and something more than concern smoldered in their depths.

"Excuse me," Eve, the paramedic said as she stepped between Greyson and Kat. "I'm going to check you out. Do I have your permission?" She snapped blue latex-free gloves into place.

"I'm ok, really..."

Greyson cleared his throat and glared at Kat.

Kat bristled, ready to argue with him, but sighed upon seeing the frustration on his face. She turned her attention to Eve. "Go for it."

Kat squeaked when the cold metal from Eve's stethoscope touched her skin and then slid down her shirt over her left breast.

Eve bit her lip to smother a smile. "Breathe deeply, if you can."

Kat sucked in a wheezing breath and glared at Greyson, who was watching over her like an expectant father.

"I'd like to transport you to Chandler Regional for observation." Eve fiddled with some gauges in the ambulance behind Kat's back. Greyson looked like he actually winced when she said that.

"Whatever." Kat hoisted herself onto the gurney and flopped back against the crunchy sheets. She ground her teeth in frustration when Eve strapped her down. Greyson grabbed her hand and squeezed it reassuringly. Her eyes shot to his.

Eve pushed the gurney into the ambulance. "Excuse us."

Greyson held Kat's hand until the distance forced him to let it go. He smiled a half-smile at her, his eyes locked with hers.

The doors of the ambulance closed and the sirens blared as the emergency vehicle pulled from the scene. Kat and Greyson's gazes remained locked until the crowd closed in behind the ambulance as it sped away.

"Boyfriend, huh?" Eve murmured as she pulled the blood pressure cuff off Kat's arm with a resounding rip.

Kat frowned. "Who?"

"Lover boy back there. Your boyfriend?"

Kat snorted. While intended to be sarcastic, it only resulted in another fit of coughing into the oxygen mask strapped to her face.

"Easy, there."

Kat took in some deep breaths. When the coughing subsided, she smiled weakly. "No, he's not my boyfriend. I'm dating his brother, Eric."

Eve's blonde eyebrows rose over her light blue eyes. Something flickered beneath their icy depths, but she quickly quenched it. "Oh, I didn't realize Eric was dating anyone."

Kat snorted. "I get that a lot."

A whisper of a smile quirked Eve's lips. "Well, lover boy back there..."

"No," Kat snapped.

Eve continued as if Kat hadn't spoken. "...seemed pretty worried about you."

Kat's sarcastic half-smile's impact was lost beneath the translucent green oxygen mask that Eve had strapped to her face. "He has a serious case of Knight in Shining Armor syndrome. He'd be the same with any female firefighter on duty, I think. Besides. He's Eric's brother."

Eve smirked. "Knight in Shining Armor syndrome?"

Kat nodded. "Since the day I started on his shift over a year ago, he's been hell-bent on keeping me out of danger, rescuing me when I didn't need or want to be rescued." She sucked in a few more deep breaths, breathless from the effort of talking. "I'm a firefighter, for God's sake. It's my job to rescue others, not be rescued. And besides, it's freaking annoying!"

A knowing smile stretched across Eve's model-like face. "I know what you mean."

Kat blinked. "You do?"

Eve nodded. "Guys have a hard time comprehending that not every girl wants to be rescued. We can take care of ourselves. Besides, some girls like the heat."

Before Kat could respond, the ambulance lurched to a stop and the doors flew open. Instantly she was surrounded by a flurry of motion and people as she was rushed into the ER. Someone, a nurse, Kat assumed, clipped a pulse oxyometer to her finger. The hallway was a blur of motion and bright overhead fluorescent lights flashing above her head. The second the gurney stopped moving, someone stabbed her with a needle and another hooked up an IV. It felt weird to be on this side of the chaos, to be the one poked and prodded and shuffled around like a bag of flour.

Before she knew it, she was in an x-ray room, posing in different positions for chest x-rays. Finally, with a pained sigh of relief, she was back in the exam room in the ER. She closed her eyes and leaned back on the gurney, relieved to finally have a moment to relax after all of the craziness.

As soon as she closed her eyes, something vibrated on the table beside her gurney. "Seriously?" Kat groaned and rifled through the opaque plastic bag of her belongings. Tucked securely in her pocket on her bunker pants, her I-phone vibrated relentlessly.

She carefully slid the phone from her pocket and studied the screen. She rolled her eyes, fully aware that the movement was lost on who was calling. She tapped the screen and held the phone up to her ear. "Hi, Mom."

"Oh my God, Kitty Kat! Are you okay? Eric just called me!" Her mom's shrill shriek echoed through the speaker like she was on speaker phone. But she wasn't.

"Mom, don't worry. I'm fine," Kat said quickly. Why the hell would Eric call her mom? He hadn't even called *her* yet to see if she was okay. Besides, hadn't he already figured out that was the last thing Kat needed when she was injured? Was it on purpose so her mom would chew her out about not being more careful? She was going to kill him when she got out of here...

"I'll be there in twenty minutes. Don't let them touch you until I get there. Understand me?"

"I don't need you to come down here, Mom. Really," Kat attempted to argue, but it was like talking to a voice messaging system. Her mother might be on the other end of the phone, but no one was listening.

"Okay, Kitty. Just hold tight. Momma's coming." And with that, she was gone.

Kat sighed and flopped back on the gurney. So much for rest.

The curtain surrounding her little semi-private room swished open and the lights flickered painfully to life above Kat's throbbing head.

"Hey, Kat." Dr. Monty, the resident hottie ER doc, said as he flipped through her chart. He pulled the x-rays from the envelope and stuck them on the lighted wall box and flipped the switch. Kat watched silently as he studied the x-rays with his dark eyebrows furrowed.

"Looks like you're going to be hanging out with me for a few days," he said and smiled apologetically at her.

Kat groaned. "That bad, huh?"

"Nah, I just wanted to keep you hostage here to keep me company." His eyes twinkled as he smiled at her. "But I do need to keep you here at least twenty-four hours, to make sure the damage isn't any worse than what I'm seeing up there. Then we can re-evaluate, okay?" He waved a hand toward the x-rays.

Kat sighed, the effort bringing on a new wave of coughing.

Dr. Monty sat down on the bed and patted her back. When the fit stopped, he searched her eyes. "You know, you could have died."

Kat bit her lip and silently returned his gaze.

"You need to take it easy. I don't mean just now, because of the smoke inhalation. I mean at work. Take it easy. You don't have to work so hard to prove yourself. You're going to get yourself killed because you don't want to show any weakness."

Kat studied his face, and all she saw in his face was pure concern of a doctor for his patient. "I know," she murmured.

3

Chapter Three

Kat squinted into the sun as she drove toward station three, trying to see the traffic light above her in the bright morning sun. Red. She glanced at her phone. The sight of no new messages made her frown.

Eric was one hell of a firefighter, but his skills in the relationship department left something to be desired. Besides a quick text to let him know she was out of the hospital, she hadn't spoken to Eric for the entire week she was off work. To be honest, she was still pissed at him for ratting her out to her mom. Two unanswered texts from him and apparently he'd gotten the hint. He never was much for being the doting boyfriend type.

Which is what she liked about him. He understood how important her career was, and how much she valued her independence. So he gave it to her in spades. Which was also probably why he'd been through his share of girlfriends before her. No one but another firefighter could understand the intense drive Eric had for his job. It was almost as strong as hers.

But the fact that he hadn't called, hadn't texted to check up on her since the first day irked her. For someone who professed his undying love for her, he sure didn't show it.

Kat's heart accelerated as she pulled her midnight blue Ford F-250 into her usual spot beneath the twisted green branches of the Palo Verde tree. The week off due to smoke inhalation had been one of the longest weeks of her life.

She worried at her bottom lip with her teeth as she pulled her bag from the passenger seat and shut the door. It wasn't that she wasn't happy to be here. She was. It was the fact that she tried so hard to prove that she was one of the guys. She trained harder, studied harder, worked harder. It was an honor to be accepted into the boy's club, but she constantly had to prove herself to them. Hopefully the incident from last week hadn't undone all of the work she'd done to get there.

She pushed open the door and stepped into the engine bay. The scent of wet concrete mixed with the lingering hint of smoke and diesel fuel encompassed her like an old friend. E-282 and L-281 were two of the prettiest rigs she'd ever worked on. They were pristine white with gleaming chrome trim and fire-engine red letters with the words "Chandler Fire Department" adorned on the side. She traced her hand along the cool paint of L-281 as she passed. She loved that rig, even though she'd almost died on it a week ago.

Her fingertips traced the lettering on the side and she cleared her throat to dissipate the niggling cough that wanted to bubble to the surface. While she tried to pretend she was fine, just the short amount of time that she sucked in the choking black fumes had burned her lungs and left a sticky residue clogging them. She was lucky Greyson pulled her back. A few more minutes of breathing in the deadly smoke and she would have been dead on the ladder.

The chill from the cold metal radiated through her body at the thought of succumbing to the smoke. How ironic it would have been for her mom to have lost both of her twins to smoke inhalation, just twenty years apart. Kat shuddered and pulled her hand from the truck and bee-lined for the stairs.

Her feet were quiet on the concrete steps as she climbed the stairs and made her way down the shiny hallway to the locker room. She stored her bag and changed out of her street clothes and into her on-duty uniform, a navy blue t-shirt adorned with the Chandler Fire logo, navy blue shorts, and her Brooks running shoes. She pulled her wavy mass of dark hair into a high ponytail before slamming the metal door shut and spinning the lock.

She meandered down the hallway, following the scent of freshly brewed coffee and the sounds coming from the TV in the lounge. The crowd cheered and an obnoxious announcer gave a play-by-play of what was happening on the field. The Cardinals were up by a touchdown with two minutes left on the clock.

She silently crossed the room and pulled a bottle of water from the fridge.

Kevin jumped from the overstuffed sofa where he was watching the game. "Kat! We missed you!" He scooped her up in a bear hug, lifting her off the ground in the process.

Kat laughed. His enthusiasm always brightened her day. He was such a contradiction. On the outside, he might have had the hard body of a seasoned firefighter, but inside he was as soft as they come. At least with regards to her, anyway. Kevin could teach Eric a thing or two...

Kevin didn't put her down, just kept his head against her neck, her body pressed against his and suspended a few inches off the floor.

"Um, Kevin? You can put me down now."

"Oh, yeah, sorry." He reluctantly lowered her to the floor. She couldn't help the flush on her cheeks as every inch of her body slid against his.

"Fuck!" Jake shouted and slammed his soda on the table. Pepsi shot up out of the can and soaked his shirt. He growled and stomped off down the hall.

Kevin raced to the TV just in time to see the playback of the Cardinal's quarterback getting sacked.

Kat bit back a chuckle. Thankfully Jake hadn't seen the exchange between her and Kevin. It was no big deal, but Jake would have thrown the entire crew into sexual harassment training if he had. She didn't want to be treated differently than any of the guys. And besides, Kevin was harmless.

Greyson, however, caught the entire embarrassing display. If looks could kill, Kevin would have dropped dead from the glare that Greyson shot at him from behind his coffee mug.

Kat's gaze caught his and he inclined his head slightly in her direction. Then he shook out his newspaper and lifted it, successfully hiding himself from her gaze. After how he'd acted at the fire last week, she'd expected things would've been different between them. Maybe... It didn't matter. He was Eric's brother, after all, and she'd obviously been mistaken. He was right back to his cold, aloof attitude towards her.

Kat's skin prickled as anger flowed over her. Greyson was a classic case of the "knight in shining armor, protect the damsel in distress syndrome" that some members of the boy's club seemed to adopt when there was a woman on their shift. She didn't need a knight in shining armor, and she damn well didn't need to be protected. She could take care of herself and didn't need anyone rescuing her.

The tension built in her body. She bit her cheek to contain the words she wanted to spit at Greyson. Instead, she spun on her heel and headed for the gym, stopping by her locker to grab her iPod on the way.

Her hand closed on the cool metal of the door handle to the gym. She wrenched the door open and stepped inside, slamming the door with more force than necessary behind her. The morning sun filtered in through the high windows and sent angular rays of light across the padded blue floor mats. The room smelled of air conditioning and Pine Sol and tiny specks of dust sparkled in the air like glitter. She set her water bottle on the treadmill and stretched each of her hamstrings in turn.

She slipped her ear buds into her ears and stepped up on the belt. Her thumb slid across the phone screen and the pounding beat of the drums and guitars soon matched the beat of her Brooks hitting the belt. She pounded away on the treadmill, her eyes locked on the window before her, watching the cars and trucks whizzing by her as they crossed through the intersection in front of the station.

Her pace quickened to match the program and the belt whizzed beneath her feet. As the miles melted away, her anger did too. Soon she could barely remember why she was angry in the first place. All she could think about was how much she looked forward to the weekend when she would be able to take her Brooks on a long trail run up South Mountain, which was one of her favorite runs.

**

Greyson quietly opened the door to the gym. He knew where Kat had stomped off to. Whenever she was pissed, she always hit the treadmill. She seemed to love the physical torture of running herself into the ground. His breath caught in his throat when he saw her firm ass bobbing gently as her shoes hit the belt. The dark department-issued shorts fit snugly against her body, the curve of her hips, the swell of her ass, the juncture between her thighs...

He cleared his throat in an effort to change the direction of his thoughts. Since Kat had been assigned to his shift, he had found it hard to focus. She was gorgeous, with her supple body and angelic face, but it wasn't her looks that drew him to her. It was her drive to be the best, to show that she was as good as, if not better than, any firefighter she was compared to. But she was Eric's girlfriend, and regardless of that, they worked the same shift. She was off limits. The best plan of action was to be as distant as possible. But almost losing her to smoke inhalation a week ago brought on feelings that he hadn't had about a woman since Sara.

"Are you supposed to be pushing yourself this hard so soon?" Greyson asked.

She practically missed a step on the treadmill and caught the handrail to steady herself, but she didn't slow down. She ripped her ear buds from her ears, but kept her gaze locked on the window in front of her.

"Don't worry about it."

He walked to the window and put one of his large hands on the glass. Frustration washed over him as he stared down at the intersection and watched the blur of color as the cars whizzed by.

God, she was so stubborn. And there was so much he wanted to say to her. But she wasn't his. And although the bastard didn't deserve her, she was his brothers. So he couldn't say a word. Couldn't tell her how almost losing her had put a crack in the wall he'd built around his heart after Sara left him. Couldn't tell her how she didn't need to push herself so hard, how she was already a better firefighter than every man on the crew. And they all knew it.

But she wouldn't appreciate him telling her that. Because that would be admitting that she was a female. God forbid. While the run had done its job in draining the anger from her body, one wrong word could bring it all back.

But he couldn't just say nothing. He sucked in a deep breath and prepared for Kat's wrath.

**

"What's your problem anyway?" Kat snapped. The program slowed, indicating that she was nearing the end of her run. *Had six miles really gone that quick?*

A sigh escaped his lips. "I'm sorry. I was just really worried about you." He clenched his hand into a fist on the window.

Kat could see his face reflected in the glass, and his eyes were closed. His t-shirt stretched taut across his broad shoulders that tapered to a V at his hips. She chewed her lip. With his tousled brown hair, caramel-espresso eyes that slightly crinkled at the corners when he smiled, and two-day old scruff, he was definitely her type. But even if she was single, they worked the same shift. Besides, he had a serious case of the Knight in Shining Armor syndrome that drove her completely insane.

"You don't need to worry about me," she said, a bit breathless from her run. At least that's what she told herself. The treadmill slowed to a walk, and she grabbed her bottle of water and took a sip.

"I know you can take care of yourself." He opened his eyes but didn't turn around.

Kat stepped off the belt, her legs a little wobbly from the sudden change in motion. She took a step towards him. "Then what's the problem?"

He spun around so fast Kat took a half-step back in surprise and her heel caught in a seam on the mat. Off-balance, she tipped backwards. His big hands snapped out and wrapped around her arms, effectively stopping her tumble onto the mat.

"Whoa, there." Greyson's voice rumbled in her ear.

His voice, so close to her, sent shockwaves through her body. Heat blossomed on her cheeks. "Thanks." She glanced up to find him searching her face, his face a few breaths from hers.

But he didn't let her go. They stayed that way, staring at each other, their breath intermingling in the tiny space between them. His fingers dug into her arms, as if willing her to move first. The little points were pain and pleasure at the same time.

"Shit," Greyson growled and released her.

She stumbled slightly, only then realizing how off-kilter he had been holding her. The skin where his fingers had pressed into her arms tingled as the blood rushed back to them.

He ran a hand through his thick hair. "Kat, I –" he started, but was cut off by the station bell ringing.

4

Chapter Four

Whatever he was going to tell her would have to wait. Kat raced for the fire pole, wrapped her arms and one leg around it and slid gracefully down to the engine bay.

She ran to her gear and stepped into her boots, shrugged the suspenders on the protective bunker pants up over her shoulders and hefted her eight-pound jacket off the hook on the wall. The tines of the zipper snapped metallically as she cranked the zipper up. She grabbed her helmet from the hook and climbed into the back of the engine cab.

"Thanks for joining us," Jake said from the passenger seat. Kevin was already strapped in beside her.

"Sir," Kat murmured.

Greyson climbed in to the driver's seat and started her up. The diesel engine rumbled to life.

The sirens screamed as they sped through the busy streets of morning rush hour in Chandler. Most cars pulled over to the side of the road on their approach, but some moronic motorists just continued on their merry way, blocking the engine's path. Greyson blared the horn and Jake got on the loud speaker.

"Please pull your vehicle to the right!" Jake shouted into the handheld and slammed the handheld back on its hook. "Assholes. Completely oblivious!" Jake growled.

Kat smiled. His demeanor was so professional when they were on a call. She knew what he wanted to yell into the loudspeaker "Get out of the way, you dickheads!" But Chief Phillips wouldn't like the complaint calls later if he did. And then the entire crew would be in serious trouble.

They pulled up to the three-alarm industrial fire and climbed out of the cab. Jake stopped by the Battalion Command to check in.

"Here's the deal guys. Station two already has guys inside. More stations are en-route. Chief wants backup inside to check for victims and ventilation. Greyson and Kevin, I want you two up on the roof." Jake made eye contact with each of the men as he rattled out the assignments.

"But Sir!" Kat argued.

"Hale –" Jake caught her eye. "Chief said you're off ladder for a while. He wants to make sure you're one hundred percent before you get back up there."

Kat glared at him and searched his misty green eyes. She only encountered the cool, professional stare of a Captain following orders. "Yes, Sir. But I won't sit this one out. Please," Kat pleaded.

Jake winked. "Good. I want you on the front line doing search and rescue with me."

"Yes, Sir!" She beamed.

"But Sir!" Greyson growled. His jaw clenched.

"Neal?" Jake's eyes narrowed.

"Sorry, Sir. It's just that Kat just came off of medical leave. Is she ready for front-line duty?"

"Well, her medical release says she's ready. But since you're *so* concerned about her well-being, you can hit the front line with her. I'll take the roof," Jake snapped.

Kat grit her teeth to the point that her jaw popped. Here Greyson was debating her ability to do her job with the Captain while she was three feet away. He was going to pay for this later. She would see to it.

"Alright guys. Dismissed," Jake said.

Kat paused momentarily to pull the fire-resistant hood over her head and strap the heavy SCBA air tanks to her back. She strapped her mask over her face and replaced her helmet. With her ax in one hand, she double-timed it to the entrance of the building. There was no way she was going to wait for Greyson to force her behind him.

"Kat!" Greyson shouted into his radio.

"Back the fuck off, Greyson," she shouted back into her radio.

The double glass doors were propped wide open and smoke billowed into the morning sky. She stepped over the crisscrossed hoses littering the doorway and into the thick smoke. The wispy tendrils wrapped around her. The hiss of air as she inhaled and exhaled in her mask filled her ears. She switched her flashlight on and squinted into the darkness. The fire hadn't taken the hallway yet, but choking black smoke poured out the doors as she passed, indicating that the rooms were fully engulfed. Water poured out of one of the rooms where a hose disappeared. Station two's guys were obviously hard at work in there.

"Hale? You ok?" Greyson's voice came over the radio.

"Yeah, I'm fine. Heading towards the stairs." *Professional. Keep this professional. You can tear into him later, when we don't have the whole world listening to our conversation over the radio and the eminent danger of flames around us. Besides, there could be survivors somewhere.*

Greyson's gloved hand tapped her shoulder. "Right behind you."

"Nice to have you along." She wanted to add "to supervise me", but she didn't.

Visibility increased as the smoke recessed a bit. They must have vented the roof. The hallway stretched out before them and Kat could make out stairs at the end. She checked each doorway as she passed.

"I think I see something." Greyson disappeared through the door-way.

Kat paused for a moment, and when he didn't say anything more, she continued her progress down the hallway.

"Found a survivor. Coming out," Greyson's voice rasped through her radio on her shoulder.

Kat's foot was already on the first step of the stairs when she turned around to see him emerge from the room with an unconscious elderly man in his arms.

"Take him out. I'm going to keep going," Kat said into her radio.

"But..." His eyes bored into hers from across the blackened hallway.

"Go! There could be other survivors!" she shouted.

He nodded and spun on his heel to carry the man from the building.

She carefully picked her way up the rubble-strewn stairs. Luckily, they all seemed to be in pretty good shape and supported her weight. She was only about 130lbs, but with the 67lbs of equipment slung on her 5'10" frame she was almost 200lbs. The stairs groaned as she climbed.

Kat wasn't prepared for what she encountered when she turned the corner.

Angry white-orange flames licked across the ceiling from the rooms, all the way down the hallway. Smoke billowed towards the holes in the roof.

"You ok in there?" Greyson's voice rasped from the radio.

"Yeah. How's the survivor?"

"Conscious. He says there were two other people in the building when the alarms went off that he knows of. One of station two's guys found one of them. The other is still MIA as is the other firefighter from station two."

Kat's blood chilled. "Eric?"

There was a crackle in the radio but no response. Then Greyson's voice came. "No, Eric's safe."

She let out the breath she had been holding. "Ten-four, I'll keep my eyes open for them."

She picked her way down the hallway, dodging flaming rafters as they crashed down before her. Her boots crunched over the charred wood as she made her way past the open doorways. The remaining doors were closed. She made it to the first door and shoved it open. A hot wave of flames and smoke billowed out of the door after her. She reeled back and slammed against the opposite door.

The flames died back and she crossed the hallway and peered into the room. Everything was engulfed in fire. If anyone was in the room, they were toast. Without a hose, there was no way she could enter the room without being a casualty herself.

She turned and kicked the door she slammed into open and jumped back, expecting flames to fly out of the room. Somehow this room was already out, like flames had come, devoured everything and extinguished itself or moved on to other materials to ignite. She cautiously stepped into the room and shoved the charred office chair out of the way to check under the desk. Nothing.

Kat glanced around for any other potential hiding spots. A closed door, likely a supply closet, in the far back of the room. A bookcase collapsed against it. The condition of the room indicated that there probably weren't any survivors back there. But the nagging suspicion that someone could be trapped behind the collapsed bookcase wouldn't abate.

She grunted and shoved crumbling furniture out of her way as she cleared a path to the door. The bookcase was hardwood, oak or walnut probably. While it was severely charred from the blast, it was still mostly intact. Piles of ash littered the shelves, resembling what were probably books or manuals at one time. She braced her shoulder against the bookcase and heaved. It rocked for a moment before settling back in front of the door.

"Damn it!" she shouted. She hacked away at the hard wood. Surprisingly, it took more work than she would have expected to chop the stubborn book case into submission.

She pulled the smaller hunks of bookcase away from the door and wrapped her gloved hand around the handle and twisted. Locked. Shit.

"Hello? Anyone in there?" Kat shouted at the door. A thunk against the door from the inside had her rattling the handle violently.

"Unlock the door! Unlock the door!" Kat shouted.

A muffled shout came from behind the door and the handle rattled. She bent down and inspected the handle. The lock was melted.

"Stand back!" Kat raised the axe above her head and brought it crashing down on the handle in a smooth sweeping motion, shearing the handle off. She reached into the opening and tried to pull the door open. The latch held.

She raised the axe over her head and started to chop at the door where it stayed firmly sealed to the jamb. Three blows and the door fell open, crashing down onto the rubble.

She squinted into the darkness. Even the light from her flashlight didn't penetrate the blackness. The firefighter from station two stumbled out with a female victim in his arms. Both were covered head-to-toe in black ash.

"What happened?" Kat asked.

"The place flashed over right after I located the victim. Barely had time to duck for cover in the closet."

"Thanks for staying alive," Kat said with a half-smile. "Come on, let's get you two out of here."

She shoved rubble out of their way as they crossed to the door, which had swung shut after she entered. She paused for a moment, studying the door. Smoke billowed from underneath it and the blackened paint bubbled like water boiling on a stove.

"Fire's taken the hallway. We'll have to use the window." She reached for her radio. "Need a ladder on the south side of the building, about halfway down. ASAP."

"On it, we'll be there in a sec. Hold tight, okay?" Jake's voice rasped through the radio.

"Ten-four. Hurry." Kat tried to keep calm. The bubbling paint on the door meant the fire was about to break through. They had less than a minute before it engulfed the room again.

She broke the window with her axe, brushing the shattered glass away with her gloved hand. Smoke billowed out of the window above her head as she peered down at the ground two stories below. They could jump if they had to, but would probably sustain serious injuries from the boulders littering the ground. The lights from the engines reflected off of the building next door, casting the entire scene in a red and blue light.

Kat breathed a sigh of relief when L-281 pulled up below them. Greyson manned the controls for the ladder as it swung towards the building. Kevin perched in the bucket as it slid up to meet them. Kat took the victim and handed her to Kevin, who scurried down the ladder with her in his arms.

"Go," Kat ordered and stepped out of the way.

"Lady's first," Martinez, the firefighter from station two, said.

"Out now!" She bellowed and shoved him towards the ladder.

He nodded sheepishly and hoisted himself onto the ladder, following Kevin and the victim down like rats escaping a sinking ship.

Sizzling and popping erupted behind her. Kat heaved herself out of the window and grabbed onto the bucket. She looked up in time to see the fire break through the door and roar at her like a lion lunging after its prey.

Kat reeled backwards as the cloud of flames billowed towards her. Her feet slipped on the window frame and her body careened backwards as the windows along the side of the building exploded from the intense heat.

Strong arms encircled her waist as she flew through the air and her feet touched the ladder.

The ringing in her ears from the explosion almost drowned out Greyson's voice next to her ear. "Got ya."

The ladder jolted beneath them and retracted, lowering them safely away from the flaming building. She breathed a sigh of relief that they managed to not lose anybody in the blaze.

She followed behind Greyson as he descended the ladder.

The moment her feet touched the ground Greyson pounced. "What the hell were you doing in there?"

"Saving lives. You would've done the same." She turned and marched over to Jake.

"Kat!" Eric's frantic voice carried above the hiss of the water rushing through the hoses. Kat's skin tingled. She knew that tone. He was pissed.

She turned in time to have the wind crushed form her lungs in a bear hug.

"Thank God," Eric whispered and squeezed her tight.

Her gaze caught Greyson's over Eric's shoulder. A look of frustration crossed his face before he crammed a hand through his hair and turned to inspect the gauges on the side of the truck.

Kat shrugged out of Eric's grasp as soon as he lessened his death grip. "I'm fine, Eric. I've got to get back to work. And you do too." She nodded towards where Martinez was sitting on the bumper of Engine 288 and breathing oxygen through a plastic mask.

Eric nodded. "Just don't do something stupid like that again, okay?"

Kat's blood boiled and she shot a scathing glare at him before turning to Jake.

"Where do you want me?"

"You fit for duty?" Jake's green eyes surveyed her.

"Yes, Sir."

"Good. Let's get those monitors back on the fire. You good to fly?" A wicked smile lit up his well-tanned face.

"Absolutely!" A proud smile spread across her face.

He raised a dark eyebrow at her.

"Um, I mean, yes Sir!"

"That's better. Go get em' Kat." He smiled and turned to Kevin.

Greyson frowned at her from behind the controls at the bottom of the turnstile as she scampered back up the ladder. She relished the feeling of flying as the ladder extended and she soared up next to the flaming building.

Kat's gloved fingers wrapped around the controls and she let the full-force of the water spray into the building. She started with one of the windows and doused it until the only thing escaping from the window was the water that she pounded it with. One by one she extinguished the flames licking up the side of the building. Working in conjunction with the other companies, they successfully put the blaze out. By the time they were done, it was nothing more than a smoldering, charred shell of a component factory.

The water thundering through the monitor receded and she felt Greyson lowering the ladder back to the truck. She unhooked her harness, climbed down the ladder and jumped from the rig. There were still miles of hose that needed to be walked out and re-laid on the truck before they could call it done.

She slid her heavy jacket from her shoulders, laid it in the cab and put her helmet on top of it. Her t-shirt was damp from perspiration and clung to her body. She longed to shed the bunker pants, but settled for shoving the wide suspenders from her shoulders so they hung from her hips. She scaled the back of the truck and felt Greyson's eyes on her as she bent to catch the hose as it was handed up.

"Great job, Kat! How'd you know they were in the supply closet?" Kevin handed a fold of hose to her.

Kat shrugged and took the hose from him. "Just a hunch, I guess."

"That's why you're one of the best firefighters I know. You trust your intuition." His chocolate eyes sparkled up at her. He was such a sweet guy.

"Um, thanks." The heat of her blush prickled across her overheated skin.

"Okay ladies, if you're done chatting, let's get these hoses put away so we can get the hell outa here," Jake said as he rounded the back of the truck.

"Yes sir," they said in unison.

5

Chapter Five

When they got back to the station the guys forced Kat to recount the rescue over and over as she made lunch. She rolled her eyes and related the details of the second floor, her thoughts about the room's condition, the bookcase, the melted door handle, hacking the crap out of both and pulling the downed firefighter and victim to safety.

"It was totally like a scene out of a movie when the windows exploded and you went flying through the air. Can't believe how fast Greyson scaled that ladder to catch you either!" Kevin laughed. "Yeah, how'd you know there was going to be an explosion, Greyson?"

"The glass was bowing," Greyson murmured and snagged a cheese steak from the pile in the center of the table before returning to his favorite recliner in the corner of the room.

"God damn, you're a good cook Hale! Why did you choose firefighting over culinary school again?" Jake slurred between bites.

"Well someone has to be able to cook in this station. Otherwise you'd all die of food poisoning if you constantly had to rely on Kevin's cooking," Kat joked and elbowed him in the ribs.

"What's wrong with my cooking?" Kevin choked.

"Tuna noodle sandwiches? Seriously?" She raised an eyebrow at him.

"Hey! That was my mom's recipe!"

"It's a good thing you're such a good firefighter..." Jake smirked. He picked up the remote and switched on the forty-two inch TV. The screen flickered to life and Kat rolled her eyes as another football game graced the screen.

"Have fun doing the dishes boys. I'm going to clean up." Kat headed in the direction of the showers. One perk of being the only girl in the firehouse meant she got the entire locker room to herself when she was showering.

She made it halfway down the hallway before Greyson's voice stopped her.

"Kat! Got a second?" His deep voice called from the doorway of the rec room. He approached without waiting for an answer, his footsteps echoing down the hall as he marched towards her.

"What's up Greyson?" Kat turned her glare on him.

"Let's discuss it in here." He opened the door to the locker room with one hand, holding it open for her. It would have been a chivalrous act were his eyes not boring into her with enough fury to melt paint.

"Fine." She stepped inside the room.

He quietly closed the door and locked it behind him.

"We need a locked door to discuss whatever it is you're glaring at me about?"

"Yeah. I'd rather not have the whole station hear us."

Kat spun on him and folded her arms across her chest. "What the hell is your problem with me Greyson?"

"Huh?" He actually looked surprised at her question.

"You've been riding my ass ever since I signed on to this shift. Is it that you don't like working with a woman? Or is it that you just don't like me in particular?"

"Wait one damn minute! I—" The confusion in his eyes sent her over the edge.

"No! I've worked my ass off trying to prove to everyone that I'm worthy of this position. But no matter how hard I work I can always tell that you don't want me here. Well, fuck you Greyson. I made the crew and I've done a damn good job and I'm not going to let you treat me like shit every chance you get. If you have a problem working with me than

I suggest you see Chief Phillips about getting reassigned." She stomped across the locker room and wrenched open her locker, yanked out her towel and hairbrush and slammed it shut.

His words mirrored the stunned expression plastered on his face. "That's not what I wanted to talk to you about. I didn't realize I gave you that impression."

The wounded look in his eyes had her mentally backtracking. Had she misunderstood the situation? Didn't he come in here to chew her ass out about something she did wrong today? She studied him, trying to read the expression in his eyes.

"I don't have a problem with you, Kat. You are a great firefighter and I'm proud to be working on the same shift as you." His molten caramel eyes searched hers.

Well if that didn't slap her in the face like an ice-cold towel.

"But I'm worried about you. I think you push yourself way too hard to prove yourself to the rest of us. You don't have to do that. We all think you are just as capable as any man on the crew, if not more so." He dropped his gaze and studied the tile.

Kat swallowed to dislodge the lump that had built in her throat as the words she had longed to hear out of his mouth came falling out.

"I'm sorry." The words were little more than a squeak from her lips.

"No, I should be the one apologizing. I had no idea that I made you feel so bad about yourself. I was just trying to keep you safe. I thought I was going to lose you after the incident on that ladder. And then today when the ceiling collapsed while you were up on the second floor, I was sure I'd lost my chance to tell you how I felt." He raised his smoldering eyes to meet hers.

"The ceiling collapsed?" At the time she hadn't noticed that the floor had been disintegrating beneath her. But now that he mentioned it, she could feel the rumbling beneath her feet as she chopped the bookcase and doorknob to rescue the victims.

"Yeah. I dropped the victim off with the medics and bee-lined it back inside to find you. But the ceiling collapsed before I made it to the stairwell. I barely made it out with the skin on my back." He rubbed at his eyes, as if he was trying to remove some debris from it.

"I'm sorry. I didn't know." She wanted to reach up and wipe the distressed look from his sculpted face, to smooth the wrinkles on his forehead as his eyebrows furrowed in frustration.

"I know. You were so intent on rescuing those people that you didn't consider your own safety. That's what impresses me so much about you. You rush in, guns blazing, your sights set only on rescuing the helpless, without a care for what might happen to you. You're too much like my brother in that aspect. You're too good at your job and you're reckless because of it. I don't want you to get hurt."

And there it was. Kat narrowed her eyes and her words ground out through clenched teeth. "I am *not* reckless."

"You put other people's safety before your own. That makes you reckless." His eyes narrowed to match her expression.

"Whatever." She glared at him.

"Are you trying to get yourself killed?" He took a step towards her.

She subconsciously backed a step away at his advance, bumping into the corner of the sink behind her. "What may look like recklessness to you is focused determination. I know exactly what I'm doing and don't need some guy with a "Knight in Shinning Armor" complex to save me."

"You've made it very clear that you're capable of taking care of yourself." He took another step towards her and their bodies practically touched.

"What are you doing?"

"Something I should have done a long time ago," he murmured and closed the distance between them. His brown eyes burned with an intensity that had Kat's stomach twisting in knots. Was he really going to do this? But Eric..."Kat, I..." He stopped, his lips mere inches from hers. His hot breath brushed across her lips and they parted involuntarily in response.

She stared up at him, confusion and longing warring against each other.

"Aw, hell." He pulled her into his arms. His mouth on hers and cut off any protest she could have uttered. The intensity of his kiss had Kat's head spinning. It was fierce and tender at the same time. His tongue teased her lips and she opened them in response. A growl rumbled low in his throat. She battled his tongue with her own, tasting him in turn. He tasted like an intoxicating blend of coffee, mint and chocolate.

Kat slid her hands up his neck and buried her hands in the soft dark waves of his hair. How many nights had she secretly dreamed about this, never even hoping it could ever become a reality?

He picked her up and pushed her back against the sink. His hands traced along her arms, leaving trails of goose bumps where ever he touched. An ache flared to life in the pit of Kat's stomach. Flames of desire licked along her skin. In the back of her mind she could hear Chief Phillip's voice recommending immediate termination. And besides, she was dating his brother...

Kat tore her lips away from his and panted to catch her breath. He buried his face in her hair and kissed trails across her collarbone.

"I'm sorry, Greyson. We can't do this..." Her body was screaming yes, and if the situation were different, her heart would be soaring. But she worked so hard to get assigned to station three, to work for Chief Phillips, she felt like she was betraying herself. And no matter how neglectful Eric was, he didn't deserve this.

"I know..." Greyson murmured into Kat's neck. "I just had to know what it was like." He pulled away from her.

"What does that mean?"

"I have wanted to do that since the day I met you Kat. It's been torture to stay away from you. When I thought I was going to lose you, I just about lost my mind. Then at the fire today I thought I was going to lose you again. I refuse to take another chance and regret not kissing you, just this once. Even if you are dating my brother."

A loud knock came from the door and the door handle rattled.

"What are you two doing in there?" Kevin's irritated voice traveled through the door. "Why the hell is the door locked?"

6

Chapter Six

Kat's eyes widened as she stared at the wood-encased glass doorway, with Kevin's form silhouetted in it.

"Shit." She scooted off the sink, brushed her hair with her hands and smoothed down her t-shirt.

"I got this..." Greyson headed for the door.

"Hey Kevin! What? The door locked? Must have caught it with my hip on the way in. I was just asking Kat if she had any eye drops. My eyes are killing me from the smoke today," Greyson said.

Kevin shoved Greyson out of the way. "Oh. Well, I gotta piss. Lemme in!"

Kat turned her back to him and quickly retrieved her eye drops off the shelf and rifled around in her purse as if she was searching for them. "Here they are!" She pulled them out, a triumphant smile on her face.

"Women and their bottomless purses..." Kevin rolled his eyes and headed for the stall.

Kat grit her teeth and narrowed her eyes at him as he passed her. She hated that kind of generalization about women, but at least he bought the whole eye drops line. Greyson was good. Very good. Kevin disappeared into the stall and the sounds of him relieving himself filled the tiled room.

"Nice, Kevin. Thanks for waiting until I left," Kat muttered.

"Want to play with the boys, you gotta act like one. Suck it up." He zipped up his fly on his way to the sink to wash his hands.

"Fuck you, Kevin," Kat replied.

"Anytime baby. Name the time and place." He caught her eye in the mirror and winked exaggeratedly.

She laughed and threw her brush at him, narrowly missing his head with the wooden end of the boars-hair brush.

"Easy there, I'm only joking!" He retrieved the brush and tossed it to her as he headed back out the door. The sound of the door closing against the jamb sent a shiver down her spine, reminding her of the gavel smashing onto the table at her dismissal hearing for dating a firefighter on the same shift.

"That was close," Greyson said.

"*That* is just one of the reasons we can't do this. You're Eric's brother, for God's sake!" Kat grabbed two handfuls of her hair and pulled gently, as if taking her frustration out on her hair would help. "And I've worked too hard to be here to throw it away when we get caught. Let's just keep this professional okay?" Her heart clenched. She wanted nothing more than to reach up on her tiptoes and kiss his soft lips again.

"I understand. I will be nothing but professional from this moment on." Greyson turned to leave.

"Greyson?" Kat asked.

He spun on his heel, hope filling his gorgeous face. "Yeah?"

"Here." She tossed the eye drops to him and turned around to gather her towel and shower bag.

"Um, thanks," he muttered and closed the door behind him.

Kat's heart plummeted. She'd been so confused about her feelings for Greyson. But he was Eric's brother. And now finding out he had feelings for her too just complicated matters more.

She took her towel and bag and headed for the showers. She slipped behind the glass door and turned the water on. Steam billowed up around her and heated the air. A sigh escaped her lips as she slipped out of her clothes.

The water streamed over her head and soaked into her dark hair. She squirted some shampoo into her hand and ran it through her hair, working it in until bubbles built on bubbles. The water ran gray with ash from the fire. She ducked under the spray and rinsed all traces of shampoo and ash from her thick hair.

She squeezed some vanilla scented body wash onto the puff. She may be playing with the boys, but there was no reason to smell like one. She fluffed the sponge until bubbles ran down her arm before smoothing it over every inch of her well-toned body. Her manicured toes shined like little ruby jewels in the water and soapsuds on the tile floor as the water ran for the drain.

She smiled. She'd worried that she'd have to lose her girlish fascinations when she joined the boy's club in order to be taken seriously, but she managed to keep the small, personal things girly. Pedicures and scented body washes and a little make-up were about all she dared. The guys didn't come in while she was showering, and unless she walked around barefoot -- which she never did -- no one saw her pedicure. They were her little secrets.

Greyson's words replayed in her head as she rinsed the bubbles from her stomach and ran the puff down her legs. Did she really put other's safety before her own? She definitely wasn't trying to kill herself, but in her effort to prove herself she had made herself vulnerable.

Kat's body tingled as she brought the puff up and hesitated over her cleft. The feel of Greyson's lips on hers was still fresh. She could still taste him on her lips. She groaned and rubbed gently, hoping to abate the ache that awoke the moment he wrapped her in his arms and crushed her lips with his.

But the pressure only built. She sighed and rinsed the suds off before turning around to rinse the conditioner from her hair. Her eyes closed as the steaming water pounded against the head and shoulders. When she opened her eyes and reached up to squeeze the water from her hair, her heart lurched. The dark silhouette of someone stood on the other side of the glass.

"Who's there?" Kat grabbed her towel and wrapped it tightly around her.

The figure bolted and she raced for the door, practically slipping on the wet tile in her haste. She crashed into the glass door and wrenched it open.

"Hello?" Kat called.

The metal on wood clank of the hallway door slamming brought her attention that direction. She raced through the locker room. Her bare feet left wet footprints on the freshly mopped tile.

She flung the door open and raced into the hallway. Fast, heavy foot-falls drew her towards the bunk room.

"Wait!"

No reply.

Rapid footsteps pounded and a metallic door slammed. The emergency exit... Kat ran past the rows of bunks, her towel flapping in the air as she ran. Whoever was peep-toming on her was going to get their ass kicked. Not cool.

The door loomed up ahead. She was in a towel, but it didn't matter. She shoved on the exit but it wouldn't budge. She rattled the handle. It was blocked from the outside. Shit.

If it was one of the guys, then they'd be missing from the rec room. Kat dashed back through the bunker and high-tailed it down the hall-way to the rec room. She skidded to a stop, her bare feet cold on the tile.

"Uh, I think you forgot something," Jake said from his recliner. Greyson sat in his usual place in the corner reading a book. Every pair of male eyes were glued to her. Except Kevin's.

"Where's Kevin?" Kat's eyes narrowed in suspicion.

Jake raised an eyebrow. "Chief Phillips called him up to his office. Why?"

"Oh, um. Nothing." The last thing she needed was for the guys to think she suspected someone on the crew to be a peeping-tom.

"It's nothing, but you're looking for him while in nothing but a towel?" Jake questioned.

"Yeah, sorry. I just remembered something that I didn't want to forget." Her body flamed, and the blush that started on her cheeks radiated from her head to her pedicured toes.

Jake nodded. Kat spun and dashed for the bathroom. She shimmied into her clothes and took off for the emergency exit again. She squared her shoulder and shoved the door with all her might.

It flung wide, like it had never been blocked. She glanced around the door, looking for anything that had been used to block the door shut. But there was nothing on the small metal balcony. She sighed and leaned against the rail.

What the fuck just happened? She leaned her forehead against her hands on the rail and closed her eyes. Had she imagined the figure standing on the other side of the glass?

Maybe. She'd been so hot with her memory of Greyson's kiss that she could have imagined it, she guessed. But the footsteps she had been following? Those had definitely been real.

Kat opened her eyes. She hadn't imagined the footsteps she had chased, or the locked emergency exit. She climbed down the emergency ladder, dropped the four feet down onto the ground, landing softly on the balls of her feet.

She knelt down and picked up the glittering object that she had seen from the emergency exit. A tiny diamond.

"Kat?" Eric's voice echoed across the parking lot.

Kat stiffened and pushed to her feet. "What are you doing here?" Her gaze flitted to everything but Eric's eyes. She wondered if the evidence that Greyson had kissed her was written all over her face.

"Hey, sweetheart. I was just in the area and thought I'd come by and say hi."

Kat frowned. He never just came by. If he wasn't working – which he always was – he was working out, or working on his Civic. Coming to visit on his day off didn't happen unless he had an agenda.

She finally met his gaze. "No, really, what's up?"

Her heart skipped a beat. He studied her with his clear blue eyes, a slight smile turning up the corners of his mouth. He was such a cutie with his short blonde hair gelled into a trendy, spikey mess, and his sharp nose leading to a set of the most kissable lips a girl could ever hope for. But as he watched her, his smile fell and he crammed a hand through his dirty blonde hair – an action that must be ingrained the Neal genetic code – and sighed.

"You always could see right through me."

Kat smirked and crossed her arms over her chest. "What's up?"

"I fucked up."

Kat smirked. She had a laundry list, but nothing she wanted to get into right now in the parking lot at work. "How so?"

Remorse twisted his features. "I've been such a bad boyfriend. I should have come to visit you in the hospital, but I was so worried you'd be mad at me about calling your mom. So I stayed away."

Kat opened her mouth to respond, but Eric hurried to continue.

"And then at the fire, I almost lost it when I heard the chief sent you inside for search and rescue. You're barely back a few hours and he sends you in!"

Her teeth ground against each other. "Don't start, Eric. I had everything under control."

"Under control? The floor was collapsing under your feet. You shouldn't have been there in the first place!"

"The structure was stable when I went upstairs!" Her nails bit into her palms where she clinched her fists.

"Fuck!" He scrubbed his head with his hands and paced a few steps. "Damn it, Kat. This isn't why I came here."

She held her ground, taking in slow breaths to calm the rage boiling to the surface. He meant well. She knew that. But sometimes he seemed to forget that she was just as much a firefighter as she was. "Why *are* you here, Eric?"

He stopped his pacing and studied her for a moment, his light blue eyes reminding her of the sky on a hot summer day. "This," he murmured and closed the distance between them.

Kat opened her mouth to argue, but his mouth covered hers, cutting her off. His arms slid around her back, tracing gentle circles over her. She melted into him, the familiar feeling of his arms around her erasing the irritation she had felt before. Her hands found their way into his hair as she desperately poured everything she wanted to feel, needed to feel, into the kiss.

A groan rumbled through Eric's chest as her fingers dug into the hair at the base of his neck. His hands shifted lower and he hooked her legs around his hips before wrapping his arms back around her torso.

Kat sighed. It felt so good to be wrapped in his arms. It'd been over a week since he'd held her like this. Not since the night before the fire that landed her in the ER. And the first person to kiss her since it happened wasn't her boyfriend. Greyson's chocolaty eyes flashed before her. Guilt twisted her stomach and she wrenched her lips from his.

"I can't do this," she panted and slid from his grasp, her legs a little wobbly when her feet hit the ground.

Eric frowned. "Why not?"

"Um, for one, I'm on duty. And two, I'm still pissed at you."

"The way you kissed me just now didn't seem like you were pissed."

It was her turn to frown. "Well, I am. Don't think that you can just march in here and kiss me senseless and everything'll be fine. Because it's not."

Eric sighed. "I know."

The sound of the alarm sounding cut off any more that Kat wanted to say to Eric.

7

Chapter Seven

She hadn't been to the bar since Dave's funeral. Kat's eyes scanned the dimly lit room until she found Greyson and Eric lounging in one of the booths in back. She avoided the leering stares of the bar usuals and quickly made her way to their booth, nudging Eric with her hip to get him to scoot over.

"Hey, sweetheart," Eric murmured and kissed her quickly before returning to his beer and watching the Cardinals on the flat screen across the room.

"Hey," Kat replied, but she knew he didn't hear her. If football was on, he was tuned out.

"Hey, Kat," Greyson murmured and watched her with a guarded expression in his chocolaty eyes.

Now here was a guy whose undivided attention she had. Kat squirmed under his scrutiny, which made her feel like she was naked before him. She tore her gaze from his when a drunken man stumbled up to their table.

"Hey, man! I know you!" the inebriated man slurred and pointed to Eric.

Eric turned his uninterested gaze on the drunk. "Don't think so."

"You're Eric Neal. We were in the same fire academy class together!"

Eric squinted at the man. "Oh yeah, Bill, right?"

The man grinned, his watery eyes lighting up. "We had some good times before I dropped out of the academy!"

Eric chuckled. "We did."

His cheery face suddenly turned solemn. "Shit. Sorry to hear about Amanda, man!"

"Who's Amanda?" Kat's eyes shot to Eric, who shifted restlessly in his seat.

He avoided her gaze and responded to the drunkard standing at the end of the booth. "Thanks, bro, but we broke up long time ago. I'm sorry about what happened, but I'm the wrong person to be offering condolences to."

Kat's frown deepened as her gaze shifted from the drunken douchebag to Eric to Greyson. But rather than avoiding her gaze, Greyson's locked with hers.

Kat cleared her throat and stared pointedly at Eric. "Who is Amanda?"

Eric took a swig of his beer and brought it down on the table with more force than necessary. "An ex." Kat waited, but he didn't offer any more explanation than that.

The drunk man snorted. "His ex that died in that house fire. Some sick fuck tied her up and set her on fire."

"Dude, you need to leave," Eric growled.

The drunken man looked shocked for a moment, and then, as if he flipped a switch in his alcohol-logged brain, he smiled brightly, patted Eric on the back and stumbled away from the table, on to the next group of bar patrons to annoy.

Kat's gaze shot to Greyson's, searching for any hope of an explanation. But he looked as perplexed and horrified as she felt.

Kat shifted her attention to Eric. "Were you planning on telling me about this?"

Eric shrugged. "I didn't see any reason to."

Of course he didn't. Because that would be something a normal boyfriend would do. And Eric didn't operate like a normal boyfriend. More and more, he operated like a bachelor who had her on the side as a booty call. "This is a bunch of crap, Eric. I have to find out that the victim at one of the scenes we worked was one of your ex-girlfriends from some drunken douchebag at a bar? Don't you think that's something you should have told me?"

Another infuriating shrug.

She scooted from the booth and flung her purse over her shoulder. "Well, when you decide to start acting like a boyfriend, call me. Otherwise, leave me the hell alone, Eric."

**

Greyson watched Kat stomp from the bar, eliciting cat-calls from some of the drunken patrons on the way out. He wanted to get up and punch each of the cat caller's in the face,but he remained wedged in the booth across from Eric.

His blood boiled at the way his brother treated Kat. She didn't deserve to be treated like that. She deserved someone who would take care of her. Someone who would be honest with her. Someone who cherished her and put her needs before their own.

Instead she was stuck with his selfish, workaholic, over-drinking, girlfriend-neglecting brother. He glanced at Eric, who was still studying the shredded label on his beer bottle.

He refused to keep silent any longer. "You know you don't deserve her, right?"

Eric sighed, "I know."

Greyson paused. That wasn't the answer he expected. He was expecting a "Stay the fuck out of it" or a "mind your own fucking business". Not "I know."

Eric's gaze narrowed on the peeling label on his beer bottle. "I know I haven't been the best boyfriend. I'm just scared, you know?"

Greyson frowned and studied his brother's face. "Scared?"

Eric nodded and raised his blue gaze to meet his. "She scares me. She makes me feel things I don't want to feel. I think about her when I shouldn't and it makes me reckless. I'm terrified she's going to get hurt on the job. I'm in love with her and it scares me to death."

"Wow." The air gushed out of him like somebody punched him in the chest. It was the first time he'd ever said he loved a girl and meant it. The first time he'd ever talked to *him* about a girl like that.

"I know. So when I found out about Amanda, I didn't want her to be scared. That's why I kept it from her." The pleading in Eric's eyes made Greyson's stomach churn.

"You know, you just let her leave the bar pissed off at you that you didn't tell her about Amanda."

Eric nodded. "I know. I'll let her cool off for a while, then I'll go find her. You know how she gets when she's all fired up about something."

Greyson nodded. He did know how she got when she was pissed. She was probably digging her running shoes out right this second. Which – Greyson glanced at the window and noted the encroaching darkness – probably wasn't the safest time to be running through the park.

He scooted out of the booth and tossed some cash on the table. "Are you coming?"

Eric shook his head. "No. I'll catch up with you later."

Greyson frowned. His brother, ever the self-centered one.

Before he realized it, he was in his truck and tearing down the road toward the park near where he thought Kat lived. While it was well lit, there were still dark places along the running track where creeps could to hide, jumping out to grab unsuspecting girls on their evening runs.

He pulled into the parking lot and killed the lights. Kat was smarter than this. So why the hell would she come here to run, regardless of how pissed off she was?

She wouldn't. Greyson turned the ignition and flipped on the headlights. The grassy field illuminated before him. He shifted into reverse and checked his mirrors before backing out of the parking lot. Maybe she had a gym membership that he didn't know about. He turned his head to back out when something caught his eye.

A person in black sweatpants, a black hoodie with the hood tied closely around their face, and sunglasses walked across the parking lot just out of his peripheral vision. Odd, considering in August the evening temperatures were easily still in the hundreds.

This person was looking for trouble.

Kat or no Kat, he wasn't letting a woman get assaulted tonight. He watched the figure move into the park and disappear into the shadows. He pulled back into the spot and quickly killed the headlights. He grabbed his flashlight from beneath the passenger seat, climbed from the truck and raced for the shadows where he saw the figure disappear.

No one was there.

His eyes strained at the darkness. They had to be here somewhere. Out of the corner of his eye, something darted between the shadows a few hundred feet away. His feet pounded the pavement as he raced toward the dark figure that was quickly getting away.

The air punched from his chest and he reeled backwards.

"Oh!" A girl's voice gasped.

Greyson flicked on his flashlight and shined it at the person on the ground. The girl had to be no older than twenty-one, in full running gear, sat on the ground, rubbing her back. "I'm sorry! I didn't see you there," Greyson said.

"It's okay. I didn't see you there either! They really need to light this track better!"

Her squeaky little girl voice triggered Greyson's protective instinct. "Go home. Now. Call 911. There's a predator in the park tonight."

The fear widened the girls eyes to the size of golf balls. But she didn't budge.

Greyson took off at a run in the direction he last saw the person in black. "Go now!"

She was up and running in the opposite direction.

Greyson prayed that she called 911 like he asked. In his haste to catch up to the suspect, he'd left his phone on the seat of the truck. But it was too late for that.

After a few minutes of hard running, he started to worry that the person had doubled back. His eyes strained against the darkness. There were too many places for the creep to hide. His flashlight beam shone like a light saber as he searched each dark spot along the path.

That's when he saw her. She'd pulled her hair up into a high ponytail and had traded her station boots for running shoes. But she was still in her station shorts and CFD t-shirt.

"Kat!" Greyson called out, his voice tinged with fear. But she couldn't hear him. His feet pounded the pavement as he raced down the path toward her.

A shadow moved in the darkness twenty feet ahead of her. It was the person in black he'd been following. From his angle he could see them crouched behind a bush just off the path. But there was no way Kat could see from her angle.

"Kat!" he roared. He pushed himself to run faster, but he was already running at top speed. But she was running too. Towards the person crouching in the shadows. He wasn't going to make it in time.

Kat passed the bush, and suddenly she was on the ground, rolling, the dark figure on top of her. A ragged scream ripped from his chest as he closed in on the rolling pair. He could hear the sirens in the distance. Thank God. The girl had called the cops.

He was on them in a matter of seconds, tearing at the person in black's arms, trying to get them off of Kat, who was laying on her back with her arms up trying to protect herself.

"What the fuck!" the person in black screamed in a female voice.

Greyson froze but didn't let go of his captive. The person's sunglasses had fallen off, but their hood still obscured their face. He pushed the hood back.

"What the hell, Greyson?" Eve snapped and shrugged out of his shocked grasp.

"Eve?" Greyson and Kat asked simultaneously.

Greyson's galloping heartbeat slowed as his brain processed the information. "Why were you hiding in the bushes?"

Eve snorted. "I was tying my shoe. I always come running here at night. I don't really like getting run into, so I moved off the path to tie it." She held her foot out to show her half-tied shoe. "I got up and got run over."

Kat rubbed her head with one hand and shrugged. "I had my ear buds in. I wasn't paying attention."

"Why are you in black sweats? It's like a hundred degrees out," Greyson asked.

"It's a thermal sweat suit. It's supposed to help you burn more calories than just running alone. It's murder to wear, but it works."

"And the sunglasses?"

"Migraine. The exercise is supposed to help them, but the lights kill me."

The red and blue flashing lights illuminated the path and the officers were on them in a matter of seconds.

Greyson smirked. "It was a misunderstanding, officers." A quick explanation of what happened and before long it was just Kat, Greyson and Eve.

He crammed a hand through his wavy hair and sighed. "Sorry for the misunderstanding, Eve. You really shouldn't be running alone out here at night. It's not safe." Greyson shot a look at Kat, who frowned at him.

"You're right. I shouldn't be out here at night. Great way to get yourself killed, right?" Eve elbowed Kat with a chuckle.

Kat frowned. "What were you doing here, anyway, Greyson?"

His gaze dropped to her shoes as if the non-incriminating answer was there. "I, uh..." He raised his gaze to meet hers again. "You were pissed at Eric. I figured you were going to run it off. But with the rash of assaults and abductions in the area, I figured I should check on you. Guess I got a little carried away."

"I'd say so," Eve grumbled.

Greyson frowned at her.

She cleared her throat and brushed the dust off her sweats. "I should get going. I'll catch you guys around. Hopefully we can avoid the full-contact football tackles next time, though."

Kat winked. "We'll try to avoid it."

With that Eve took off at a jog in the opposite direction of the parking lot.

Greyson swallowed hard when Kat turned and stared at him, a confused look on her face. "What was that, Greyson?"

He opened his mouth to respond, but no words came to his rescue. The truth was he was worried about her. Plain and simple. He thought about her more than he should, considering she was his brother's girlfriend. But regardless of the fact that it wasn't his place to worry about her, he wouldn't have been able to sleep until he knew she was home safe and sound. He sucked in a deep breath and his eyes searched hers. "I told you. I was worried about you, what with the recent crimes in the neighborhood. It's dark. What if that *had* been the suspect they've been looking for?"

Kat frowned and picked at the ends of her ponytail. "That never even occurred to me."

Greyson nodded. "Can I walk you to your car?"

Kat stared at him like he'd stunned her into silence or something. "Yeah, thanks."

They walked slowly toward her truck in the well-lit adjacent parking lot. Neither of them talked. They just listened to the crickets chirping around them and the ocean-like rush of the traffic as it raced by on a nearby street.

Kat opened the door to her truck and paused, her gaze searching his face.

Realizing that this was the last opportunity he'd have to be alone with her, Greyson found his voice. "You know he doesn't deserve you." He paused, trying to find the words. Her mouth fell open, but she didn't respond. She just stared at him with those gut-punching gorgeous blue eyes of hers. "He doesn't. But he loves you."

Pain flitted across her features for a moment. "I know."

He reached up and cupped her cheek in his palm. "God, I just wish..."

Her eyes searched his face as she waited for him to continue.

He stroked his thumb across her bottom lip. He sighed at the tremor that he felt go through her at the touch. It was the same one that went through him. But she wasn't his. And this was wrong. "It doesn't matter what I wish. You're not mine." His words were little more than a pained whisper. "Just know that Eric loves you, regardless of how much of an asshole he can be. Deep down he's a good guy."

Kat sighed. "I know. And thanks, Greyson."

That caught him off guard. "For what?"

"For caring enough to come out to make sure I was okay. It means a lot to me."

Greyson nodded. "Anytime."

She stood on her tiptoes and laid a gentle kiss on his cheek before climbing into the cab and backing out of the spot. He watched until the red tail lights disappeared around the corner.

8

Chapter Eight

Two days later, Kat sat in the rec room, twisting the tiny diamond in her fingers. In the midst of the chaos of the situation with Greyson and Eric, she couldn't forget what the little rock meant. What were the chances that this was the peeping tom's? Was it reasonable to assume that someone else could have lost the diamond there?

"What've you got there?" Jake asked and knelt beside her.

"A rock," Kat muttered. She wasn't going to supply clues to potential suspects.

"Pretty rock."

"So, when are you getting married Jake?" She raised her eyes to meet his.

Surprise flitted over his sculpted features and he scrubbed his closely-shaven head with one hand. "Oh, I don't know. I kind-of like the single life, you know? So many chicks have the firefighter fantasy. I like to think that I can fulfill that fantasy for a few lucky ladies before I settle down." He winked at her.

She smiled. He talked a big game, but he was by far the most monogamous of the group. When he met a girl he really liked, he was done for, at least until he decided she wasn't his Mrs. Right, or she got possessive and the firefighter gig got to her.

Kat rolled the tiny diamond around in her palm. A half-carat, maybe less? She didn't know. But the tiny, insignificant little rock was Kat's only clue to the identity to the person who had been watching her. Maybe.

"Besides, whatever girl I do decide to settle down with has some stiff competition to compete with in the kitchen, considering I get to devour your cooking every day." He nodded towards the kitchen. "Speaking of, isn't it your turn?"

She heaved herself from the chair and pocketed the diamond. "Seems like it's always *my* turn..."

The moment the steaming stew hit the counter, the alarms rang. The drive to the scene felt like it took ages. They knew what to expect from dispatch's briefing, but each and every drowning or near-drowning call was a test of a firefighter's skill. The kid had gotten out of the house and ended up in the pool. The baby sitter found the child floating in the water and called 911.

Kat's skin tingled as the sirens screamed. Calls involving kids were the hardest. But it was all part of the job. They pulled up to the sprawling English Tudor-style house and Kat was out of the door and running before the rig even stopped. The gate was open and she dashed inside, skidding to a stop beside the sobbing pre-teen as she clutched the limp child in her arms.

Kat knelt before her and took the child from her and laid him on the ground. "I'll take it from here. Good job."

The girl backed away and into a neighbor's arms. Her muffled sobs barely registered in Kat's ears as she began CPR.

With quick movements, she lifted the child's chin to open the airway and leaned in, her ear close to the child's mouth, checking for sounds of breathing. Nothing. Her eyes scanned the child's chest. No movement. No breath brushing against her cheek.

Her chest tightened as she leaned forward, plugged the child's nose with her fingers and breathed two breaths into his blue-tinged mouth and checked for a pulse. Nothing.

No!

She felt the notch between the two halves of the child's rib cage, measured two fingers up, put one hand over the center of the child's chest and carefully pumped. Shallow and fast. Thirty pumps. Two breaths. Thirty pumps. Two breaths.

Greyson's big, warm hand landed on top of hers on the child's chest and seamlessly took over pumping while Kat replaced her mouth-to-mouth technique with the air bag. Two breaths. Thirty pumps. Two breaths. Thirty pumps.

Tears burned Kat's eyes as she watched Greyson tirelessly pump the limp little boy's chest. He couldn't have been more than three years old.

Kat pressed against the carotid artery to check for a pulse. Nothing. Jake brought over the automatic defibrillator and placed the pads on the child's chest while Greyson continued pumping.

"Clear." Jake commanded.

It was like everything in the world froze for the second between when Jake said clear and when the pads shocked the child's heart. His little body tensed as the volts coursed through him.

Kat put the mask back on his little face and puffed two breaths. She leaned over and checked for pulse. Still nothing. Tears burned her eyes.

Please God don't take this child. Please.

"No!" Greyson growled and started pumping the child's chest again. "Don't give up!"

Jake's calm yet strained voice cut through the air. "Clear."

Greyson pulled back and Kat caught a sheen of tears in his eyes. He winced as the little boy's body tensed from the shock.

A little cough was all it took to make the tears spring free and roll freely down Greyson's cheeks.

"Thank God." Greyson murmured and brushed the child's black, fluffy hair from his face. His little brown eyes opened and a tiny wail escaped his lips.

Kat breathed a sigh of relief as his shrill cry filled the air. She felt like she hadn't breathed since her feet hit the ground when she bounded out of the rig.

Within a few minutes they had the little boy strapped securely to a gurney, a tiny oxygen mask over his nose and mouth, and loaded him into the ambulance.

"Good job, guys." Jake patted Greyson on the shoulder as he passed. Not a word was said the entire way back to the station. Or at lunch, as they slurped up cold beef stew in silence.

Kat snuck a glance at Greyson every so often. His eyes never left the bowl of stew, which sat untouched before him. What was going on with him? It was no different than any other call they'd been on. The kid survived. With what appeared to be no ill-effects.

"Are you okay, Greyson?" Kat's voice broke the silence, and two pairs of bewildered eyes turned to her.

Slowly, Greyson raised his bloodshot gaze to meet hers. The torment in their depths made her heart bleed.

The chair's legs screeched across the tile as Kat kicked it back as she stood. "Let's take a walk." It wasn't a request. And it didn't matter that Jake and Kevin were watching them with wide, confused eyes. She had to soothe the pain evident on his face.

Greyson nodded and stood. "We'll be right back." He didn't wait for Kat as he marched from the room.

Kat glanced at the two guys still sitting at the table. There wasn't an eye on her. They just studied their lunch like it held the secret of life beneath the stew's thick chunks.

Her footsteps were quiet on the shiny tile as she approached Greyson, who stood at the end of the hallway and stared down at the street below through the window.

"Come on." Kat gently grasped his hand and led him towards the stairs.

"Kat, we shouldn't..." He started to pull his hand away.

She smiled and held tight. "Trust me." When they reached the engine bay, she grabbed her radio from her bunker gear and clipped it on to the waistband of her pants. "Just in case."

He reluctantly followed her out of the station and into the adjoining park. The scent of freshly cut grass was heavy in the warm afternoon air. They silently wandered around the playground, past the pond and under the shade of a grove of evergreens, just out of sight of the station.

Kat fumbled with words in her head before finally settling on: "What's going on, Greyson? Are you okay?"

"I'm fine." His tone was as distant as his gaze.

She caught his arm and pulled him to face her. "I'm serious. What's going on?"

His gaze finally lifted to hers, and her heart clenched at the sheen of tears in his eyes. "We almost lost him, Kat."

She nodded, swallowing the lump in her throat. "I know."

"No, I mean, he was dead. It was a sheer miracle that he came back to us. A three-fucking-year-old kid almost died on my watch." He kicked a rock, which skittered across the pond.

Kat watched him silently, contemplating the words to say to make everything okay. But there wasn't anything that could be said. He was right. They had almost lost the little boy. She settled for the words she kept telling herself since they left the scene. "But we didn't lose him."

"I know. But..." He swallowed hard, his Adam's apple bobbing. The emotions churning in his heart was evident on his strained features. He was blaming himself for almost losing him.

"It wasn't your fault."

He sighed. "I know."

Her eyes searched his. "I mean the one you couldn't save. It wasn't your fault."

His shocked gaze shot to hers. "How did you know about that?"

"Jake."

The breath left his chest in a giant whoosh. He leaned back against a tree and slid down, wrapping arms around his knees and hiding his face in them. "He shouldn't have."

"I asked."

He lifted his gaze to hers. "Why?"

"I wanted to know more about you. There's something about you. I just..." She shrugged. "Have you talked to anyone about it?"

He shook his head. "The crisis team said it would just take some time to come to terms with it." He sighed. "But I just keep putting myself in those parent's shoes. Keep thinking about how I would feel if I had lost a child. There is nothing I can do to bring their kid back. Nothing I can do to make it be okay. Their life is shattered. And it's my fault."

Kat blinked away the tears that sprung to her eyes as she watched this big, manly firefighter pouring his heart out to her. "I'm so sorry." A single tear trailed down her cheek. She didn't brush it away. "But you know, it wasn't your fault. We deal with people's lives on the line every single call. We're not going to be able to save everyone. You did the best you could."

He sucked in a deep breath, as if he had been holding it for a lifetime. "I know."

She held her hand out to help him up. He caught her hand, but instead of getting up, he pulled her down to straddle his hips.

"Greyson, what are you—" Kat gasped.

His caramel eyes bored into hers. All traces of tears in his eyes were erased, replaced by something unreadable in their chocolaty depths. "Thank you," he whispered.

Kat snorted. "For what? I didn't tell you anything you didn't already know."

"Just hearing it come from your lips somehow made it hit home."

She glanced at the tree, the grass, the ducks on the pond. Anything to keep from meeting his eyes. "Well, I'm glad I could help then."

Then his head was dipping towards hers, and she lost all sense of time and space. She could taste him on the air, and wanted nothing more than to help him forget, at least for a short time, the horrors of his past. As wrong as it was, her eyes fluttered closed and her body strained against his as she impatiently waited for his lips to meet hers. Her heart and mind warred against each other, guilt and desire battling for control.

Jakes voice crackled through the radio on her hip. "Sorry guys, we just got a call. Get to the station, STAT."

**

Kat brushed the crumbs off the threadbare couch before sitting on the edge of it. She sighed and looked around the cluttered living room. It was every bit the stereotypical bachelor pad, complete with empty beer bottles and pizza boxes. Outdated issues of Men's Health and Sports Illustrated were strewn across the coffee table. No wonder why they always ended up back at her place. Eric's place made her kind-of nauseous.

"Sorry about the mess, babe. I meant to clean up before you got here," Eric called from the pass-through window in the kitchen.

Kat nodded. Of course he did. He always meant to do it. He just never actually did it. Which went for a lot of things, including their relationship. But she really needed to talk to about what had happened on her shift. That was why she was there in the first place. The drowning call had really thrown her for a loop. She needed to clear the air between them, maybe get their relationship in a place to where she could comprehend why Greyson affected her so. Guilt tingled along her spine at the thought of Greyson's lips on hers, and how her heart missed a beat when he dipped his head towards hers at the park.

Eric sauntered out from the kitchen carrying a bottle of Moet and two glasses. And he had a single red rose clenched between his teeth.

A smile stretched across her face while guilt churned her stomach. For once he'd actually surprised her. "What's this?"

He grinned widely and cleared a spot on the cluttered coffee table before setting down the champagne. He pulled the rose from his mouth and handed it to her with a flourish. "It's an apology."

Kat couldn't help the giggle that escaped her as she accepted the sweet-smelling flower. "For what?"

She watched as he popped the cork on the bottle and poured two bubbling glasses full of the sparkling champagne. He handed her a glass and knocked a rumpled sweatshirt off the couch and sat beside her.

He studied her face with a somber expression. "For being such a shitty boyfriend."

Kat sighed. That was the understatement of the century.

He put a finger against her lips. "Let me show you how sorry I am." He leaned in and pressed his lips against hers. The kiss started off tentative, as if he expected her to push him away. She wanted to talk, but he was insistent on clearing the air between them first. At least in his eyes. She needed this, needed to remember the feel of being wrapped in his arms. The image of Greyson's face flashed before her eyes, but she quickly squashed it back into the corner of her mind.

He didn't break the kiss as he shifted off the couch and swung her up into his arms, carrying her with finesse toward his bedroom. He lowered her to the bed, breaking the kiss only long enough to pull his shirt off. Then he went to work on the buttons on her shirt. Somewhere on the edges of her desire-induced fog, a phone rang in the distance.

Kat frowned when Eric pulled away, the air-conditioned breeze rushing in to cool her desire. "Just let it go to voice mail." She reached for him to pull him back down to her lips.

Eric frowned and kissed her gently. "It'll only take a second."

And with that she was alone in his bed, her shirt half-open, her lips tingling with the memory of his kiss. The minutes ticked by, and Eric didn't return. His voice echoed down the short hallway, but she couldn't make out what he was saying. But he didn't sound happy.

She quickly slid off the bed and re-did her buttons as she tiptoed toward the hall.

His next words, in hushed tones, froze the blood in her veins. "You have no proof that I had anything to do with that." A pause. "Don't fucking threaten me." Another pause. "You need to leave me the hell alone. That was a one-time-mistake. Never. Happening. Again. Besides, I have a girlfriend now, remember?" He ended the call and slammed down the cell and Kat raced back to the bed.

A moment later Eric returned and leaned over to kiss her. "Sorry about that. Now, where were we?"

She let him kiss her for a moment, but his words rattled around in her head. That call couldn't have been about Amber's death. It couldn't. Could he have been involved in her death? A tingle of doubt skittered over Kat's skin and Eric touch felt like snakes slithering over her skin.

Kat pushed gently against his chest and tore her lips from his. She had to think of an excuse to get out of there. She had to have time to think away from his distracting caresses. "I have to go," she said apologetically and slid from underneath him. She didn't look back at him as she quickly made her way to the bathroom.

She turned the lock and flicked on the lights. Like the rest of his apartment, the bathroom was no less disgusting. After a minute, she flushed the toilet and turned on the water, splashing some over her face as she stared at her rumpled reflection in the mirror. Could he really have been involved with his ex-girlfriend's death? Her sweet, neglectful, loving boyfriend? His tortured expression when he knocked her over in the parking lot after Dave's funeral came to her mind. No. He was Eric. He was an incredible fireman. He saved lives. He didn't take them. There was no way her Eric could have been involved in something so horrible.

Satisfied with her conclusion, she smoothed her hair and wiped smeared mascara from under her eyes. She leaned on the counter to get a better look at herself in the mirror. Her hand brushed a tube of toothpaste which fell to the floor with a thunk.

Kat picked the toothpaste off the floor and opened the drawer to put it away. Crammed at the back under a discarded comb and razor refill cartridges, the little leather-bound book stood out in the chaos. Her hand shook as she reached for it.

She opened the cover of the book and read through the names and addresses. Kat smiled. It was just his address book, although who kept paper address books anymore? She flipped through the pages, absently noting the people she knew, and the people she didn't. She flipped to the next page. The book turned to a block of ice in her hand. A name was crossed out. Amanda Harris.

Kat jumped when a knock sounded at the door. "You okay?" Eric's concerned voice called through the wood.

Kat shoved the book in the back pocket of her jeans and quietly closed the drawer. She unlocked the door and stepped out to face Eric. He gazed at her with those clear blue eyes and her stomach flip-flopped. Could she really be gazing into the eyes of a killer?

"I have to go," Kat murmured.

Concern twisted his handsome features. "Are you sick?"

Kat nodded. It was the honest to God truth. She felt like she was going to throw up. She side stepped him and snatched up her discarded purse off the couch. The blood red rose lay crushed on the floor by the end table where his cell phone lay.

He caught up to her and wrapped her in his arms, laying a soft kiss on her lips. "Feel better, okay? Call me when you get home."

She nodded, unable to find her voice. She had to get some air. Now. She was in her truck and halfway down the street when the tears came.

9

Chapter Nine

The aftermath of a house fire is always the worst part of the job. It was like doing construction in hell. Ash fluttered around Kat as she ripped down pieces of drywall in the hallway. The smoldering shell of a house was a total loss, and while it was a tragedy for someone to lose everything they owned in a house fire, it was the body under the sheet in the smoldering bedroom that caused Kat's skin to crawl.

It was the fifth house fire in their jurisdiction they'd fought where a woman had been tied to the bed in the past month. The M.O. was the same. A woman in her mid-twenties, naked (as far as they could tell), tied spread eagle to her bed. The arson investigators had determined the source of the blaze was always in the bedroom, candles on the bedside table.

"God damn, what a mess," Eric grumbled beside her as he prodded the smoldering pile of what used to be a couch in the living room. Flames ignited and flared. He quickly extinguished it with his hose.

She pulled on a rafter with her bar and the teetering log crashed before her, ash billowing up around it. Flakes of ash drifted through the air like dirty snowflakes.

She couldn't hold her tongue any longer. "So... Who were talking to the other night?"

He glanced toward the bedroom for a moment, the movement so quick she would have missed it had she not been watching him intently.

"No one important." His axe chopped a charred side table with a resounding snap.

"Oh," Kat murmured. Her stomach churned.

"Is that why you left?"

"Maybe." She poked at a pile of ash in the corner. It wasn't the truth, but it was as close to the truth as he was going to get right now. At least until she knew his role in all this.

"I'm sorry, Kat. It really wasn't anything important. I'm sorry I answered it and ruined our night. Forgive me?" He shot her one of his killer "how can you be mad at this face" smiles. His ice-blue eyes sparkled at her, his soot-streaked dimples deepening with his grin.

She sighed. If only she could forget what she'd learned. She found six names in his book, all crossed out. All women. Who were these women and why had he crossed them out? Her call to arson hadn't been returned, but she had to know the other victim's names.

"You guys about done over there?" Greyson's smooth voice rattled from the radio, shaking her from her mental CSI trip.

Eric still studied her. She wondered if he could tell that her heart skipped a beat every time she heard Greyson's voice. She reached up to her radio and pushed the button. Her eyes held Eric's as she spoke into it. "Yep, just finishing up. Arson here?" Eric's eyes hardened. The look in his eyes sent a chill over her skin and she turned to rip down another piece of drywall.

Greyson's voice rattled through the radio again. "Yeah. They're waiting for the all-clear." His deep voice sent chills over her skin. Stupid Greyson. Why'd he have to incite such wicked responses in her body? She had no right to respond to him like she did.

"I'm done. Eric you good to go?" She glanced around. He was nowhere to be found.

"Yeah, be right there," Eric said from the bedroom. "Fuck! Did you see the victim?"

"What the hell are you doing?" Kat snapped her head around and found Eric standing over the charred corpse of the woman, the sheet lifted by one corner so he could see her face. "Put that down. You're going to botch the arson investigation!"

"No, I'm not. I just wanted to see how bad the damage was." He peeked under the sheet and tsk'ed. "Sad. Looks like she might have been pretty, too. What a waste." He shook his head and dropped the sheet back onto the body like it was contaminated.

"That's fucking sick, Eric."

"Sorry," he muttered and made his way back down the hallway.
**

Greyson watched Kat as she pushed her salad around her plate, her eyes glued on the unappetizing lettuce. Things had been weird between them for a few days now, ever since their kiss in the locker room. She seemed more withdrawn. Greyson shifted uncomfortably in the hard plastic chair and glanced at Eric, who picked at his own sandwich beside her. The nape of his neck tingled with the realization: had she told him about the kiss?

Better to face this shit head-on. He slammed his fork down on the table and glared at them. "What the fuck is going on with you two lately?"

Kat raised her dazed gaze to meet his and he flinched at the pain in their stormy depths.

Eric returned his glare. But neither responded.

"Listen, if you two have your panties in a bunch about what happened last week, let's just have it out here and now. All this sulking is ridiculous."

Kat's eyes widened with fear and she sucked in a startled breath. Shit. Maybe she *hadn't* told Eric after all.

Eric's face screwed up in confusion. "What the fuck are you talking about?"

"Uh," Greyson fumbled to think of something that happened last week that he could use as an excuse, but came up blank.

He let out a relieved breath when Eve's familiar voice called out from across the sandwich shop. "Hey guys!"

"Hey!" Greyson said with a bit too much enthusiasm.

Eve and Chris slid into the table next to Kevin and Jake. "What are you slackers up to today?" she asked and took a bite of her sandwich.

"Shenanigans and debauchery. You know, the usual," Greyson replied.

Eve grinned. "You're so lame."

Greyson sighed and hung his head exaggeratedly. "I know."

Eric pushed his chair back and got up. "Looks like the other guys are ready to leave." He nodded toward the rest of the guys from station two, who were clearing off their table.

Eve sighed. "Bye, Eric. Call me later, m'kay?" She winked. She actually winked.

Greyson glanced at Kat, but she hadn't noticed. She was staring out the window behind him with a blank expression on her face.

Eric glared at Eve, his jaw clenched tightly. Greyson could almost hear Eric's teeth grinding. "Really, Eve? That's pretty tacky, hitting on me with my girlfriend sitting right next to me."

Again, Kat doesn't even notice.

Eve smirked. "She seems like she's preoccupied with somebody else anyway." She inclined her head towards Greyson.

"Fuck off, Eve," Eric snapped.

Now *that* got Kat's attention. Like a sharpshooter, her gaze shot flitted from Eric's to Eve's and back again. Confusion and something else washed over her features as she studied him.

"Sorry," he mouthed and leaned down to kiss her. "I'll call you later."

Kat nodded and lifted her cheek to receive his kiss, her gaze finally catching Greyson's as his lips brushed her cheek. He shot another glare at Eve before disappearing out the door after the rest of his crew.

A moment later Eve's radio crackled to life. "Paramedic 8 please respond to 180 E Chandler Boulevard for medical aid."

Eve murmured "Paramedic 8 to medical aid" into her radio. They stuffed their lunches back into a bag and raced out of the restaurant.

Kevin got up to dump their trash while Jake headed toward the iced tea dispenser.

Kat let out a sigh like she hadn't taken a breath since Eric sat down beside her.

Greyson frowned. "Is everything okay?"

She brought her gaze to his. She looked exhausted. "I can't talk about it."

He took her hand in his. "You know you can talk to me, right? If you're upset about what happened between us –"

She pulled her hand from his like he'd burned her. "It's not about that."

He waited for her to continue.

She shook her head. "He's your brother. You're better off not knowing."

Suspicion and anger tingled through his blood. What had Eric done to her? But the pain and fear in her eyes stopped him from pushing the subject. For now.

10

Chapter Ten

"Fiah tuck!" The toddler squealed as Greyson hoisted him into the truck. He pointed to the controls, explaining what each of them did in kid-friendly terms. "Siwens!" The boy squealed.

"He loves fire trucks, especially since his dad left." The little boy's mom made sure to emphasize the word *left*.

He absently half-smiled at her and focused his attention on the kid. "You want to be a firefighter when you grow up?"

The little boy nodded. "Like daddy!"

"Oh, your daddy is a firefighter?"

The kid nodded his red head again.

"Well here, this'll help you get started, then." Greyson grinned and reached behind the seat and pulled out a CFD badge sticker and a little plastic fire helmet. "Now you're a Junior firefighter!"

The little boy stared at the hat in amazement. "Thannnk youuuu!"

Kat grinned and leaned against the side of the truck beside Kevin. "He's great with the kids, huh?"

Kevin snorted.

Greyson's voice filtered down from the cab, and soon Kat had a hard time paying attention to anything but his voice. "Sorry, ma'am, but it's against the rules. I am flattered, though."

The mom pouted as she helped her son down. "Well here's my number if you change your mind."

Kat stifled the giggle when the desperate housewife handed her phone number to him. Greyson smiled uncomfortably and handed the card back. "Sorry, ma'am, I really can't."

She frowned, which made her overly-tanned face wrinkle like leather left out in the sun too long. "Your loss." With that she ushered her toddler to their waiting SUV.

Kevin nodded towards her retreating form as Greyson stepped down from the rig. "Damn, Greyson. You could have tapped that ass."

"Not my type." Greyson closed the cab door and walked towards the Randall's entrance. "Coming?" he called over his shoulder.

After some debate and a little more searching, they made their way to the registers with enough food to feed a small army. Or, a shift of hungry firefighters.

"Hey guys!" The perky cashier said. Her sandy blonde hair was piled in a bun on top of her head, sprays of hair falling around her freshly washed face. Her hazel eyes locked on Greyson like a heat seeking missile. "Looks like you guys are having a party at the firehouse today!"

"Nah, just feeding a handful of hungry firefighters." Greyson smiled and handed over the cash while Kat, Kevin and Jake bagged the groceries.

"Sounds like fun. Wish I could come!" She blushed and handed the change to him.

Greyson's eyes dropped to her hand that lingered on his as he took the change. "Uh, thanks." He pocketed the change and grabbed the bags from Kat.

"I've got them..." Kat snapped and snatched the bags back. She hadn't missed the flirtatious looks the jailbait cashier was shooting at him. She swallowed hard to fight the jealousy that bubbled to the surface. If women threw themselves at him, there was nothing she could do about it. Besides, he wasn't hers to be jealous for.

He raised an eyebrow at her and then shrugged. "Okay."

Miraculously, they managed to not get a call for a few hours, which meant an uncharacteristically uninterrupted lunch followed by some outside physical activity and team building, which meant flag football at the local park with station two.

Kat's skin tingled at the thought of having to spend more time with Eric. Until arson called back and gave her the names of the other victims, she couldn't abate the tingle of suspicion every time she saw him.

Kat pushed the terrifying thought to the back of her mind and fought a smile as she watched Greyson's tanned, muscled legs pump as he tore across the field, his long legs taking up huge expanses of grass in a single bound, the football tucked securely under his arm like a baby. She shoved against Flores and tried to dart around him to complete the play. His meaty hands clamped onto her hips.

Kat jumped back and glared at him. "What the hell was that?"

Flores held his hands up innocently. "Sorry. Forgot we were playing flag and not full-contact." His eyes told a different story.

Her eyes narrowed and her jaw clenched. "Don't let it happen again."

A slight smile twitched across his face. "Yes, sir."

During the brief moment that the exchange occurred, Greyson lost his flag.

His angry strides ate up the grass as he marched up to them. "What happened there, Kat?"

Kat glared at Flores for a moment before turning her attention to Greyson. The frightened look in Flores' face was priceless. He thought she'd tell Greyson about the little incident. Little did he know she fought her own battles.

"Nothing. Sorry," Kat snapped.

"Okaaay." Greyson's gaze darted from Kat's face to Flores' like he knew something was up.

"C'mon. Let's kick their asses already," Kat snarled.

"You can kick my ass any day, Hale," Flores mumbled under his breath as he walked away.

Out of nowhere, Eric shoved between them. "Excuse me, what did you say?"

"Uh, nothing, man," Flores stammered.

"You touch my girlfriend again and you're a dead man, Flores." Kat's skin tingled at Eric's choice of words.

She shoved between them and pulled Eric's face to look at her. "He's not worth it, Eric. Let it go."

Eric nodded and marched away, shrugging off Martinez when he tried to console him.

Flores purred in her ear. "For playing in the boys club, you sure do let the boys fight your battles for you."

Kat paused mid-stride, then shook it off and marched away. Like she told Eric, he wasn't worth it. She wouldn't give him the satisfaction of a response.

They huddled and came up with a play to win the game. Jake, who was playing quarterback, would pass to Greyson. Kevin would play interference while Greyson went the distance. If he ran into trouble, he'd pass off to Kat.

Kat hiked the ball to Jake and then made a mad dash down the field. Flores tried to keep pace, but his thicker limbs didn't give him the speed advantage that Kat had. Kevin blocked two of the other company's guys while Greyson raced around them towards Kat. Eric raced after Greyson. But rather than snatching the flag – which was in easy reach of Eric's hand – he tackled Greyson to the ground.

Kat caught up with them as Greyson shoved Eric off his chest.

"What the hell, Eric!" Greyson growled and brushed the grass off his t-shirt and station shorts.

"Sorry," Eric grunted.

Kat wasn't the only one that noticed the smug smile plastered across Eric's face.

Before she could blink, Greyson was in Eric's face. "You got a problem with me, little brother?"

Eric butted his chest against Greyson's. "Actually, I do!"

"Well fucking spit it out and quit acting like a spoiled little kid."

"Me? Acting like a kid? You're the one being childish. She's *mine*,

d as she tried to shove between them. "Wait just a

son's face was mere inches from Eric's. "You're *so*

huh?"

nd. Mine. Do I need to put a ring on her finger to

d. "Like she needs to be married to an asshole fire-

re about the job than her!"

Kat barely dove out of the way in time to avoid Eric as he lunged for Greyson. The pair rolled across the grass, exchanging blows, the gut-wrenching thumps as their fists connected with each other's bodies echoing out across the park. Kat watched, unsure if it was that she was unable or unwilling to stop them.

Jake and Eric's captain dove into the fight, each muscling a bruised and bleeding brother into their arms. "That's enough, guys!" Jake bellowed.

Kevin shoved between Eric and Greyson, putting a hand on each brother's chest. They struggled against their captain's restraining arms, eager to get back to beating the shit out of each other. "Take it easy, guys!"

"No! I'm fed up with him constantly trying to weasel his way in between Kat and me. *She's mine!*" Eric shoved against Kevin's hand.

That was it. Kat had heard enough. She marched in between them, nudging Kevin out of the way with her hip. "This is fucking ridiculous, Eric. Greyson is not trying to steal me from you. If anyone should be jealous, it sure as hell isn't you! You should be more worried about what *you* are doing to push me away than anything Greyson is doing to get between us!"

Pain flitted across Eric's features. "I'm sorry –"

"Save it. You should be apologizing to your brother. Your *brother*, Eric. Blood is thicker than water. Act like it!"

"I don't want to apologize. I want to knock his teeth out." Eric lunged at Greyson again, practically breaking free of his captain's hold, were it not for Kevin jumping in again and putting two restraining hands on Eric's chest.

Kat's blood hummed with adrenaline. She was ready to call both of them assholes and leave the whole dirty mess, but the sight of the diamond-studded class ring on Kevin's right hand braced against Eric's chest made her pause. She took a tentative step towards him, intent on inspecting the ring. Her breath caught in her throat at the tiny hole where a stone was missing.

Anger and betrayal welled up inside of her. Was there anybody she could trust? "Let them go. If they want to kill each other, go for it. I'll be waiting in the truck." Kat marched off without a backwards glance.

**

Her bag came down with a thump on the coffee table as Kat barreled into the house. The phone rang one last shriek then went silent, just as she reached for the phone. Kat sighed and looked at the caller id. The number was local, but she didn't recognize the name. She picked up the phone and dialed her voice mail.

Kat rifled through her bills as she absently listened to the three messages. Two were her mom, fifteen minutes apart. Both wanting to know if she was alive and why she hadn't returned her calls. Kat hit the button to delete the messages.

The final message she assumed was another from her mom. Her fingertip hovered over the delete button until she heard an unfamiliar voice come over the speaker.

"Miss Hale, this is Paul Anderson of the Chandler Fire Department Arson Unit. You called with some questions about the victims of the recent arson investigations. While normally I can't give information like that out, considering you were on the crews that worked the fires, I believe I can give this information without breaking any rules."

Kat frantically dug Eric's black book out of her bag and flipped to the pages with the crossed out names. She held her breath as Mr. Anderson said the first name: Melissa Tovrea. Kat's eyes scanned the list. Her fingers felt like ice when she found the name. Like Amanda, her name had been crossed out. Kat gasped, unable to catch her breath. Two. She barely heard the rest of the names as he rattled them off. But there they were, each crossed out in blood red ink.

Tears burned Kat's eyes as the reality hit her. Her boyfriend, the guy who she at one time had seen herself spending the rest of her life with, was a murderer. "No," she gasped. It couldn't be. It couldn't be.

He was exceptional at his job as a firefighter. He took an oath to protect life. Not to take it. His handsome face flashed before her, his ice blue eyes pleading. Was this really the face of a killer?

Kat nearly dropped the phone when it rang to life in her hand. She didn't even look at the caller id screen to see who it was. She held it up to her ear.

"Yes?"

"Hey, sweetheart."

Her blood chilled. "Eric."

"You're still mad, huh?"

Kat blanked. Mad? She just found out her boyfriend was likely a murderer. Mad didn't even begin to cover it. She squeaked out something unintelligible.

"I understand. I shouldn't let Greyson come between us. Can we meet to talk about this?"

Kat nodded, unable to find her voice.

"Hello, Kat?"

"Sure." Her voice sounded ragged.

"Good. I'll be over in a few."

That snapped her out of her fog. "No!"

"Um, okay?"

She cleared her throat and tried to calm her galloping heart. "I'll come to your place."

She could hear the frown in his voice. "Okay, I'll see you in a few. I love you."

"Uh huh." Kat hit the end button and dropped the phone on the counter. What the fuck was she doing? She should call the police and let them take care of it.

But deep down, she still loved him. She couldn't do that without giving him a chance to tell her something that would somehow explain what was going on. Even with the evidence in her hands, she couldn't bring herself to believe it. She'd given him over six months of her life, and her heart as well. Tears burned in her eyes. Could it be true that she really didn't know him at all, the entire time they were together?

The drive to Eric's apartment took forever. Not because he lived so far away from her, but because she turned around. Twice. Both times she talked herself into turning back around and facing this head-on. No matter what happened, she had to do this.

Eric met her at the door and pulled her into his arms. Kat shrugged out of his embrace and marched into his apartment, determined not to let his charm distract her from her mission: to find out the truth. She gasped at the smell of pine sol and firewood. His apartment was spotless. He'd even lit a fire in the fire place. A dozen roses lay on his highly polished coffee table.

"Wow," Kat murmured. He'd done this for her.

"Thought I should start acting more like a grown up and less like a spoiled, selfish bachelor."

"Eric, about that..."

Eric shushed her and led her to the couch. He handed her the bouquet. The sweet scent drifted over her and she closed her eyes to savor it.

She felt him push her hair back from her face, and she fought the urge to open her eyes and look at him. He was so good at making her melt into a pool at his feet when he turned on the charm. Which was probably why he managed to hold on to her. She just couldn't resist him.

Her eyes fluttered open when he pressed his lips to hers. She pulled back and scooted away on the couch.

"Please don't, Eric. We need to talk."

He nodded with a disappointed look on his face. "If this is about what happened between me and Greyson, I promise it'll never happen again. Look." He reached into his pocket, but she put her hand on his, stopping his movement.

She shook her head. "It's not about that." She reached into her bag and pulled out the little black book and handed it to him, her eyes searching his as realization dawned on his face.

"What? Where did you --" Confusion flitted across his face as she watched him mentally search his apartment for where he had kept it. Realization dawned on his face, and his eyes hardened as he stared at the tiny leather-bound book in her hand. He grumbled under his breath and scrubbed a hand through his spikey hair. "Listen, I can explain that."

Kat waited for him to continue.

"I've had that since high school. It doesn't mean anything. I should have gotten rid of that thing a long time ago." He reached for the book, but she avoided his grasp.

"Why are there names crossed out?"

He frowned and studied her. Then he shrugged. "They're ex-girl-friends, Kat. They don't mean anything to me. That's why they're crossed out."

Kat waited for him to continue, to give her some indication that he wasn't involved in those girl's murders. Hope inflated in her when he started to speak.

"Is that why you've been so weird lately? Because you're jealous?" He shook his head in a frustrated gesture and then took her hands in his, the book clenched between them. "They don't mean anything to me, Kat. If it will make you feel better, I'll get rid of it."

Kat frowned. That wasn't how this conversation was supposed to go. He was supposed to say how he had nothing to do with their deaths. Not accuse her of being jealous. "It's not that, Eric."

He snatched the book from her hand and tossed it into the fireplace. "There. Gone. See? They mean nothing to me. You are the only thing that matters to me, Kat."

Kat gasped as she watched the book sail through the air and land in the flames. The book quickly caught fire and Kat watched in horror as the only piece of evidence she had of Eric's possible involvement in the murders went up in flames.

Eric pulled her to face him. "I love you, Kat. Only you. Forever." He leaned in and pressed his lips to hers. Tears burned her eyes as the words she longed to hear from him finally came from his lips. But it was too late. Without breaking the kiss she felt him shift to kneeling on the floor before her.

She pulled away and watched in horror as he pulled a box from his pocket. "Eric, don't."

He held out the box to her, a hopeful look on his face. "Marry me, Kat."

Kat shot up from the couch, practically knocking him over in the process. She couldn't breathe. It wasn't supposed to happen this way. Not this way. It was too late. "I can't see you anymore, Eric."

Tears burned her eyes and blurred her vision as she raced for the door. The picture of Eric standing in his doorway, watching her with a heartbroken expression on his face burned into her brain as she tore from the parking lot.

11

Chapter Eleven

Kat bent and dunked the brush into the bucket of sudsy water and sloshed it onto the side of the rig, rubbing in wide swirling motions. The suds ran down the side and pooled onto the asphalt. Sweat trickled into her eyes as the scorching Arizona sun beat down on her. She wiped it away from her face with the back of her hand.

She tried not to think about Eric. She had to let him go. She couldn't turn him in. She had no proof. Eric had burned the only evidence she had that he was connected with the murders. But she couldn't forget that each of the girls in that book that had been crossed out were his ex-girlfriends. Now that she was in that category, could she be next?

And to complicate matters, Greyson seemed to be completely in the dark of his brother's actions. She caught a glimpse of him out of the corner of her eye. How could he be related to a potentially cold-blooded killer?

She wiped the sweat from her brow again. Normally she didn't mind washing the rig, but it was so hot she decided to try a new tactic to speed up the truck-washing process. She picked up the bucket of soapy water and splashed it onto the side of the rig. She squealed as it splashed back at her, dousing her from head-to-toe in bubbly white soap suds. Her soaked t-shirt and shorts clung to her body.

She spun around at a chuckle that came from behind her. Greyson stood shirtless before her, his tanned, muscled chest and abs standing out in definition. He looked like he belonged on the cover of surfer boy weekly rather than standing in front of her with a hose and a bucket in hand.

"The hose probably would have been better for that, although I like the result." His eyes blazed as they raked over her wet t-shirt clad breasts. Her nipples beaded against the damp material under his gaze. "Here." He handed the hose to her.

"Thanks." Kat reached to take the hose from him. His hand closed over hers on the nozzle and he hesitated. His eyes locked with hers. She worried against her bottom lip with her teeth when his eyes dropped to her mouth. "Greyson, don't..."

"Kat..." he murmured, his voice thick. His eyes narrowed and his lips parted. Her breath caught as he lowered his lips towards hers.

She turned her head to the side and spoke. "I broke up with Eric yesterday."

Greyson's face lit up, but he nodded solemnly. "I'm sorry."

Her surprised gaze shot back to his, his face just a breath away. "No, you're not."

He half-chuckled. "You're right, I'm not."

Kat sighed and took a step back. "There's something I haven't told you about Eric, Greyson."

He held up a hand, effectively stopping her words. "Don't. Don't talk about my brother. I don't care. I don't want to hear his name right now." Greyson crammed one big hand through his tousled hair. His mouth was set in a grim line.

Frustration welled through her body. She wanted to throw something at him, scream at him to listen to her. So she used the only weapon she had and turned the hose full-force on him.

"What the f..." he choked out. He tried to shield himself from the spray with his hands, which ricocheted some back towards her. She turned her head to avoid getting hit in the face with the overspray but kept up the attack. That'd teach him to brush her off when she was trying to tell him something important.

The surprise on his face brought on a bout of laughter that brought tears to her eyes. But she couldn't drop the attack or she'd be in for it.

"Stop that!" he growled and lunged for her.

She ducked to the side and swung the nozzle of the hose back in his direction. She couldn't help the girlish giggle that escaped her lips.

"Kat!" He dove for her again.

Her heel connected with the curb behind her and she lost her balance. His thick arms wrapped around her waist as they tumbled onto the grass.

Kat laughed and tried to roll away. But his arms stayed firmly planted around her body, his face a few inches away. His hot breath puffed against her lips.

"That wasn't very nice Kat." The rumble of his deep voice vibrated against her body, which was pressed against his hard form.

"You deserved it." She tried to wriggle free, but the friction of her body against his only succeeded in making an ache deep in the pit of her stomach flare.

"Did I?" He smiled a mischievous half-smile. His chocolate eyes darkened.

"Yes." Her heartbeat quickened at the way he watched her tongue dart out of her mouth to wet her lips.

"Well you deserve this..." He lowered his lips to hers.

Kat opened her mouth to protest when his lips touched hers. But the heat simmering deep in her body roared to life. His lips were soft against hers and she could feel the hesitation behind his actions.

God. She'd secretly wanted this since that day in the locker room. And now that she was free, there was nothing to stop her except the whole career jeopardy thing. And that niggling issue that her ex-boyfriend might be a cold-blooded murderer. But for the moment, she gave herself over to his kiss and the desire clouding her judgment.

She wrapped her arms around his neck and buried her hands in his thick, dark hair. The hesitation shifted to fierceness as he devoured her with his lips, tugging and tasting her. His tongue prodded against her lips and she opened them, willingly accepting the invasion of his tongue and fighting back with her own.

His hands traveled over her body, trailing over her ribcage, lightly tracing over her breasts, up to her collarbone to cup her face between his warm palms. A growl of satisfaction rumbled deep in his chest when she slid her hands to his shoulders and dug her nails into the hard flesh.

Kat gasped against his lips as he slid one hand down and firmly cupped her breast. It strained against his hand, the nipple pebbling beneath his touch. Her body ached for him to touch every part of her. She clutched at his shoulders and arched against his hand.

The echo of footsteps in the engine bay broke through the fog that his kiss and touch had immersed her in. A groan emitted from his lips and he pulled away, standing up quickly and pulling her with him. She swayed on her feet and tried desperately to catch her breath. He smoothed back his hair with one hand. Kat attempted to straighten her soaked shirt. God only knew what she looked like right now.

The lightly scattered gray hair on the top of Chief Phillip's balding head emerged above the battalion command truck. He rounded the bumper and closed in on them with long, determined strides.

Oh, God. Had he seen them making out in plain daylight on the grass in front of the station? Had some innocent bystander witnessed their PDA and called the Chief? Her blood pounded in her ears. This is it. The determination on his face made her stomach flutter.

No! He can't fire me! I've worked too hard, given up everything else that matters to me to be here. I'm not going down without a knock-down, drag-out, bloody fight.

"Hale!" Chief Phillips' his dark eyebrows furrowed as he approached.

"Sir?" Kat closed the distance between them. She always met challenges head on. This would be no different.

"I've got a bone to pick with you, Hale." He stopped a few feet away from her, his feet spread shoulder width apart, at military ease. His background as a Navy firefighter never left him and he commanded himself, and his battalion, like they were in the military. And he always treated her exactly the same as any male in his command. She respected him for that. Since the day she and her brother had been pulled from the fire that devoured their tiny three-bedroom house by firefighter Phillips from station three, she knew she wanted to be a firefighter just like him.

"Yes, sir?"

"What the hell were you doing out there this morning? I got six reports from bystanders commending me on the courageousness of my crew at the scene, specifically the female firefighter." One corner of his mouth turned up slightly.

Kat blanked. She'd expected him to reprimand her, fire her even, for making out with Greyson. Turns out he didn't even see.

"Huh?" she asked stupidly.

"The car accident this morning, Hale. The rescue from the overturned car with the two small children trapped in the back seat?" The smile he was fighting won and took over his entire face.

"I was just doing my duty sir, any one of us would have done the same." Well maybe not exactly the same – she had taken the loose interpretation to 'protocol' when she scaled the vehicle and pulled the two little ones to safety.

"Not quite, Hale. You didn't follow standard protocol. While you rescued the kids before the car burst into flames, you could have gotten yourself killed. Next time, follow proper safety precautions upon arriving at the scene, or I'll be forced to put you on administrative leave." His words may have been sharp, but the smile in his eyes still remained. He'd become like a protective father to her. He said these things because he had to, not because he wanted to.

"Yes, Sir. Thank you, Sir, for giving me another chance."

"Dismissed," Chief Phillips said.

Kat spun on her heel and grabbed her bucket and hose.

"Oh, and Hale?"

"Yes, Sir?" Kat stopped mid-stride.

"Great job out there today. Your quick thinking saved the lives of two little kids. Their family contacted us and wants to meet you to thank you personally."

Kat's cheeks flamed. Chief Phillips never handed out praise, even to his favorite firefighters.

"Thank you, Sir."

He nodded and went back into the station. Kat turned and picked up the bucket.

Greyson stood next to the rig, a scowl marring his beautiful face. Kat's stomach fluttered. She turned on the hose and sprayed the side of the rig.

"I'm sorry." She focused on the suds as it ran down the side of the truck.

"I'm not." He closed the distance between them, turned her and pushed her up against the wet truck and crushed her lips with his. Water soaked into her clothes and ran down her legs. She braced her hands against his chiseled chest, his hot skin soft like velvet beneath her touch, yet his muscles hard like stone. He began to pull away.

Kat wrapped a hand around the nape of his neck and pulled him closer. Her heart pounded at the chance that they could be caught. How would they explain why he had her pushed up against the rig, wrapped in his arms, her lips swollen from his kiss?

She didn't care. She sucked his lip into her mouth and bit gently. He growled and shifted her towards the step up and slid his hand down her thigh. With a sharp motion he hooked his hand beneath her knee and lifted it up around his hips. Kat groaned when his hard shaft prodded at her from beneath his shorts. Were they not clothed, he'd already be buried deep inside her.

She wrenched her lips away from his scorching kiss.

"Greyson, stop." The words escaped her lips, but her heart and body screamed "keep going". Her body ached where his hardness pressed against her.

He sucked in a ragged breath and nuzzled her neck, planting soft kisses along her collarbone.

"We can't do this, not here." Kat pushed against his chest. His skin burned where her hands touched, and she wanted nothing more than to explore every inch of his naked flesh, to see if the rest of him was the same combination of soft and hard.

"I know," he sighed.

Kat sat down on the step and tried to slow her frantic heart. She clenched her thighs to try to abate the ache that built there, but it only made it worse.

"Shift change is in a few hours..." Greyson murmured.

"And then what?" Kat glanced up at him through the curtain of her dark eyelashes.

His grin made her heart clench. "I'm taking you on a date."

"I'll have to check my schedule." Kat fought a smile.

"Whatever you've got scheduled will have to wait." He took a step towards her.

"Okay, okay!" Kat held up her hands to fend him off. "You know this is an *extremely* bad idea right?"

"I know. I don't care. But I'm going to go crazy if I can't do that again." His eyes smoldered as he gazed down at her, causing the ache between her thighs to intensify.

Kat bit her lip.

"Chow's on!" Jake called from the doorway to the station.

Her stomach lurched. "Right there!" she called back.

Greyson's eyes searched hers, a wide smile on his heart-wrenchingly beautiful face. She stood on her tiptoes and planted a soft kiss on his lips. Then she turned and ran for the station door, her heart soaring ahead of her.

12

Chapter Twelve

Greyson had taken three bites of his sandwich when the alarms sounded. They were on-scene within a minute, since the scene was just down the street from the station. Greyson angled the truck in front of the four cars blocking the intersection. Kat grabbed the medical kit and approached the man sitting on the ground clutching his chest.

He surveyed the scene. Pretty severe damage to the four vehicles, but the worst injury was probably some broken bones and whiplash. But the man with chest pains on the ground was worrisome.

Engine 288 and Medic 8 pulled up a moment later. The crews descended on the scene, checking vital signs of everyone involved. Eve crouched beside Kat and surveyed the elderly man. Within seconds, she had him loaded up in her ambulance and was racing toward the hospital down the road.

Eric bumped shoulders with Greyson as they passed on the way back to their trucks to reload their gear. "You still pissed about the other day?"

Greyson shook his head. "Nope."

"Good."

"Kat told me." Greyson murmured as he made his way back to the cab to stow his gear.

Eric's hand snatched out and grabbed ahold of Greyson's shirt as he passed. "Told you what?"

He paused long enough to disengage Eric's clenched fingers from his shirt. "That you two broke up."

Eric's face twisted in pain. Greyson felt a momentary twinge of regret for hurting his brother, but he quickly pushed it back. "You didn't deserve her. It was only a matter of time before she sent you packing anyway."

Eric scowled. "How many times do I have to tell you our relationship is none of your business?"

"You don't have a relationship anymore." Against his will, a proud grin stretched across Greyson's face. "And it's my business now."

"What the fuck is that supposed to mean?"

"I'm taking Kat out tonight."

The air gushed from Eric's chest like Greyson had physically punched him. "No."

"Believe it, little brother. You had your chance to be with the most amazing woman in the world. And you fucked it up. Now you get to step aside and watch how a real man does it."

"You hurt her and I'll rip your heart out," Eric growled.

"*You* are telling this to *me*? You already hurt her. If anybody should be getting his heart ripped out, it's *you*. That girl loved you and you couldn't get your head out of your ass long enough to realize how good you had it. And now you've lost her."

Eric just stared at him like he had reached into his chest and was holding his bleeding heart in his hand. Greyson swallowed the lump that grew in his throat at the sight of his brother in pain. The last thing he wanted to do was cause him pain. But Eric was a grown man and had to take care of his own messes. "I'm sorry if this hurts you, Eric. But I can't stay away from her anymore." With that he climbed into the driver's seat on L-281 and slammed the door, unable to turn to watch his brother emotionally implode.

**

A handful of medical calls and car accidents took up the rest of the shift, and before Kat knew it they were back at the firehouse and she was packing up her stuff to leave for the day. She bit back a smile as she pulled her purse out of her locker and slammed it closed. Her stomach fluttered at the thought of what tonight held in store for her.

She couldn't help but consider what it would be like going out with Greyson since the moment she was assigned to his shift at station three. Now it was becoming a reality. If she were wise, she wouldn't allow it to become a reality.

If someone found out, they could both be terminated, and at a minimum one would get transferred to another shift, if not another station entirely. And if Eric found out, it could destroy whatever was left of his humanity.

Door hinges creaked as someone came into the locker room.

"Hey, Kat!" Eric said as she turned to face him. His eyes sparkled and he had a wide grin plastered on his too-handsome face.

"What are you doing here, Eric?" She slung her Coach purse over her shoulder and marched for the exit. Suspicion tingled over her skin.

"What are you doing tonight?" He stumbled to match Kat's pace as she raced from the locker room and towards the stairs.

"Does it matter? We broke up, or don't you remember that?" She stomped down the stairs.

He kept pace with her as she rushed down the stairs and out to the parking lot. "I was hoping we could talk about it. I love you, Kat." The remorse on his handsome face made her heart hurt. But he was a liar, and potentially a murderer.

"I'm sorry, Eric. I just can't do this anymore." She yanked open her truck's door and tossed her purse on the passenger seat.

His shoulders slumped, the twinkle in his eye dulled, the corners of his mouth turned down. "Please, Kat." Eric braced his hands either side of her on the open door and on the car body.

She shook her head, tears filling her eyes. "No, Eric. Please, just let me go." With that she heaved herself into the cab and yanked the door from his hand, slamming it shut before him.

With a heartbroken look on his way-too-handsome face, Eric nodded and walked around to the driver's side door of his car. A second later he peeled out of the parking lot, leaving a little puff of burnt tire smoke in his wake.

Kat sighed as the familiar scent of cherry air freshener and new car plastic overwhelmed her senses. She slipped the key into the ignition and smiled when it purred to life in her hands. She carefully pulled out of her spot and eased onto the road and headed for her house.

She hadn't hit the first light when her phone vibrated on the seat beside her. She looked at the screen and her heart flip-flopped. It was Greyson.

She tapped the screen. "Hello?"

"Hey Kat, you left yet?" Greyson's smooth voice came through the speakerphone.

"Yeah, just pulled out of the lot." The clicking of her turn signal matched the frantic pounding of her heart. "Eric was here. He wanted to talk things out."

Silence.

"Hello?" Kat asked, half afraid that he'd hung up on her.

"I'm here. Did you talk to him?"

"I told him to let me go."

Another pause. "That had to be hard, I'm sorry."

"It was. But anyway, I'm on my way home now."

"I just got into the car. Jake caught me to discuss something."

"Oh, well have a safe drive home." *Maybe he forgot about the whole date thing.*

"Thanks. So what time do you want me to pick you up?"

Her skin tingled. "Pick me up for what?"

"Our date, silly. Don't pretend that you haven't thought about that kiss for the past four hours." His voice somehow managed to smolder even through the crackle of the cell phone speaker.

"I have thought about it, and I really don't think that going out on a date is such a good idea…" Her brain screamed it was the right thing to do, but her heart lurched in protest.

"I know. It's crazy and wrong and we'll probably both regret it, but we'll never know unless we give it a shot right?"

"I guess you're right."

He chuckled. "Of course I am."

She stiffened. It was like Eric all over again. Telling her what to do, when to do it, without giving her any say in the matter.

"No. Really. We shouldn't go out tonight," she ground out through clenched teeth.

"Please, Kat?" he pleaded.

The ice that had started to frost over her heart at the thought of Eric melted into a pool in her lap at Greyson's plea. "Fine."

"Thank God. I'll come and get you at eight?" he asked, almost tentatively.

"Yeah, that works." *This was such a bad idea…*

"Um, Kat?"

"Yeah?"

"I don't know where you live…"

Kat laughed and gave him directions to her house.

13

Chapter Thirteen

The drive home felt like it took hours. By the time Kat pulled up in front of the house, she only had an hour to get ready before Greyson picked her up.

She turned off the alarm and Diesel, her beloved boxer, jumped excitedly around her, but she didn't have time to stop to greet him. She scratched his ears for a moment before she dashed through her cozy one-bedroom cottage, shedding her clothes as she ran to the bathroom. A quick shower, blow dry, mascara, blush and some tinted gloss and she was almost ready to go. Except for her clothes. She stood before her gaping, yet disappointing closet in the sexiest bra and panties she owned. She didn't have much to choose from. But the red and black pin-stripe material with a red ribbon cinching up the sides of the boy-short panties to little bows actually weren't bad. The majority of her underwear was purchased for practicality, what would be most comfortable under her bunker gear. Thongs were about as sexy as she got.

Kat sighed and surveyed the pitiful selection of her closet. The problem with dating another firefighter was that he's seen her at her worst: hot, sweaty and covered head-to-toe in ash. And he liked it that way. So she never found it necessary to dress up all girly for dates with him. Besides, he never really took her anywhere that required a dress code nicer than a t-shirt and jeans.

She definitely needed to go clothes shopping on her next night off. There wasn't much to choose from. The red silk blouse with a pair of low-slung jeans and strappy sandals? No too teenager-on-a-date-ish. The light blue sundress? No, too springy. She flipped hanger after hanger, her touch increasingly rough as she slammed the hangers of black and navy blue aside.

"Aaaah!" Kat shouted in fury at her closet. She whipped around and plopped on the bed with an oomph and buried her hands in her tousled hair. The wisps of smoke from the vanilla candle on her dresser danced and swirled in the fading light.

What the hell was she supposed to do? She took in a few calming breaths and approached the closet again. The red silk blouse and jeans would have to do.

She reached for the silky red shirt and brushed something soft hanging amongst a nest of black shirts. The material was different than the utilitarian cotton blend shirts. She cocked her head to the side and parted the black masses. There it was, on a black plastic hanger like the rest of her clothes.

She'd bought the dress the day Eric hinted to taking her to a romantic dinner at a nice restaurant that night. Which was *so* not like Eric. They'd dated for six months, and they'd talked about getting married a handful of times, even if only in the hypothetical sense. So it was completely reasonable to think that he was going to propose. Which was why she went out and splurged on the silky little black dress in her hands -- because she refused to be proposed to while wearing a t-shirt and jeans. Damn him for finally proposing, but only after finding out that he might in fact be a murderer.

Kat pulled the black plastic hanger out of the closet and turned it back and forth. It was a gorgeous dress that had cost a small fortune and had never seen the light of day. Well, this much pretty shouldn't go to waste, and what better way to christen it but on her first date with Greyson?

She pulled the silky black cocktail dress from the hanger and slipped it over her head. The straps just covered the red striped bra straps. The bust of the dress was gathered just underneath her full breasts with a black satin bow. The silky chiffon skirt flowed out from the empire waist in soft pleats.

She felt like a naughty angel in it. It was perfect.

Shoes!

Now that was an aspect of her attire that she hadn't let become utilitarian. She surveyed the shoe rack that hung on the back of the closet door. There they were, in all their gleaming glory. The black patent leather Jimmy Choo 'Loxley' peep toe pumps. The ultra high heel and ankle strap would be perfect. Greyson was well over 6'4", so he'd still be taller than her, even with her four-inch heels.

Kat reverently took the obscenely expensive shoes off of the rack. She'd saved a long time on her firefighter's salary to afford those shoes. And now she would finally get the chance to wear them. She gingerly slid them on her feet and fastened the straps around her ankles. She turned to look at her reflection in the mirror and froze.

It had been forever since she'd felt pretty. Being a firefighter wasn't about feeling sexy. It was about saving people's lives. But the sexy seductress that stared back at her from the full-length mirror didn't care anything about what she did for a living. This woman was gorgeous, her breasts straining against the gathered bust of the dress, the skirt falling in gentle pleats over the soft swell of her hips, her tanned legs going on for miles past the hem of the almost-too-short skirt, the priceless shoes making her legs look even longer.

Kat brought her gaze back to her face and gasped at what she saw. A healthy blush flushed across her cheeks. Her dark blue eyes framed by a thick curtain of dark lashes, her mahogany hair falling in soft waves around her face and down well past her shoulders, curling over and around her breasts and shoulders.

Confidence filled the gaping holes in her self-esteem. She straightened her shoulders and stared proudly into the mirror.

The sound of the doorbell ringing and Diesel's frantic barking made Kat's stomach twist in knots. Was it really time already? Was Greyson already here and she was actually going to have to go through with the 'date' thing? *Holy shit.*

With a deep breath for courage Kat turned and made her way to the door, quickly picking up the clothes she had strewn around the house in her haste to get ready. She ducked into the laundry room and deposited the offending material into the washer.

The doorbell rang again. Kat bit her lip. *Pushy much?*

"Diesel! Chill!" Kat commanded as she opened the door, nudging the boxer back with her Jimmy Choo-clad foot.

"Greys..." Her heart leapt into her throat when she saw who was standing on her porch.

"Hey Kat," Eric murmured.

"Oh, um, Eric." What the fuck was he doing here?

"You didn't have to get all dressed up just for me." An evil glint lit up his eyes. He reached up and grasped the top of the door, effectively erasing any thought to close the door in his face without snapping some fingers off.

"Why are you here, Eric? I asked you to leave me alone."

"I can't stay away, Kat. I love you. And I know you love me too." He stepped one boot inside the door frame.

A chill of fear tingled down her spine. "We broke up, remember Eric? You need to let me go."

"I'm so sorry, Kat. Please give me another chance." He licked his lips in what she assumed was supposed to be a seductive move.

"I'm sorry, Eric. But it's best for both of us this way. You know it never would have worked out." She meant every word of it, down to her soul. As much as she loved Eric, she had to let him go.

"Please don't push me away, Kat." He gave her the big puppy dog eyes. The ones that had worked so many times before on her.

This time she couldn't let them melt her. He was a potential arsonist who killed his ex-girlfriends. And she potentially was next. She straightened her shoulders and looked him in the eye. "I'm sorry. You need to go, Eric. I have other plans." She pushed against the door to shut it.

"Oh, yeah. Your other plans. Greyson told me about them." He pushed his weight against the door, shoving it open a bit further. His ice-blue eyes raked over Kat's thigh-length cocktail dress. "That dress was meant for *me*."

Another shove against the door that held firm against Eric's wide shoulders. "No, it wasn't."

"Please, Kat. Let me show you how much you mean to me." He stepped through the doorway and took a step towards her. The overwhelming stench of alcohol blew in through the open door.

Her stomach twisted in knots. She had to get him out of her house, before things got bad. "You're drunk, Eric. You really need to leave." She backed up, putting the couch between them.

"I can't." He took another step towards her.

The lump that had been growing in her throat from the moment that she opened the door and saw Eric's face threatened to choke her. "You're drunk. Go home."

He shook his head. "No."

"What do you want?"

"To remind you why you love me. To remind you how it feels to have me buried deep inside you, one last time. I want to hear you scream my name as you cum. I can see in your eyes that you still want me. Your eyes just got darker listening to me talk about fucking you. Tell me you don't want me Kat." He took another step toward her so he stood just on the other side of the couch. The front door was still open.

"I don't want you, Eric." She locked her blazing gaze with his. She wanted there to be no misunderstanding in her words or her gaze this time.

"Yes, you do. You just don't want to admit it."

"What the fuck do I have to tell you to get you to understand? I don't want you. You lost your chance with me. Please go." Her voice teetered on the brink of hysteria.

"Don't say that, Kat."

"I'm sorry, Eric. Please. You need to leave."

"Ever since that day in the shower, I knew I could never, ever give you up, and I'll do whatever I have to in order to keep you." His icy blue eyes bored into hers.

Kat gasped. "That was you? But..."

"The diamond? I dropped Kevin's missing diamond there just in case, to throw off anyone who might suspect it was me." He smirked. "It was pretty fucking hot when you started fingering yourself in the shower. I knew you knew I was watching and were doing it for me. You're such a little nympho. Just let me show you why you should chose me over Greyson. I promise you'll be begging me for more." He licked his lips and dropped his gaze to her cleavage as he spoke.

With his attention momentarily distracted by her boobs, she made a mad dash for the door.

"No!" He dove for her, wrapping his steel grip around her waist as they crashed to the floor and slid into the table by the door. The glass vase of irises fell to the floor and shattered, scattering sparkling bits of glass over the hardwood floor like tiny diamonds.

"Don't make it be like this," he begged.

"Please, Eric. Don't do this!"

"I'm doing this because I love you, Kat. I can't just let you go." He got up and easily held her captive with one well-muscled arm as he closed and locked the front door. She writhed to escape his iron grasp to no avail.

She swallowed the lump in her throat. *This can't be happening.*

He swung her up into his arms, one arm around her back, the other under her knees and carried her towards the bedroom, wavering slightly in his inebriated state. If it had been a month ago, before she'd learned what she had about him, it would have been an incredibly romantic move from him. But now it only sealed the terror that had its vise grip over her heart.

"Put me down. Please, don't do this."

He didn't respond, but gazed down at her with his icy blue eyes. Desperation and pain were etched across his features. He didn't look up as he purposefully strode towards the bedroom.

"Please stop." She struggled in his arms, but he held her so tightly against his hard chest that she couldn't move.

"Trust me, Kat. You used to trust me. What happened to that?" He gazed down at her.

She swallowed hard. Yes, she used to trust him. This was the guy she had, at one point, thought was *the one*. Now she was potentially about to become his next victim.

He gently laid her in the center of her four-poster bed. "Stay," he commanded and went to her dresser and opened the top drawer. He pulled out two pairs of thigh-high stockings and held them up before him, as if he was mentally measuring their length. Kat used his momentary distraction and jumped off the bed and ran for the door.

"I told you to stay!" he roared as he grabbed her hair and flung her back on the bed.

She scrambled back against the headboard. Tears of pain sprung to her eyes and her scalp throbbed where he practically ripped the handful of hair from the roots.

"Oh God, Kat. I'm so sorry. I didn't mean to hurt you." He knelt on the bed before her and cupped her face in his hands. He leaned in and pressed his lips to hers. He tasted like cheap beer and cigarettes, but for a moment she forgot everything except how he used to make her feel. And then she felt the nylon tighten against her wrist.

Kat gasped. "What are you doing?"

Eric brought a fingertip to her lips. "Trust me," he whispered.

Kat shook her head. "I can't."

Pain flitted across his features.

She sucked in a deep breath for courage and slowed her breathing. There was no escape. She'd have to consider other ways of convincing him to let her go.

"You don't have to tie me up." She tried to channel every sexy, feminine molecule she had into her voice. She gazed up at him and batted her thick lashes.

"Mmm, now that is the reaction I wanted to see out of you, baby." Eric dropped to his knees on the bed beside her. He lowered his mouth to hers in a savage, sloppy kiss and slid his hands over her.

She fought the nausea that almost consumed her at his touch. Maybe if she pretended she didn't know what she knew about him, maybe she could pretend it was before all this crap went down, she could get through this. But she was about to be raped by her ex-boyfriend.

He trailed his hands over her torso and down her hip as he lapped his tongue over her lips. She clenched her lips closed against his invading tongue.

"Come on baby, open for me," he murmured against her lips and slid his hands further down her chiffon-clad thigh.

She gasped when his hand slid to the inside of her thigh and under her dress between her legs. He took that as her surrender to him and he thrust his tongue into her mouth.

Her heart leapt into her throat as he slid his hands under the hem of her dress and stripped it off her in one swift movement, breaking the kiss just long enough to raise it over her head. Then his hands were back on her, eagerly exploring her unwilling bra and panty-clad body. His fingers found her satin-covered mound and pressed against it roughly.

"Mmm, I can tell you want me. I'm glad you chose this outfit for me. Perfectly suiting for what I'm going to do to you."

She grit her teeth and closed her eyes and focused on Greyson's face before her. But rather than seeing his sexy half-grin that melted her, his face was twisted in anger. He was angry that she wasn't fighting back. With renewed resolve to protect herself at all cost she froze and opened her eyes.

Eric sensed the change in her demeanor and slid his hands up her arms and caught her wrists, pinning her to the bed.

"What's wrong?"

Like he fucking didn't know. "You're trying to rape me. What the fuck do you think is wrong?"

"You can't rape the willing, baby. And you're wet for me. So even if your mind is saying no, your body is saying yes." He slipped the loop of nylon thigh-high around the bed post, tying it so tightly that the nylon bit into her skin. He followed suit with her other wrist and each of her ankles. In a moment she was tied spread eagle to the bed. He stood and surveyed his handy work.

"Please don't..." Kat whimpered, but her voice fell on deaf ears.

"Mmm, this whole bondage thing is way underrated." He murmured and dropped his pants.

14

Chapter Fourteen

Bile rose to her throat again and she coughed at the stinging taste of stomach acid.

"Oh, God." Her throat singed from the terror that built inside her.

"Don't worry. You know you love this part." He knelt on the bed beside her.

"Please don't, Eric. I'm begging. Isn't that what you want? For me to beg? I'm begging you. Please don't do this!" Kat pleaded, tears streamed down her cheeks.

"Don't cry, Kat. I promise I'll be gentle. You'll love it as much as I will and you'll wonder why you fought it so hard." He trailed his fingers over her shapely calf, up her thigh, over her flat stomach. His hand traced over her breasts and Kat turned her face away.

"Look at me."

She shook her head. He may be holding her body captive, but her heart and mind were hers. He couldn't touch her there.

"God damn it, Kat, look at me or so help me..."

The unuttered threat made Kat grit her teeth and turn her fiery glare on him.

"That's better. Now I want you to keep your eyes open the whole time. Don't you dare close them."

He slid his hands back down her body, pulling her bra down to expose her breasts over the top of her bra. He licked each one before he dropped his hands down and slowly untied the lacing on her hips with his fingers. The panties fell away, leaving her completely exposed.

He gasped and trailed his long fingers over her shaved mound.

"Mmm. See? I knew you wanted this. You're fucking amazing, Kat." He slid a finger inside her.

Kat stiffened and clenched her eyes at the invasion.

"Keep them open."

She opened her eyes and glared at him. Greyson, Greyson, Greyson. She mentally chanted. Think about Greyson. He'll help you get through this.

Eric dipped his head and tasted her. Under any other circumstances this would have been incredibly erotic. But being tied unwillingly to her bed, her ex-boyfriend's head forcefully between her legs caused the nausea to overwhelm her.

The doorbell rang just as Eric delved his tongue inside her. Diesel's nails tore across the hardwood floor and his insistent barking and jumping at the door brought Eric's head up.

"Fuck!" he growled and stood up. "Stay right there." He winked at her before yanking his pants up and tiptoeing down the hallway.

The moment his back disappeared down the hallway Kat writhed at her bindings. They not only held, but tightened.

A muffled yelp and Diesel's barking stopped. Kat gasped, her heart tearing in two at the thought of Eric killing her dog.

Heavy footsteps tore down the hallway.

"Leave it to my brother to fuck everything up," he growled as he ran back into the room.

Hope rushed through Kat's body.

"Greyson!" she screamed as loud as she could. "Greyson help!"

"Damn it, Kat!" He crammed a hand through his hair and looked down at her with a mournful expression.

The pounding at the front door intensified. "I'm so sorry." Eric leaned down and pressed a kiss to her lips. "I love you so much." He cupped her cheek and stared into her eyes.

For a moment, she saw the man she had fallen in love with.

"Goodbye, Kat," he whispered and climbed quickly out her bedroom window without a second glance.

She breathed a sigh of relief and closed her eyes. Thank God Greyson had showed up when he had, or who knows what would have happened. Her relief dissolved and her eyes popped open at the faint scent of smoke.

She gasped in horror when wisps of smoke curled up from the trash can next to her dresser. Her gaze darted to the top where her vanilla-scented candle had been.

"Oh my God, Greyson!" Kat screamed.

Flames flickered to life over the rim of the trash can and quickly licked up the gleaming wood on the side of the dresser.

"Greyson!" Kat screamed. She thrashed at the nylon, trying desperately to rip it from the bed or her wrists. The material tightened more. Kat could feel the intense heat of the flames as it burned up the wall and ignited the ceiling. A few more seconds and the bed would catch fire too.

Diesel's disoriented whine drew her attention to the doorway. He wobbled in, blood trailing out of his ear.

"Diesel! Outside! Quick!" If she was going to die, at least her sweet boxer wouldn't die with her.

He whined again and jumped up on the bed beside her.

"Get out of here!" Kat screamed. But her faithful companion growled and chewed at the hose holding her wrist to the bed.

"Greyson!" Kat screamed again, her voice now hoarse. The smoke choked her and she coughed violently. Her eyes burned and the hairs on her arms singed from the intense heat. But it wouldn't be the severe burns that would kill her. It would be inhaling the super-heated gas that would burn her lungs beyond repair. Less than a minute. That was it.

The pounding stopped. Kat's heart sunk. Had he given up? Could he have even heard her?

Kat struggled for consciousness. Her lungs ached for clean air. Her eyes burned and watered. As the blackness closed in, something shattered in the distance and Greyson's face appeared in the heat waves before her.

**

Greyson brushed his hands down his black button-down shirt and wiped each boot on the back of his black pants as he approached Kat's door. This was really happening. They were really going out.

Guilt niggled at the back of his neck for a second when he thought of his brother. But the bastard didn't deserve her. He cared more about the job than he did about her. It was about time that Kat had a guy treat her well. And he was just the guy for the job.

He glanced at his watch and sucked in a deep breath as he pushed the doorbell. He was a little early, but hopefully she'd see that as a positive trait. He quickly ran his hands through his hair and stepped back and waited for her to open the door.

No response.

And then he heard it. His name, screamed in terror, in Kat's voice. His blood solidified in his veins.

He dove for the door knob and shook it. Locked. He pounded on the door until his fists ached. "Kat!" Greyson shouted. He tried to look in the living room window, but the curtains were pulled tight. Another terrified scream sounded like it was coming from somewhere towards the back of the house.

He took off around the side of the house. The gate was locked, but he scaled the wall easily. His heart skipped a beat when he caught the scent of smoke on the air. Without hesitation, he grabbed one of her wrought iron patio chairs and heaved it at the sliding glass door. The glass shattered and smoke billowed from the gaping opening. Kat's boxer stumbled out.

"Kat!" Greyson crawled into the room beneath a blanket of thick smoke. What he encountered made his stomach roil more than the taste of the smoke in the air.

Kat lay spread-eagle on the bed, tied to the bedposts with tight knots around her wrists and ankles. She was naked save her bra that had been pushed down around her torso. Angry white-hot flames trailed up the wall and onto the ceiling. Tendrils of flames licked along the top of the headboard, dangerously close to Kat's hands. Her eyes were open, staring unfocused at him.

He crawled onto the bed and made quick work of cutting her binds with his pocket knife and pulled her limp body to the floor. She coughed, the sound weak beneath the roar of the flames.

Smoke choked him and he fought to control his coughing as grabbed her dress from the floor and stuffed it against her face. Her slight weight was nothing as he dragged her out the door beneath the billowing waves of black smoke. The intense heat from the flashover chased them out the shattered door. He stumbled as he scrambled to get distance between them and the inferno.

He lowered Kat to the grass a safe distance from the house. Her eyes fluttered open and she coughed, an irritated, ragged cough that reminded him of the scene so many months ago when he thought he almost lost her. And he'd almost lost her again.

He coughed hard before he found his voice. "Kat?"

She shook her head and coughed again, but sat up on her own. Greyson helped her into her dress and scooped her up into his arms.

Kat struggled to find her voice between bouts of ragged coughing. "Diesel?"

He nodded to the disoriented boxer, who followed close behind. "He's okay."

Kat leaned her head against his shoulder. He dialed 911 into his phone and hit send. A few words with the operator and help was on its way.

Once they were a safe distance from the house, he lowered her to the curb.

"What the fuck happened?" Greyson's eyes searched hers.

"Eric forced his way into the house." She coughed hard before continuing. "He said he wanted to show me how much he loved me, and how he couldn't let me go. I told him to leave. He tried to rape me."

The second the word rape escaped her lips her body trembled uncontrollably.

The breath punched from his chest and his stomach churned. "My *brother* did this?" His jaw clenched and his eyes narrowed.

Kat nodded and tears filled her blue eyes.

"Oh God, Kat." He pulled her into his arms. Tears burned his eyes as he stared at the raging inferno of Kat's house. His brother. His friend. His blood. A rapist and a murderer. His blood ran cold at the thought.

**

It felt good to be nestled in his lap, wrapped in his strong, protective arms. She mourned the wonderful night that was originally ahead of them. Instead the night would end in tragedy. Her home and all of her possessions were gone. Eric was somewhere on the loose, potentially stalking his next victim.

Diesel whined as the wail of the siren from station three approached.

The guys from station three piled out of the engine and unfurled hoses and began pumping thousands of gallons of water onto the house.

The ambulance pulled up a moment later.

"Why are they here?" Kat glanced at Greyson.

"Just to check you out, you know, make sure he didn't hurt you." He stroked her cheek with the back of his hand.

"I'm fine. I told you he stopped when you got here. He didn't get the chance." Please God, don't let them ask what he did to her.

"Hey, Kat," Eve said somberly as she pulled her medic kit out of the ambulance.

"Hey, Eve."

"Can you walk?"

"She doesn't have to. I'll carry her." Greyson stood up, all the while keeping her in the safe cocoon of his arms.

"Diesel, stay," he commanded. Diesel whined but laid back down on the sidewalk.

"I can walk. Really, I'm okay," Kat protested.

"Still." He gazed down at her with a pained expression.

She sighed and allowed herself to be carried to the ambulance. He climbed up and set her gently onto the gurney and pulled the sheet over her.

"Thanks." Kat gazed into his eyes. The pain in his gaze made her heart hurt. Was he beating himself up because he couldn't save her from Eric in time? Did he feel responsible?

"Thanks, Greyson. Now, if you'll excuse us," Eve murmured and tilted her head towards the closed doors.

Greyson nodded and stood up.

Kat grabbed his hand in a death grip. "Please, don't leave me." Kat caught Greyson's shocked expression.

"Um, okay." Eve swept her blonde ponytail over her shoulder. As she checked Kat's vital signs, she started with the standard questions.

"Are you experiencing any pain?" Eve asked.

"Yes."

"Where?"

Kat held up her wrists. The nylon was cinched tightly against her skin. Kat kept her eyes locked with Greyson's. He was the only thing keeping her from going completely to pieces.

Eve pulled her scissors from her medic kit. Kat winced when the nylon tightened against her tender skin as the scissors slid into place. A small snip and the first wrist was free.

"Wow! You really must have put up a fight," Eve murmured as she surveyed the damage. The skin was rubbed raw where the knots had chafed against her skin.

"Yeah," Kat murmured.

Eve made quick work of the rest of the restraints, slipping the material into a zip-loc bag for the forensics team. Her wrists were worse than her ankles, but there was a deep red, angry band circling each. Eve applied antiseptic ointment and wrapped them with gauze.

A knock at the door brought everyone's attention to the rear of the ambulance. Eve opened the door a crack, murmured a few words and then allowed Officer Mendoza of the Chandler Police Department into the ambulance.

"Kat, I need to ask you some sensitive questions. Are you sure you want him here for this?" Officer Mendoza asked. His dull brown eyes searched Kat's.

"I want him to stay, please." Her heart pounded.

"Okay. But I don't want his presence here to impact your answers. I need complete honesty here, okay?"

Kat nodded.

"Were you sexually assaulted tonight?"

"Yes," Kat murmured. Kat caught Greyson's gaze and held it.

"Do you know who the person was?"

"Yes, it was Eric Neal. My ex-boyfriend." A single tear slipped down her cheek. *What a fucking mess.*

Eve grunted. Officer Mendoza shot a silencing glare at her and she blushed and went back to her paperwork.

At the officer's prompting, Kat related the details of how Eric forced his way into her home and tied her down. The details were unclear as to how the candle ended up in the trash can. Greyson's eyes darkened with anger and his jaw tightened as each new detail was revealed.

Officer Mendoza cleared his throat. "I'm sorry to have to ask, but I need all the details. After he tied you to the bed, what did he do?"

Kat swallowed. The lump that had built in her throat since she started to relay the details of the attack grew until she could barely breathe. She stared at her hands, which were folded in her lap. The bandages barely covered the angry red welts that were beginning to swell.

"He took my panties off and pulled my bra down and licked me." Another tear rolled down her cheek.

"What?" Greyson roared.

Officer Mendoza shot an angry look at him.

"He licked you?" Officer Mendoza repeated.

"Yes. He was taking his time. He forced me to watch while he licked me." Kat sucked in a deep, cleansing breath.

"Then what happened?"

"Greyson showed up and rang the doorbell. Eric apologized and said he loved me, then climbed out the window." Kat clenched her jaw, trying to stifle the chattering of her teeth. Her entire body trembled uncontrollably.

"Did he rape you, Ms. Hale?" His brown eyes searched hers.

"No." She held his gaze.

Greyson let out a relieved breath.

"How did you get out of the room?" Officer Mendoza glanced at Greyson.

"Greyson broke my sliding door and drug me out." Kat raised her tear-filled eyes to meet Greyson's furious gaze. His jaw clenched and the look in his eyes was murderous.

"Thank you, Miss Hale. Your information will aid us in catching Mr. Neal," Officer Mendoza said and exited the ambulance.

"We don't need to transport you, but if you want us to, we can take you to the ER for a check-out," Eve said.

"Everything I said was the truth. He did not have sex with me. I don't need a rape exam." Kat's eyes locked with Eve's pale blue ones.

Eve shrugged. "They have counselors too. Even if you don't need the exam, if you need someone to talk to..."

"Thanks, Eve. I'll keep that in mind." Kat slid off of the gurney. "Can I go home now?"

"Um, Kat, your house is toast, remember?" Greyson said.

"Shit," she growled. "I'm going to fucking kill that asshole if I ever get my hands on him."

"There's our feisty little Kat." Greyson shot her a sideways smile. "I was afraid we lost her."

15

Chapter Fifteen

"Y ou can have the bedroom, I'll sleep on the couch," Greyson said as he opened the door to his second-story condo on the San Mateo golf course. He let go of Diesel's collar and the boxer furiously sniffed off in the direction of the bedroom, his nails clicking on the hardwood floor.

"No way, I'm fine on the couch. Besides, you're too tall to sleep there."

He turned on the lights and Kat gasped. She expected the quintessential bachelor pad, complete with uneaten pizza and beer cans littering the floor. Just like Eric's. Instead, Greyson's apartment looked like something out of a magazine. Light tan walls, white trim and honey maple hardwood floors gave the apartment a warm glow. A huge oriental rug stretched across the floor in the living room, flanked by a black leather sectional and a massive TV. Huge prints of paintings by Alex Grey graced the walls that towered to twelve-foot high cathedral ceilings.

"Wow. This place is gorgeous. How'd you get the TV up the stairs?" Kat asked with a smile. She stood just inside the door, but didn't come any further into the room.

"Thanks, and you wouldn't believe it if I told you," Greyson said, his eyes sparkling.

"Try me."

"Let's just say that it didn't come in through the door okay?" Greyson winked.

"The balcony? Damn, that's hardcore."

Greyson chuckled and flicked on the lights in the kitchen. Even the cabinets had lights in them, showing off a set of black dishes through the glass fronted cabinets.

"You've got some great taste. Alex Grey, right?" Kat walked over to the psychedelic Alex Grey painting of TOOL's 10,000 days Album cover.

"You like TOOL?" Greyson raised an eyebrow at her.

"Aenima was my favorite album," she said with a sideways smile, her eyes riveted on the black and gray swirling pattern of a face before her.

"You're amazing." Greyson crossed the room towards her.

"Why?" She turned and her chiffon dress, still permeated with smoke, swirled around her hips.

"Because after all you've been through tonight, you can gaze at an Alex Grey painting and tell me which album was your favorite. Like what happened didn't affect you at all."

"It affected me. Trust me," she grumbled. "Hey, can I borrow your shower and some clothes?"

He nodded and took her hand tentatively in his, like she might bolt at any moment.

"You're gonna get through this. You're the strongest person I've ever met." His eyes searched her face.

She nodded and dropped her gaze. It was like he was staring into her soul, and she just couldn't deal with anyone getting close to her right now.

"Come on," he said softly and pulled her towards the bathroom. A wet sloshing noise echoed out into the hallway, and he reached around the doorframe to flip on the switch.

"Diesel!" Kat gasped. Her sweet, dumb boxer was lapping water greedily from the toilet.

"Oh man," Greyson laughed.

"Diesel out!" Kat's cheeks flamed. "Sorry about that."

"It's no biggie. I'll give him some water and food while you take a shower okay?" He pulled some fluffy white towels from the closet. "There's a clean robe on the hook on the other side of the door, and you're welcome to anything in my closet you want. It's just through that door." He pointed to the bedroom.

"Thanks, I really appreciate it."

Greyson disappeared back into the kitchen and she closed the door behind her. She kicked off her Jimmy Choo's, the only item that made it out of the fire that she would ever want to wear again. The vanilla marble floor was cool on her bare feet. She turned on the water in the shower to let it warm up while she got undressed.

She padded over to the sink and stood on the fluffy white floor mat and gazed into the mirror. She actually didn't look too bad for having been through hell and back. Her mascara was smeared down her cheeks, her skin blotchy with smeared ash. The once-black dress was smeared with gray streaks, and streaks of soot smeared across her neck and chest.

She sighed and turned on the water, which splashed into the carved marble sink. She wet a wash cloth and reached up to wipe the mess from her face. The bandage around her wrist caught her attention. She reached down and pulled the gauze away from her wrists one at a time. Angry red raised welts emerged from the gauze.

"The police better get to him before I do, because I'm going to fucking kill him." She ground her teeth and bent over to tear the gauze from her ankles. Angry welts graced each of her ankles and matched the mess on her wrists.

She reached down to the hem of her dress and ripped it over her head. Officer Mendoza had asked for her to surrender her clothes to them for evidence, so unfortunately, she couldn't burn it like she wanted to. That fucking dress had brought her so much heartache. It was like it was cursed or something.

She folded the cursed dress and sat it on the counter and followed it with her bra. Her panties had been lost in the fire. She avoided her naked reflection as she went back to the shower and slipped under the spray.

The scalding water felt good against her skin, but stung like a bitch on her wrists and ankles. She stood under the steaming spray and let the water soak into her thick hair. She cocked an eyebrow when she saw her favorite Victoria Secret vanilla body wash and her favorite shampoo on the shelf. He didn't seem like the metrosexual type, so why did he have Victoria Secret body wash in his bathroom? Was it an ex-girlfriends?

The thought of scrubbing her body clean of any memory of Eric's touch overpowered her jealous streak. She reached for the shampoo first, and thoroughly scrubbed the ash from her hair before she reached for the body wash and squeezed it out into the wash cloth. She massaged it into a lather and went to work scrubbing every inch of her body until it was pink, removing at least a few layers of skin in the process.

But she could still feel Eric's slithering touch over her body. It just wouldn't come off. She scrubbed harder and harder, until angry red streaks marred her once tanned skin. A sob caught in her throat and she fought to maintain her composure. She crammed her fists against her eyes to stem the flow of tears. The bastard didn't deserve her tears. But her body betrayed her. She slumped against the cool marble wall and slid to the floor under the rhythm of the water beating down on her.

She sobbed like she had never cried in her life. Not even when her brother died. Because she had always maintained control. But in the situation with Eric she had no control. He took everything from her. And he tried to kill her, with the very thing that she had to face on a daily basis. She was almost the next victim on his growing list.

Kat rocked back and forth under the steaming spray, her head resting against her knees, her arms wrapped around her legs and held them tight to her body. She tried to calm herself, but the tears just kept coming. Tears for every woman who hadn't survived Eric's attack. Tears for the women that he could be doing the same thing to right now.

A gentle knock on the door brought her head up.

"Kat? Are you okay?" Greyson's concerned voice traveled through the wooden door.

The tears came harder. Even her relationship with Greyson was now soiled by what Eric had done. How could he ever look at her the same way after knowing what his brother had done to her? Could she ever look at him the same knowing that he was related to a monster?

The bathroom door opened and Greyson stepped into the room.

"Kat, honey..." He opened the shower door, reached in, and turned the water off. He grabbed one of the fluffy white towels and wrapped it around her wet, naked body and kissed her head softly as he gathered her into his arms and nestled her against his chest.

Kat sniffled and wiped the tears away from her face. Her skin stung at the gentle touch of the fluffy towel against her body from her furious scrubbing.

**

Greyson gazed down at the naked woman in his arms. He'd fantasized so many times about this, but the situation was all wrong. She shouldn't be crying because of her close call with being raped and burned alive. By his fucking brother. She should be smiling up at him with her stormy blue eyes dark with desire. He sighed as she buried her tear-stained face in his chest.

He slowly walked down the hallway to the bedroom and paused to hit the light switch with his elbow. The recessed can lighting flickered to life and cast the room in a cozy glow, lighting up the corners of the room where he had strategically placed potted palms and a beige overstuffed leather recliner.

Crisp with white linens on the cherry sleigh bed matched sheer white curtains that were pulled shut over darkened floor to ceiling windows on either side of the bed. He bent to set her down on her feet on the fluffy white rug, but she clung to him, refusing to let go. His heart ached at the haunted expression in her deep blue eyes.

"I'm so sorry." He brushed his lips softly across her forehead, hoping to smooth the lines of worry from her perfect face. Her red-rimmed eyes were a bit puffy from crying her heart out in the steaming shower. Her creamy skin was marred by angry red streaks that went the length of her arms and legs, as if she tried to scrub her skin off. Her wrists and ankles had swollen raw welts from the restraints the bastard used on her.

If he ever got his hands on his brother, he would squeeze the last breath of life from his body. How he could hurt the woman he supposedly loved like this made his blood boil. He was his brother, but it was suddenly like he never knew him at all.

Instead of placing her on her feet, he laid her gently in the middle of his bed. The fluffy white duvet puffed around her like a cloud. She leaned back against the pillows and pulled the towel around her tightly.

Greyson stood back and gazed at her.

"Do I look that horrible?"

"You look like an angel who's been through hell."

She blushed and dropped her gaze.

"I'll be right back." Greyson disappeared down the hallway.

"No! Greyson!" Kat shrieked.

He came back into the room carrying his medic kit.

"Oh." Kat relaxed back against the bed.

"I figured if you weren't willing to go to the ER to get checked out, I could take care of you here. These are deep enough that they'll scar if we don't treat them. Are you okay with this?" He pulled her hand out and turned it back and forth, inspecting Eric's handy work. His eyes hardened. He looked up and his worried gaze searched hers.

Kat nodded her consent.

He pulled out a roll of gauze and a large tube of antiseptic ointment. As gently as he could, he smoothed the ointment across the angry wound encircling her wrist. He un-wrapped a length of sterile gauze and gently wrapped it around her wrist, smoothing it down and taping it to secure the end.

She watched him intently as he worked. For such large, strong hands, he was incredibly gentle. Only the sting of the antiseptic caused her a twinge of pain.

He treated her other wrist the same way, followed by each of her ankles. He held her foot in one warm hand as he gently wrapped the gauze around the damaged skin. When he finished with her other ankle he gazed up at her, the look in his eyes so tender it brought tears to hers.

"Is there anything else I can do to make you more comfortable?" Greyson's eyes locked with hers.

"Thank you, for everything." Kat snuggled against the pillows, as if she were suddenly overcome with fatigue. It was probably post-traumatic stress causing the drowsiness, but she could hardly keep her eyes open.

"You're welcome." He reached down and pulled the comforter over her towel-clad body. Her soft, steady breathing told him she was already asleep.

He let her sleep and went back into the kitchen. Diesel had discovered the ivory throw that was draped over one end of the black leather sectional and had turned around in it until it was twisted into the perfect dog bed in the middle of the couch.

He pulled out a glass, filled it with water and took it back to the bedroom, stopping by the bathroom to grab some aspirin on the way by. If she woke in the night she'd probably need some pain relief from the abrasions that mottled her perfect skin. He wasn't sure which was worse, the damage Eric had done to her with the restraints or how she had scrubbed her skin raw, probably trying to remove the memory of his touch.

He stepped silently into the room and tiptoed to the bedside table, setting the glass and the medicine down on the shiny wood. In the minute since he had left, Kat had managed to throw the comforter and the towel off. She lay curled on her side, the gentle curve of her naked ass taunting him. Her arms were crossed over her chest and tucked under her cheek, the swell of her full breasts pressed against her elbows.

She looked so innocent and helpless lying naked in the fetal position in the middle of his bed. How many times had he imagined how she would look, naked in his bed? But definitely not like this. Angry red streaks trailed up and down every inch of her supple body.

Fury boiled up inside him as he reached out to gently pull the comforter over her again. He'd make sure his brother found justice. No matter what.

16

Chapter Sixteen

The leather couch was great for mid-day naps and watching the game, but not the best idea for sleeping an entire night. Greyson flopped over again and pulled the blanket up to his chin. His feet stuck off the end at an uncomfortable 45-degree angle. Diesel lay snuggled against his pillow above his head. He ground his teeth and stared up at the cathedral ceiling. The slats of skylight sent little shafts of moonlight down into the room.

This was definitely not how he pictured this night. It was supposed to be their first date. They were supposed to go to a romantic Italian dinner. He was supposed to buy her flowers. They were supposed to walk around downtown Scottsdale and make fun of the yuppies. Then they were supposed to end up back here, removing articles of clothing from each other as they made their way toward the bedroom. And the night was supposed to end with them naked and spent in each other's arms.

Instead he was sleeping on the couch, his skin sticking to the butter-soft leather, and Kat was naked in his bed, nursing wounds from Eric's attempt to rape her. Just the thought of his brother sent his blood boiling.

He had been completely blindsided by his brother's actions. Since they were little, he'd looked out for Eric, made sure he was doing what he was supposed to be. He was honest and sincere and couldn't even bring himself to kill a spider. He'd always catch it in a glass and take it outside and let it go. He was one hell of a fireman and his job was paramount. Granted, as a result of his dedication to his career as a fireman, he was neglectful of his girlfriends, but he was never abusive.

So how could his brother, who he'd been so close with growing up, attempt to rape and then murder his ex-girlfriend? He racked his brain for anything he might have missed that could have clued him in to this. Nothing stood out. Sure, he'd been a bit more withdrawn since Dave's death, but what firefighter wouldn't after losing his partner in the line of duty?

Greyson's skin tingled. Could that have sent Eric over the edge? Or, was it the fact that he told him that they were going out tonight? His chest constricted with panic. It was *his* fault that she almost died tonight. He had sent his brother over the edge by asking out his ex-girlfriend the day after they broke up. What the fuck had he done?

Greyson thought back to the other arson scenes. They were pretty similar to what had happened to Kat. Was Eric responsible for those too, or was this just an eerie coincidence?

His chest tightened more as the panic set in. Kat could have been the next unidentifiable body. The thought made his stomach churn. He pushed up from the couch and buried his head in his hands, tugging his hair.

She could be gone. She could be little more than a pile of ash in her burnt-out four-poster bed. He would never have had the opportunity to see the way her eyes flashed with defiance when she thought he was having a bout of 'Knight in Shining Armor Syndrome'. Or the little dimples she got in her cheeks when she smiled. Or the spread of blush when their skin brushed. Or the little flecks of gold in her eyes when she gazed up at him after he kissed her, her lips swollen from his kiss.

His groin hardened at the thought of kissing her again. He wondered if her eyes would darken with desire as he buried himself within her warmth. He longed to feel the sharp sting of her nails as she dug them into his back as he took her. To make her scream his name as he came in her. To make her utter those words that he never wanted to hear out of a woman's mouth. He shook his head. She wouldn't appreciate him thinking about her like that, especially not tonight. Not after what happened.

He loved how strong she was. Her defiance. Her independence. Her self-control. Her determination. Her commitment to saving lives. His heart lurched as the realization hit him like a bucket of ice water dumped over his head. He loved her. He flopped back on the couch with a sigh. Diesel stirred and whined before curling back into a ball at his head.

After all his attempts to avoid commitment he'd gone and fallen in love. And with the one woman he couldn't have. It was against the rules to date a firefighter on the same shift at the same station. And up until today, she was his *brother's* girl. Besides, he'd vowed to never get married or have kids, to save them from the possibility of leaving them behind when he died in the line of duty. Everything screamed it was wrong. That he shouldn't allow it. If he followed his heart, he'd be risking everything to be with her. His career. Her career. His heart. His brother.

But his brother was already gone. He'd jumped off the deep end and it was *his* fault. Guilt tingled along his spine and he crammed his hand through his hair. But as wrong as it was, he had fallen in love with his brother's girl. How the hell did that happen?

He rubbed his eyes with the heels of his palms and sighed.

He knew how she felt about her career at station three. She wouldn't do anything to jeopardize that position. She'd worked harder than every man on that shift to get her position, and every day she went above and beyond the call of duty to prove that she deserved the right to be there.

She'd never give it up for him. Besides, who knew if she would even want him after what happened with Eric? And even if she could put that aside, she'd never sacrifice her career for him. He'd never ask her to do that. She wouldn't be the same person if she did. What he loved about her the most was the one thing that she'd have to give up to be with him.

He should end this now, before anyone got hurt, before things got messy. For her sake, he should just let her go. Push her away, make the decision easy for her by never giving her the choice.

His heart ached at the thought of never touching her again, of watching her every day and never giving in to what was in his heart. Could he do that? Could he be strong enough for both of them by keeping his distance? For her he would. He'd risked his life by running head-first into burning buildings trying to protect her. He would rip his bleeding heart out with his bare hands if it meant keeping her from harm.

A blood-curdling scream had him up and at a full-run for the bedroom, the clatter of Diesel's nails on the hard wood close on his heels, his growls reverberating down the hall.

Kat sat in the center of the bed, clutching the comforter to her heaving chest. Tears streamed down her face and she stared at him with wild eyes.

"Kat! What happened? Are you okay?" Greyson frantically searched the room.

She forced herself to slow her breathing so she could speak.

"It was just a dream. It was just a dream," she chanted. He wondered if she was saying that to him or trying to convince herself of that fact.

"Shhh honey," he murmured and tentatively sat on the bed beside her. "It was just a dream. Want to talk about it?"

She sniffled and nodded. He grabbed the box of tissues from the nightstand and handed it to her.

"Thanks." She took three tissues from the box and dabbed at her raw eyes and wiped her nose.

"What was it about?" He reached up to brush a strand of hair from her face.

She flinched. "Sorry!" she gasped when she realized what she had done. Tears sprung to her eyes again. She sobbed into the tissues.

"It's okay." He drew her into his arms and rocked her gently as she cried into his shoulder. His chest was damp from her tears, but they didn't let up. Her shoulders shook as she sobbed against him. "It'll be okay, Kat. I promise you. I'll make this right."

"Thank you." She wiped her face with the tissue again. "Sorry I'm such a mess. I didn't think it would bother me so much!"

"You've been through hell, Kat. It's okay to let it all out. Do what you need to do to deal with it." His jaw clenched. "What was your dream about?"

"Eric," she sighed. "It was a replay of what happened tonight. But instead of you ringing the doorbell and stopping him, he finished what he started. He raped me and then burned me alive." She shuddered.

"Oh God, Kat." He didn't know what else to say. The same dream had been on replay through his mind when he fell asleep. That's why he couldn't sleep. He didn't want to shut his eyes and see her that way.

"Are you okay now?" He pulled away a bit to study her face.

She sniffled and nodded. His heart wrenched. She looked so innocent. He wanted nothing more in the world than to kiss away the tears that fell down her cheeks.

He sucked in a deep breath and shifted to nestle her back into the bed, tucking the comforter around her still naked body. He scooted back and one foot touched the floor when her hand clamped onto his arm.

"Please don't leave me." Her stormy blue eyes locked with his.

His heart ached at the pleading in her eyes. He nodded and laid down on top of the comforter beside her. The air in the room was cool from the ceiling fan, and his thin boxer briefs did little to maintain his body heat. Goosebumps pricked along his skin. He shifted to get up.

"Please?" The fear was plain in her voice.

"I'm just getting a blanket, I'll be back." He smoothed her hair from her forehead.

"Come here." She lifted the comforter for him. Moonlight filtered in from the windows behind the bed and illuminated her naked body in an ethereal blue-white shimmer. His shorts tightened around his hips as his body reacted to the sight of her beautiful body.

He chewed his lip and slid under the comforter beside her. He tucked her into his shoulder, careful to keep her hips a safe distance from his jutting hard-on.

She sighed and the soft curve of her ass nuzzled against him. He gritted his teeth and tried to get his mind off of the naked woman nestled comfortably in his arms. She fit perfectly against him, like she was made just for him. *Thoughts like that will get you nowhere*, he thought.

She shifted again until her entire body pressed hard against his. Her back molded against his chest, her hips snugly tucked into his. The bottoms of her feet rested on his shins.

Her body was on fire and scalded his skin where they touched. He desperately wanted to run his hands over her, to feel the silkiness of her tanned skin under his rough palms. He settled for putting his hand on her flat stomach and marveled at the way it practically spanned her from hip to hip.

Her silky skin was firm like a ripe peach and the contours of her abdomen begged him to stroke his fingers across her, to trace the muscles on their path lower. But he kept his hand frozen, pressed firmly against her stomach. His cock twitched as she brushed her hair from her neck. He was so close he could lean forward and kiss her neck without either of them having to move. He longed to run his tongue across her collarbone, to lay kisses along her sternum between her breasts before worshiping each one of them in turn.

Her even breathing told him she was asleep. He took the opportunity to nuzzle her neck and prayed that she wouldn't wake up while he was indulging himself. This would be the one and only time he'd ever have her naked in his arms. He had to have something to remember her by.

He sucked in a deep breath to help gain control of his raging thoughts. Her scent, a mixture of vanilla and something sweeter, drifted from her hair and set his body aching. How was he supposed to get any sleep like this, with her nestled in his arms all night, when he wanted to roll her onto her back and make love to her, make her forget the horrors of earlier and replace them with ecstasy-filled ones?

He clenched his eyes shut. Rage overwhelmed him at the thought of what his brother had done and successfully quenched the burning ache between his legs.

Kat sighed and rolled over. She snuggled into his chest, pressed her face against his neck and threw a leg over his hips. He bit back a groan. Her firm breasts pressed against his chest, her hard nipples teasing the scattering of hair across his chest.

Her leg pulled him tight against her hips. He could feel her heat through the thin material of his boxer briefs. His cock strained painfully against the fabric, like it was desperately trying to break free and bury itself deep within her warmth. It pulsed in his shorts and he knew he couldn't handle any more.

"Kat?" Greyson whispered.

"Mmm," she murmured and nuzzled closer. He almost lost control when she pressed a kiss against his neck, just beneath his jaw.

"Jesus, Kat, you're killing me here," he growled and brushed her hair back from her face.

"Hmm?" She opened her eyes and gazed up at him with the most innocent, sleepy expression that almost brought him to tears.

"Uh, I need..." He didn't know what he wanted to tell her he needed. What he really needed was to bury himself deep in her wetness while he shouted that he loved her from the rooftops.

Her sleep-clouded blue eyes gazed up at him. The way she worried at her bottom lip with her pearly white teeth forced him to dip down and kiss her lips softly. The kiss held none of the raging need that roiled in his body, only the tenderness that he knew she needed.

She smiled against his lips and snuggled against his chest again. Almost instantly her breathing slowed and her shoulders rose and fell softly.

He gazed down at her sleeping form, snuggled so perfectly in his arms. While he wanted to replace the horrific memories of the night with hot sensual ones, she was more important than any need he had. This would be the only night that they would ever lie like this. And he was content to just have her snuggled in his arms.

17

Chapter Seventeen

Kat opened her eyes to the golden rays filtering in through the sheer curtains flanking windows on either side of the bed. Fear seized her and it took a moment to recall where she was, or why someone was curled around her. A well-tanned, muscled arm wrapped snugly around her torso. Her arm lay on top of it, their fingers entwined. The angry streaks from her attempt to scrub off the feeling of Eric's touch on her skin had faded, and the only mementos from the horrors of the night before were the gauze bandages that encircled her wrists.

Kat disentangled herself from Greyson's embrace and padded naked to the closet. She avoided the reflection in the mirrored door as it slid open on oiled tracks. She surveyed the walk-in closet and selected an oversized white button-down shirt and a pair of plaid boxers and carried them to the bathroom.

She smiled as she quietly shut the door behind her and noticed the toothbrush still in the wrapper and the tube of toothpaste. He'd thought of everything.

She quickly showered and brushed her teeth before slipping into the shirt and boxers. She felt bad for taking his clothes without asking, but he'd told her that she was welcome to whatever she wanted to use in his closet. The shirt hung loosely on her shoulders and she had to twist the waistband on the boxers up several times to get it to stay on her hips. Even then, they still hung low on her hipbones.

Diesel whined and scratched at the door. She opened it and followed him to the kitchen, where he showed her where Greyson had stashed the food. She put a cup of kibble into his dish and started a pot of coffee while he snarfed it down.

The seductive scent of hazelnut coffee drifted over her and her heart clenched. It was the way Greyson tasted when he kissed her. She poured the steaming brew into a mug and inhaled deeply, savoring the tingle that coursed over her body from the memory.

Diesel scratched at the front door and whined pitifully. She let him out and stood in the doorway, leaning against the doorjamb and nursing her coffee as he sniffed around the grass. After he was satisfied with peeing on every tree and bush within ten feet of the stairs she whistled gently. Diesel's head popped up and he listened for a second before he went back to sniffing the bumper of a white car parked a few doors down. She whistled again.

Rather than coming like he always did when she whistled, the hair on his haunches raised and he snarled at the car.

"Diesel!" Kat called.

At her command he turned and raced for the door, muscling her back into the condo.

"What the hell is wrong with you silly dog?" She practically tripped over him as she shut the door behind her, throwing the deadbolt and the security lock.

He growled at the door.

"Diesel hush," she whispered.

He whined and circled before plopping down against the door on the mat.

She shook her head. "Weirdo."

She put her coffee mug in the sink and tiptoed back into the bedroom and gazed at Greyson's sleeping form. His forehead was knit with what looked like anger. She wondered what he was dreaming about. If his dreams were anything like hers had been, she could understand the look. The scene from last night had played on a horrifying loop throughout the night.

She felt incredibly guilty waking him up. He looked so innocent and exhausted, snuggled on his side, one arm tucked under his cheek, his chestnut hair tousled into playful spikes from sleeping on them. His two-day old shadow along his jaw line made her body ache to have the prickly stubble tickle her neck as he nuzzled it. He'd had a long night, and from the shadows under his eyes, it looked like he'd had a longer night than she had. She should just let him sleep and slip out. She could call him later to thank him for his hospitality. After waking up naked in his bed, she figured that would be the easiest, least embarrassing scene for both of them. He had to be disgusted by her now. She was tainted.

She leaned down and gently pressed her lips to his. They were soft and warm and the stubble from his slightly overgrown facial hair tickled her face. She wanted so much to continue, to turn the kiss from a good-bye kiss to something more. Something deeper. But it wasn't right. Not now, not after what happened with Eric.

She sighed and started to pull away when his hands cupped her face. Her eyes popped open and encountered his chocolate eyes, still disoriented from sleep, intensely gazing into hers. Her lips opened to whisper an apology, but his eyes closed and he slanted his lips across hers, his tongue delving into her mouth.

Her body clenched with desire. She sighed and knelt on the bed before him and slid her hands across his cheeks, savoring the way his stubble tickled her palms. Her eyes fluttered closed.

A rumbling growl erupted from his chest and he rolled her onto her back. Fear seized her for a moment and she froze. Images of Eric forcing her onto the bed flitted through her mind. She opened her eyes and her body instantly relaxed at the sight of Greyson's face.

He hovered over her and crushed her lips with his fiercely, his tongue battling with hers as he devoured her. She buried her hands in his hair, clenching it tightly in her fists, so tight it had to hurt. But she wanted him closer. She pulled at his bottom lip with her teeth and then soothed it with her tongue. Even with his lip in her mouth he wasn't close enough. She pulled away and panted to catch her breath.

"Greyson, I..." Kat murmured.

He nuzzled against her neck. The sensation of his prickly beard against her over-sensitized skin sent tendrils of need curling through her body.

"Mmm," he murmured against her neck, "that's quite a way to be woken up."

She smiled and stroked his hair.

"Are you okay?" He pulled away from her and gazed into her eyes, his elbows propped on the bed on either side of her head.

"I will be. Thanks for everything you did last night." Her heart ached at the way he gazed down at her. "I should probably go."

"You don't have to..." He made no move to let her up.

"I know. But I don't want to be a burden. I should get a hotel room and I'm sure my cell has a bunch of missed calls from my insurance company." She turned her head to hide her face.

"You're not a burden, Kat." He shifted off her.

The wounded expression on his face made her stomach churn. "You've already done so much for me."

"I wish you'd stay."

"Why?" Her gaze searched his.

"Because I..." He leaned over and pressed his lips softly to hers. Her lips parted slightly and he delved his tongue into her sweetness. She tasted like coffee, hazelnuts and something sweet and dark. She wrapped her arms around him, crushing her breasts against his chest. Her hands trailed over him, as if she were trying to memorize each sinewy cord of muscle on his arms, his chest, his stomach. He froze when she hooked her thumbs under the waistband of his boxers.

"Kat?" He glanced at her in confusion.

"Please, help me forget about what happened last night. Give me new memories. Sweet ones. Hot ones. Wet ones," she purred and punctuated each type with a lap of her tongue across his lips.

He crushed her lips with his, biting gently at her tongue when it delved into his mouth. He slid his hands up her arms, over the rolled-up sleeves of his shirt. He'd fantasized about how she'd look in his clothes. She looked a million times better in real life. Her thick mahogany hair cascaded over her shoulders and covered her full breasts that heaved against the buttons of his white shirt. Her full lips were a rich pink and slightly swollen from his kiss. He wondered if other areas of her body would swell from his kiss. The thought sent a rush of blood to his pants and his body strained against the thin material of his boxers.

She smiled against his lips as she felt his hardness press against her stomach. He was so much bigger than she'd ever imagined. Was she really going to do this? Could she really erase the horrible memories of the night before with one morning of amazing sex? Besides, this could seriously jeopardize everything she had worked so hard to attain at the department. Could they keep it professional at work and keep their relationship a secret?

It didn't matter. Right now the only thing that mattered was being with Greyson. She pulled back and brought trembling fingers to the button just above her breasts. She felt like a teenager, doing this for the first time. But it was the first time for her. The first time that she'd allowed herself to throw caution to the wind. The first time she'd let someone else take control. Because she'd never felt this way about anyone before. Even before she found out what Eric had done, she never felt about him the way she felt about Greyson. The realization hit her like a lead weight in her stomach.

Her hands stilled on the button she was trying to ease from the hole. She loved him. It was true. She'd been in denial of her feelings for him for so long that it felt commonplace to push the feelings into the corner of her heart. But now that she'd admitted to herself that she loved him, the feelings crashed over her like waves beating the sand.

She shook her head to clear her thoughts. Focus on the here. The now. It didn't matter how she felt about him. This couldn't continue. She knew this. She'd already come to terms with the fact that she could never let him know she loved him if she valued her career. Because if those three little words fell from his lips and she'd be putting in her request for transfer.

He watched patiently as her fingers deftly undid the rest of the buttons with renewed determination. She leaned back on the bed and gazed up at him, her eyes smoldering with desire. He swallowed the lump that grew in his throat. The words he wanted to say were lodged right behind the lump, and all would be lost if he uttered them.

He shifted his body over hers and kissed her tenderly before laying a trail of kisses down her jaw line, to her neck, pausing to pay special attention to the delicate skin just above her collar bone. He loved the way she trembled as his breath puffed gently against her skin. He kissed her shoulder as he pushed the material of his shirt over it and down her arms. Her full breasts popped free and her dark nipples stood erect in the cool morning air. His hardness pressed stiffly against his shorts.

She gasped as the shirt fell free of her breasts. He continued to lay trail of kisses down her chest. Her back arched when his tongue trailed a lazy circle around her areola. His hand cupped her other breast, teasing the hard pebble of her nipple between two fingers. She moaned at the tugging sensation that traveled from her nipple to the wet juncture between her legs.

He smiled as she arched against him and sucked the hard nipple into his mouth greedily. She stifled a moan and clutched at his shoulders.

"Mmm, you like that?" he murmured against her nipple.

"Yes!" she cried as he paid the same attention to her other nipple.

"God, Kat, you're gorgeous." He laid a path of kisses down her stomach. He still had her breasts captured in his palms and was twisting and tugging on their taut peaks. Her breath came in pants, and a little gasp of pleasure escaped her lips with each twist or flick of her nipples.

"Please." She didn't know what she wanted. She wanted him to continue paying attention to her nipples, but the ache between her legs increased by epic proportions.

"What do you want Kat?" He gazed up at her from where he was nuzzling her bellybutton.

"You. I want you Greyson. Now!" She couldn't handle any more of his attention without spontaneously bursting into flames.

"I know." He smiled down at her, his eyes crinkling at the width of his smile. He was smiling like a school boy hearing that the girl he had a crush on liked him. He didn't care. As long as he didn't tell her he loved her everything would be fine.

She couldn't help but smile at the mischievous grin that crossed his face when she demanded that he stop taunting her and give her what she wanted.

She squirmed under him. "Greyson, please." She spread her legs and wrapped them around his torso, hoping that he would get the hint.

"Shhh. Patience, love. I want to savor every inch of you first." Shit. Had he just called her love? His jaw clenched at the almost-slip.

"Oh God, Greyson, please! I need you!" She writhed against him.

"Shhh." He released her breasts from his torturous caress and hooked his fingers in the waistband of his boxers on her hips. It was one of the hottest things he'd ever seen. Just the sight of her flat stomach, the gentle swell of her hips in his boxers had almost been his undoing. But this was about her pleasure, not his.

He slid the boxers down slowly, kissing each inch of newly exposed skin as the fabric was pulled down. He paused above her mound.

"Are you sure?" He gazed up at her. Last chance to change her mind.

She returned his gaze through heavy-lidded eyes filled with desire. "Fuck Greyson! Yes I'm sure!"

He smirked at the language that fell from her sweet lips.

She writhed against him in frustration. She wanted him in her now, and he was taking his merry sweet time. She half considered forcing him to his back and climbing on top.

He stripped the boxers from her hips and pushed them down her legs. The sight of her hairless pussy was too much. He wanted to make love to her slowly, giving her every pleasure before he even considered getting any for himself, but the sight of her naked had his cock straining against his boxer briefs.

His eyes trailed over every inch of her exposed flesh. Her full breasts, their dark peaks, the jut of her ribs, the ridges of her abdominals, the gentle swell of her hips, her long tanned legs. He swallowed hard. God how he wanted to be inside her right now.

Her voice brought his eyes to hers. "Grey, please!" Her eyes smoldered with desire.

He smirked at the nickname. She was the first person to ever call him Grey and get away with it. He loved the fact that she was so desperate for him that she'd resorted to nicknames.

"Mmm, while I love hearing my name on those sweet lips of yours, I'd rather be tasting them." He crawled over her and pressed his lips against hers.

"You're cruel," she whined against his lips.

"Oh, am I now?" He traced the tip of his tongue against her lips and found the tight peaks of her nipples with his fingers, caressing and pinching playfully.

She arched against his touch and cried out. This was complete and utter torture. He was intent on driving her insane. The need in her body burned hotter and hotter, threatening to engulf her at any moment.

"Do you want me Kat?" he whispered against her lips.

"Yes!" She gasped as he tweaked the sensitive buds.

"Tell me what you want me to do. You're in control. Tell me." He slowly slid his hand down her flat stomach and cupped her wet mound. Her hips thrust against his hand of their own accord.

"Please, please."

"Do you want me to do this?" He kissed his way down her chest and sucked her nipple into his mouth. At the same time, his long fingers parted her folds. She gasped and spread her legs wider. His fingers found the tight nub at the top and he rubbed gently against it.

She gasped and writhed against his hand as he deftly stroked her clit. Each stroke increased the tension in her body until she couldn't stand any more.

"Greyson!" she screamed as the need peaked in a white-hot explosion of sensation. Her body trembled and she rode the waves of pleasure as they washed over her.

Her eyes fluttered open and her breathing calmed. "Holy shit." She gazed down at him where he ran tongue in circles over her nipple. He barely touched her and she came harder than she had in her entire life.

"You haven't seen anything yet." His caramel eyes burned intensely and held her gaze as he slipped a finger inside her.

She gasped with surprise as the hot tendrils of need unfurled in her like a flower in bloom, her body instantly ready for a second round of the pleasure that she found at Greyson's fingertips. She closed her eyes at the intimacy of having him watch her as his fingers delved inside her.

"Open your eyes, love." Shit. He'd just called her love again. He was walking the edge of a very sharp knife here...

Her eyes fluttered open and she gazed at him with half-closed eyes. His heart ached at the vulnerability in her eyes.

"Watch me. Know that it is me that is pleasuring you. Let everything else fade away."

"Okay," she whispered and watched as he slid between her legs. His face was level with her slit, his fingers still buried deep within her. She stiffened as he started to lower his mouth to her. Eric had kissed her like this, but rather than revulsion like she felt when Eric touched her, the desperate need she'd experienced a few moments ago flared to life, hotter than before.

"Oh, God," she squeaked as his tongue traced over her clit. She shifted her legs farther apart and almost came again as he dipped two fingers inside of her while sucking on her clit. His fingers thrust in and out of her and he rubbed her sensitive nub with his tongue. His eyes still held hers, and it was as if he was staring into her soul. Her gasps turned to breathy pants as he increased his pace.

"Please take me," she begged and implored him with her eyes. She couldn't take any more of this exquisite torture.

Her body sung as his gaze narrowed with desire. He got up and quickly shed his boxers. Finally! Her eyes widened at the sight of him standing at attention. The mushroom head was thick and smooth, the thick shaft pulsing. She yearned to take it into her mouth to see if it tasted as good as it looked. But not now. Now she wanted to feel him inside her. She'd have time for that later.

He went to the dresser and pulled out a foil wrapper and quickly sheathed himself. Then he slid over her and positioned the throbbing head of his cock at her wet cleft. Just the feel of how wet she was made him almost lose control. Slow. This is for her pleasure, he thought.

At his hesitation she reached down and wrapped her fingers around his thick, hard shaft. It was just like she thought it would be. He sucked in a shocked breath and clenched his eyes shut. Through the thin latex she could feel the veins pulsing under her fingers. She had to have him in her. Now. She arched her hips against him, causing the tip of his shaft to slip into her wet opening. She let go of him and ran her hands over the corded muscles of his biceps.

"Jesus, Kat." Her name was like a prayer on his lips as he pushed inside her.

Her eyes fell closed and she gasped at the excruciating pleasure of his thick shaft entering her. He stretched her as he slowly filled her. She moaned and writhed against him, each movement causing tiny sparks of ecstasy to ignite in her core.

Nothing she experienced before could ever have prepared her for how it felt to have Greyson buried deep inside her. Her muscles clenched around him. It was like she was a virgin, experiencing sex for the very first time. Every touch, every sensation was new, so much more intense and powerful than anything before. He barely slid inside and she already felt the white-hot pleasure of her orgasm licking along her skin.

"Greyson." She shifted her hips beneath him, pulling him deeper into her core.

He stiffened. "Are you okay?"

Her eyes fluttered open and the intensity of his gaze on her made her clench harder around him. "Please don't stop." She caught her bottom lip with her teeth.

A growl rumbled through his chest and his biceps flexed beneath her fingertips as he pulled back and filled her again. She arched her hips off the bed to meet each powerful thrust and punctuated each with a tiny moan. Each withdrawal, each entry, intensified the sparks of ecstasy that tingled through her. The aching pressure built in her core, each thrust brought her closer to the white-hot inferno that threatened to consume her.

He took her full breasts in his hands. His eyes locked with hers, and he swore he could see her love for him in the stormy sea of her deep blue eyes. Was he imagining it? The words came to his lips. He viciously gnawed on his bottom lip to keep them from passing his lips. Instead he twisted the hard peaks of her nipples between his fingers gently. Her breasts bounced in his hands as he pounded into her. I love you, he thought. Each thrust sang his love for her. I love you, I love you, I love you.

"Greyson!" Her body arched off the bed as the scorching inferno of her orgasm overwhelmed her.

He caught her and wrapped his arms around her as he pounded his release into her. He clenched his eyes shut as his seed shot into her. I love you. He stiffened. Fuck. Had he said that out loud? Unable to support them any longer, he collapsed onto the bed, practically crushing her, his breath puffing against her neck.

She let out a satisfied sigh and stroked his shoulder, tracing his shoulder blade down to his tight butt. Rather than being suffocating, his weight on her felt right. He was still lodged inside her, and even in its flaccid state it stretched her. She wriggled against him, the little fireworks of ecstasy still ricocheting through her body.

"I must be crushing you." Greyson shifted onto his side, taking her with him so she was still wrapped in his arms. Were this not his condo, with any other woman, he'd be up, dressed and halfway down the street by now. But with Kat he wanted to stay this way forever. Naked, wrapped in each other's arms, his manhood buried to the hilt in her wet pussy. His heartbeat thundered in his ears.

She smiled. "That's okay, I was enjoying it." Her hands trailed up his chest, the light scattering of wiry hair tickling her palms. "God Greyson, if I had known it could be like this..."

The words sprung to his lips again, but he crushed them by crushing her lips with his. Don't fuck it up, Greyson.

"Me either," he murmured once he had control over his emotions again. That was safe enough, letting her know it was incredible without telling her how he truly felt. He was trying to protect her. From Eric, from him, from the world, and ultimately from herself. Someday she'd thank him for not fucking it up for her.

They fell asleep in each other's arms for what felt like a few minutes and hours at the same time. Diesel's ferocious barking and scratching at the front door woke her from the most peaceful sleep she'd had in years.

"Diesel!" Kat shouted and grabbed Greyson's shirt off the floor as she bounded from the bed. She shot Greyson an apologetic look as she turned to run down the hall to quiet the obnoxious boxer.

"Diesel! What the hell's the matter with..." she stopped short. He was lunging at the door, his massive paws hitting high on the door, rattling the handle. Beneath his feet was a large manila envelope, which had obviously been crammed between the door and the jamb.

"Diesel, hush!" Kat commanded. He whined but complied, turning in a circle and plopping in front of the door once more.

"Greyson? Someone put an envelope under your front door," she said as she walked back down the hallway to his bedroom. She flipped the envelope over and looked at the bold handwriting in elegant calligraphy in all caps. FOR KAT. "Wait, it's for me?" She sat next to him on the bed.

"Who would've known you're here?" He took the envelope from her and flipped it over in his hands.

"No one. I haven't called anyone since we left my house." Her stomach churned as she took back the envelope.

"Maybe we should take it to the police station before you open it."

"No, I just want to get it over with. You're here to protect me, right?" she said with a sideways smile.

"Absolutely."

She slipped her finger under the flap and slid it across. The sound of paper ripping felt ominous.

"It's pictures." She dumped the contents of the envelope out onto the bed. A folded piece of ivory parchment fell out on top of the pile. She tentatively lifted the expensive paper and unfolded it.

Written in graceful flowing calligraphy in blood red ink, the words sent ice water shooting through her veins.

Kat,

You should have died in that fire. But, since you didn't, I look forward to the opportunity to try again. You weren't the first, you won't be the last. But you will be among them. Trust me.

To think you chose the lesser of the Neal brothers. How pathetic.

Hopefully Chief Phillips doesn't see these before I see you again. That would just be tragic...

E

Her hands shook as she read the last line. Acid rose in her throat as she turned to the pictures. All dark haired, blue-eyed girls, all in their mid-twenties, naked and tied to a bed, flames licking along their skin, their glassy eyes staring sightlessly back at her. Five girls in all, taken before the blazes reduced them to the charred corpses they put out. She flipped to the final set of pictures. Nausea overwhelmed her and she dropped the pictures.

Greyson stiffened as Kat dropped the pictures and dashed for the bathroom. Her retching echoed down the hallway. His skin tingled with anxiety as he reached for the pictures. At the bottom of the stack, beneath the gruesome death pictures of girls tied to their beds, the same way that Kat had been, was a stack of pictures. Taken from outside of his window from the greens of the golf course. Kat, asleep, naked in his bed. Him in his boxers, her naked thigh draped over his. His head between her legs. The last picture of him on his knees between Kat's legs, her breasts in his hands, his cock halfway inside of her. From the clarity and angle they must have had a telephoto lens.

Greyson growled and dropped the pictures on the bed and raced for the window. The green was empty.

18

Chapter Eighteen

"He didn't show up for his shift today. They went to his apartment and it was like he left in a hurry. But no one in his neighborhood recalls seeing anything out of the ordinary. No one saw anything. No one heard anything," Chief Phillips said from the head of the conference table.

"Kat, I am putting you on desk duty until this whole bloody mess is cleared up. It's too dangerous to have you out there with this going on."

"Please don't." Kat stared at the wood grain patterns on the honey maple conference table.

"It's for the best, Kat." He used the gentle fatherly tone that he only used when they were behind closed doors.

"If you want to protect me, send me out there. Pretend like nothing's different. Let me do my job. Keeping me in a cage does nothing to protect me. It will do more damage than if Eric got his hands on me again." She raised her tear-filled eyes to his. Her back stiffened in anger that her emotions would betray her when she needed to be calm and reserved.

"Is that really what you want?" His deep brown eyes searched hers. The fatherly concern that gazed back at her made her homesick.

"Yes. I'll go crazy if you put me behind a desk until he's caught."

"Fine. If you can promise me that you'll be beyond careful from now on. We're going to go on the buddy system. Kat never goes anywhere alone. Ever. One of you will be with her at all times. Got it?"

Greyson shot up from his seat, sending his chair clattering onto the floor behind him. "But Chief!"

"You have something to say, Neal?" Chief Phillips raised a dark eyebrow at him.

"Sir." He took a deep, calming breath. "I mean no disrespect, but the safest place for Kat is desk duty. Eric could be anywhere, and he knows Kat's personality. He knows she'd never allow you to desk her." His eyes locked with hers.

Were it not for the tortured expression in the smoky depths of his eyes, she'd have cussed him out for being a blatant example of Knight in Shining Armor Syndrome. But after their morning together, she couldn't bring herself to think of him like that anymore. He really was trying to do what he thought was best for her. But it wasn't his job to protect her.

Her eyes remained locked with Greyson's as she spoke. "Please, Chief. I understand Greyson's concerns, but I can't just hide in a corner while the boys protect me. I can take care of myself."

Chief Phillips cleared his throat, effectively breaking the standoff. "Greyson, your arguments are duly noted. But we need to let Kat take the lead on this. I will do this, however: you're her partner. You will have her back on every call. How does that sound to everyone?"

Jake and Kevin nodded and murmured their agreement. When they learned about Eric's attack on her, each had reacted differently. Jake punched his fist through the drywall in the rec room. Kevin stared into space and didn't return to the living for an hour.

"This is fucking ridiculous!" Kat flinched when Greyson pounded the table with his fists. "This is your life we are talking about here Kat! Eric almost killed you!"

"I know. But I can't just cower under the covers until he's caught. I won't let him win. I can't let him win." She clenched her fists, so hard that her nails bit into her palms.

"Fine. I accept the assignment." The triumphant look in her eyes at his acquiescence made his heart lurch.

Chief Phillips stood up. "Good. Let's get to work then."

The screaming of the alarm sounded in the hallway. The thunder of boot-clad feet pounded the shiny tile floor as they dashed for the pole. Kat made it first and slid gracefully down and hopped out of the way. One by one they pounded into the padding at the base of the pole.

It felt so good to be back. It was like nothing had happened in the past twenty-four hours. Except for the nagging dread that simmered deep in her stomach as she hefted the suspenders of her bunker pants over her shoulders and shrugged into her heavy jacket. *Head in the game, Kat.*

She grabbed her helmet and crammed it on her head as she dashed for L-281 and climbed in. Kevin was already strapped in beside her. So much had changed over the course of forty-eight hours. She wished she could turn the clock back and not open that door. Or even further back and never said yes the first time Eric asked her out. Tears burned her eyes as her mind replayed every interaction with Eric since the moment she met him. Why hadn't she seen the warning signs?

"You okay?" Greyson asked from the driver's seat

"Yeah. I'm good." She stared out the window at the streetlights flashing by. She blinked at the tears that threatened. *Head in the game.*

The red and blue lights of the engine reflected off of the blackened stucco of the small three-bedroom Santa-Fe style house. Flames barreled high into the air, licking at the power lines draped overhead. L-281 was the first responder and the blaze raged un-checked. E-282 and E-288 pulled up seconds later.

"Get the power off on those lines!" Jake commanded as they barreled from the cab. Kevin took off at a breakneck run towards the power supply control box.

"Kat, you and Greyson are front-line. I'll throw Kevin up on ladder for ventilation. Let's get some water on this thing!"

Kat climbed up on the back of the rig to pull out the hoses with the scream of sirens echoing in the distance. Within a few seconds two blue and white Chandler Police Department patrols screeched in front of the scene. Black-uniformed officers started taping off the area surrounding the fire, successfully pushing back the gawking bystanders.

She hauled the heavy length of hose towards the door of the tiny house with Greyson and Jake pulling up the length behind her. She crammed her mask on and called into her radio. "Ready!" The hose unfurled beneath her as it filled with water. The thick canvas casing tightened in her hands.

"Let's do this," she said and pulled the nozzle back, releasing the pounding spray into the blazing doorway. She loved the hissing screams of the flames being tamed into submission. Her body sung as she forced the flames back. It was the one thing in her life she could control right now. While the rest of her world was crashing down on her, at least here, in the thundering blaze, she was in control of her destiny.

One small step at a time, they marched into the flaming house, wielding the spitting anaconda of the fire hose. Kat wanted to push through fast, squashing the flames into submission before her as they searched for victims. The power trip had her head spinning and she didn't want to lose it. Each incandescent orange tongue of flame looked like Eric's face sneering at her. She bit back a rabid scream as she aimed the spray at the blazing couch.

"Take it easy, Kat," Greyson shouted from behind her. The sounds of the other firefighters from 282 and 288 crunched behind them.

She nodded, but didn't concede. This is mine. I'm in control, she thought.

They made their way into the first bedroom and Kat kicked the door open. Thick, choking smoke rolled out of the door and billowed up on to the ceiling and into the hall. Angry white-hot flames licked up the walls, but the bed was already extinguished. The sight of the charred four-poster bed brought bile to her throat. Her blood coagulated in her veins like honey. It was like she was back in her house when Eric tried to set her on fire.

Maybe going full-force the day after Eric's attack wasn't such a good idea after all. She felt her mind wandering from the determined focus that was vital to surviving while fighting fires. Bad idea. Bad idea. Kat reeled backwards and ran into Greyson's hard form.

"You okay?" he asked through his mask.

She shook her head.

"Is your equipment malfunctioning?"

She shook her head again.

"I'm not ready for this." She handed him the nozzle and took the length of hose from him.

"Don't let him win. This is your life. You give up he wins! Do you hear me, Kat?" Greyson shouted and shoved the nozzle back into her hands.

She shook her head, the tears rolling down her cheeks.

"You're not giving up. I'm right behind you. We'll do this together."

Her eyes widened, but she nodded and turned around. He pressed his body against hers and held the length of hose behind him. Just the press of his body against her shook her from the mental torture that the thought of Eric had brought.

He mimicked her steps as she pushed forward into the room, extinguishing the flames as they advanced. The crunch of their boots on the charred floorboards was muffled by the intense hiss of the flames as they went out under the intense spray. It wasn't until the room was dripping in black-tinged water that Kat stopped to survey the bed.

Nausea overwhelmed her as she stared down at the charred figure in the bed.

She was tied up the same way as Kat had been, naked, arms and legs spread eagle. But she had one more tie around her neck, pulled tight like a noose. Her sightless eyes bugged slightly from her charred flesh. The vividness of her dreams paled in comparison to the actual aftermath of Eric's handy work. This had to be Eric. Had he done this just so that she would see it?

"Oh, God." Kat turned from the gruesome scene before her. Greyson's stricken expression brought a fresh wave of tears to her eyes.

He reached up to his radio. Kat stopped his hand.

"I have to finish this. I have to finish what he started."

"You sure?" His chocolaty eyes searched hers.

She nodded.

They pushed down the hallway, battling the blaze back with the pounding spray from their hose. Kat was relentless and took her fear and anger out on the blaze. At least the worst was behind her. She owed it to the girl in that room to finish this. She'd make sure Eric was caught. She wouldn't allow the house to go up in flames and destroy all of the evidence that he might have left just because of the roiling of her stomach.

As they battled the flames back into the master bedroom, it was if the floorboards beneath her had fallen through. There, in the bed, was a second victim. Trussed up the same way as the first, down to the noose around her neck.

She sunk to the floor as her knees gave out. Greyson caught the writhing hose a moment before it collided with her facemask.

"Two..." She gasped. He hadn't even let the smoldering ashes of her house cool before he set to work on his next victims.

She wanted to throw up. But that wouldn't help these poor girls. They needed to have their deaths avenged. The determination from mentally picturing Eric being brought to justice filled her and she pushed up from her knees. How could she ever have been in love with a psychopathic murderer?

"I'm good," Kat shouted and tried to take the nozzle from Greyson. His jaw was set in a tight line.

He shook his head.

"Give me the hose, Greyson. I'm fine." Her clear blue eyes locked with his. Something clicked in his gaze and he nodded and handed the hose to her.

They battled the blaze down to the last glowing ember. And when arson arrived, she was ready for them.

19

Chapter Nineteen

Kat watched the garage door on the engine bay rattle closed behind the truck. After talking to arson, she'd been in a daze since the moment they climbed into the cab and sped back to the station. She couldn't close her eyes without seeing their charred faces, the sightless eyes, the tortured expressions.

Damn Eric. Damn him for taking the one thing in her life that meant the most to her and turning it into something she feared. She could see his sneering face before her, hiding in a dark corner somewhere, waiting to strike.

Fuck him. She wasn't going to live her life in fear, waiting for him to jump out and grab her like some real-life boogie man.

"How you doin' Kat?" Jake asked. She jumped and caught a glimpse of his green eyes as he turned the corner and started shrugging out of his bunker gear.

"I'm alive." She shoved her hair back from her face.

"And thank God for that." Jake had taken Eric's betrayal particularly hard. He and Eric had been good friends. Did he feel responsible for what happened to her?

"Sir?" Kat asked.

"Hale?" He glanced over his shoulder at her as he hung his jacket on the hook.

"It wasn't your fault." She glanced at him and hung her helmet up.

"Yeah it is, at least partially." His eyes stayed locked on his jacket on the hook. "He was my friend. I should have seen the warning signs. I just thought it was his jealous streak. I mean, you're a beautiful woman Kat. It would be silly to think a guy wouldn't be jealous having every hot blooded man in the city gawking at you."

Kat blinked and warmth crept onto her cheeks. This was surprising coming from Jake's mouth. He was such a hard-ass. And those were not words of a hard-ass.

"Don't, Kat. Don't blush. I just meant it as a matter of fact. I'm not coming on to you... Fuck," Jake stammered.

She bit back a smile. "I understand, Captain."

He turned and raced from the room like the alarm had rung.

She shook her head and shrugged out of her heavy bunker jacket and hung it on the hook. Her fingers hooked under the suspenders of her bunker pants when a pair of strong hands stroked her shoulders.

She gasped and spun around, practically falling over her boots that she had kicked off.

"Sorry, I thought you heard me come up behind you." Greyson held his hands up defensively.

"Sorry. Apparently I'm just a bit jumpy." She sighed and turned back around. She shrugged the suspenders off her shoulders and shoved the pants down her legs. The crisp air-conditioned air felt good against her overheated skin. Her shirt and shorts were damp with perspiration and stuck to her body.

"It's understandable." He shrugged from his jacket and toed off his boots. The red suspenders of his bunker pants splayed across his broad shoulders.

Kat nodded and tucked her pants around her boots beside the rig.

"Do you want to talk about it?" He positioned himself in her line of vision. Apparently he'd noticed that she was avoiding his gaze.

"No, I want to forget. I don't want to think about it anymore." She blinked furiously at the tears that filled her eyes.

"I know, I do too." He gathered her into his arms and stroked her hair as her tears fell onto his chest.

She snuggled against his damp chest for a few moments, relishing in the feel of his strong arms around her. It felt so safe, so right to be wrapped in his arms. It was too bad they worked the same shift. Maybe something could have been there if they hadn't.

Her eyes drifted to the clock on the wall. It was just past two-thirty in the morning. The rest of the guys were probably already sacked out in their bunks by now, trying to rest up before the next call. It was the slow time. The bars had been closed for a while, so the car accidents were dying down. Most of the nine to fiver's were still in bed and wouldn't get up for the morning rush hour for a few hours yet.

She didn't want to try to sleep. She knew what would haunt her dreams. And there was no way she was ready to face that train wreck.

"I'm not going to bed, but I should go shower," Kat murmured against his chest.

"Me too."

She stiffened in his arms. Did he mean like, together? She leaned back and gazed into his soot-streaked face. His two-day old shadow held little bits of ash. Dirty wasn't a good look for most men, but on him it was sexy. His heart-wrenchingly gorgeous eyes burned with intensity.

"Kat."

No talking. Don't ruin it... Kat thought. She stood on her tiptoes and pressed her lips softly against his. He crushed her against his chest, his tongue thrust into her mouth, his hands running frantic trails across her back.

His grunt of disapproval as she pulled away brought a smile to her lips. She shot a flirtatious smile at him and sauntered towards the stairs. *This is a bad, bad idea.*

Greyson watched her as she disappeared up the stairs. In a heartbeat he was out of his bunker pants and clamoring up the stairs after her. He wasn't sure what she had in mind, but he was game. Anything to forget what he'd seen.

He tiptoed past the bunkroom and peered inside. Kevin and Jake were snoring loudly. Between the two of them, it sounded like a snoring concert. How he got any sleep with the two of them around was anyone's guess. He smirked and continued down the hall. His heart skipped a beat when he caught a glimpse of Kat's well-rounded backside disappear into the locker room.

The blue-white light of the fluorescents flickered to life as Kat pulled her favorite vanilla scented body wash from her locker. She kicked off her shoes and padded across the cool tile into the shower stall, still fully clothed. She set the body wash on the shelf and turned on the spray. She stifled a squeal when the icy water shot from the showerhead. At least she knew that if the guys were so tired they'd hit the sack without showering, they'd be too tired to bother them.

A shiver of anticipation tingled through her. *Were they really going to do this? What if they got caught?*

It didn't matter. She wanted to forget, and Greyson's embrace was the most effective at helping her do that. In love or not, it didn't matter.

The click of the lock on the door behind her brought butterflies fluttering to life in her stomach. Her heartbeat mirrored the echo of his boot steps across the tile as he approached.

"Kat?" The timbre of Greyson's voice sent chills over her skin as it echoed in the tiled room.

"In here." She was fully clothed in the shower. She rolled her eyes. It had been a while since she had done the seduction thing.

The dark shape of his body on the other side of the glass made Kat take a step back and she squeaked as her butt came in contact with the steaming hot spray from the shower. For a brief millisecond, the memory of Eric watching her shower flashed through her head. She squashed back the memory as fast as it flashed before her.

His hand stilled on the door, his fingertips wrapped around the top of the glass.

"Come in." She hoped he didn't notice the tremor in her voice.

He pulled the door open and stepped bare-foot into the shower.

Her name came out on a sigh from his lips as he crossed the distance and pulled her into his arms. His lips crushed hers as he pushed her back against the cold tile of the wall. The intoxicating fragrance of a mixture of wet lavender and vanilla drifted over him.

She gasped as the cold from the tile seeped through her shirt. Steaming water ran in rivulets over their heads and soaked into their clothes. She buried her hands in his hair, holding him tight against her as he plundered her mouth. His lips were hard against hers, devouring her with a ferocity that was absent from his previous kisses. Even when they had made love, it hadn't held the desperation that she could taste in his kiss.

He ran his fingertips gently down her arms, tracing each of her fingers before his hands wrapped around her waist. He pushed his hips against hers, his arousal straining in his soaked pants and against her hips. She felt so good pressed against him, the heat of her skin radiating through her clothes.

Desire sparked deep in Kat's body as she felt his hard length pressed into her stomach. God, she wanted him in her. Now.

When his hands caught the hem of her shirt, she raised her arms to help him rip it over her head, their lips breaking from their feverish kiss momentarily to allow the soaked material to pass over her head. The water quickly soaked through her lacy white bra and her dark nipples peaked against the thin material. She pulled him back to her lips, pressing the aching buds against the hard planes of his chest.

The sight of her soaked bra-clad breasts almost sent him over the edge. Her rosy nipples stood at attention against the flimsy material and begged for him to kiss each one in turn. He almost obliged when she yanked him back against her and crushed them between him. The little beads of pleasure pressed firmly against him. He slid his hands up her flat torso and cupped the soft mounds through the lace.

She traced over the muscles in his back, scratching and caressing in her quest to get as close to him as possible. When she came in contact with the hem of his shirt, she tugged at it desperately.

A satisfied half-smile crossed his face as he broke away from her kiss and leaned back to oblige as she wrenched the shirt from his shoulders. She was on fire tonight. And he planned on fanning those flames.

"Slow down, love." He placed a gentle kiss on her lips.

"No." She fumbled with the button on his pants. Her stormy blue eyes locked with his as the button released.

Greyson caught her hand before it disappeared beneath the soaked material of his pants.

"Are you sure we should do this? Here?" His eyes searched hers.

Kat nodded and pushed the material down his hips. His manhood brushed her wrist as it burst free of its restraint. He kicked his rumpled, soaked pants towards the door.

"Mmm," she murmured with satisfaction and wrapped her hand around his firm shaft. She smiled when he flinched, but it instantly grew and throbbed in her hand.

"Kat," he growled and crushed her lips in a fierce kiss. The feel of her hands on him was almost unbearable.

She gasped with pleasure as his arms slid around her, one hand quickly releasing the hook on her bra. Her breasts bobbed free in the steamy air, the pert nipples straining for his touch. Her knees buckled when his hands cupped her naked breasts and tweaked their tender tips. She couldn't stifle the moan that escaped her.

He released her lips and gently pressed her against the cold tile wall. The contrast of the chilled tile and the heat from Greyson's body and the steamy shower had her trembling in his arms.

A wicked grin crossed his face as he hooked his fingers in the waistband of her pants. Her breasts brushed his face as he bent to push her pants and panties from her hips. He couldn't help but suck one hard nipple into his mouth while he slid her pants from her body.

She gasped and shuddered against him as he sucked her nipple into his mouth. Her nails bit into his shoulders and she gnawed on her bottom lip to stifle the moans that threatened to erupt from her.

"You're such a tease," she whispered and gazed down at him through half-closed eyes.

"Oh, am I now?" He pushed her back against the icy wall.

The blood rushed to her cheeks at the smug smile that was plastered to his face. The steaming water streaming over their heads had washed the soot from his hair and face. He looked like a model for Old Spice. Rustic and sexy, with just a shadow of a beard. Looking at him brought the desire in the pit of her stomach flaring to life again.

The smug smile changed as his eyes locked with hers. Something deeper. Something more. A lone butterfly of hope fluttered in her heart at the look he gave her. But this was just sex. There wasn't supposed to be anything else there. Not for him.

He leaned in and gently pressed his lips to hers, pulling her into his arms, her entire body pressed against his. He wanted to go slow, to give her time to recoup, but the feel of her naked, wet body pressed against his was too much to bear.

She gasped when he hooked his hands under her knees and brought her legs around his hips. His hardness prodded against her wet opening. She clung to him and scratched his back gently.

"Oh God, Kat." He pushed her against the tile and sunk into her warmth.

She cried out as he entered her, gasping at the conflicting sensations of the searing heat as he slid inside her and the iciness of the tile at her back. He caught her mouth with his, effectively silencing her moans.

His heart clenched when he pulled back to gaze into her flushed face. Her high cheekbones, her lush lips, swollen and red from his kiss, her dark hair hanging in dripping waves off of her shoulders, her deep blue eyes wide with surprise as he took her against the wall.

"I l..." Greyson murmured. Fuck. He'd almost done it again. He pulled back and rammed his thick shaft inside her sweet juncture. He clenched his jaw and slid slowly in and out of her wetness, her muscles clenching and releasing excruciatingly as he invaded her.

She gasped at the pleasure that flooded over her with each thrust, the position causing him to hit that secret area, that place that she didn't think even existed. Tingles of ecstasy licked over her and built with each movement of his hips.

"Greyson!" Kat screamed as the fireworks exploded before her eyes.

"I love you," Greyson whispered against Kat's hair as she screamed in ecstasy. When the words finally fell from his mouth it was as if a huge weight had been lifted from his shoulders.

Hard pounding on the hallway door brought both of their heads up.

20

Chapter Twenty

"Kat! What the fuck's going on in there? Are you okay?" Kevin hollered through the door. The pounding intensified.

"Shit!" Kat whispered as Greyson slid her back down to the floor. The friction from their naked, wet bodies sliding against each other caused a sliver of heat to curl around her insides. But the insistent pounding at the door was like a bucket of ice water being dumped over her head.

"Sorry Kevin! I'm fine! Just a sec!" Kat shouted at the door. "Shit! What are we going to do?" she whispered.

"Don't worry. Just get the door. I'll stay out of sight." A brief kiss and he was gone.

She picked up their soaked clothes and stuffed them into the bottom of her locker before grabbing a towel and tucking it securely around herself. She padded to the door and cracked it open.

The door narrowly missed her face as Kevin barreled into the room.

"Where's the cock sucker?" Kevin shouted as he searched the locker room.

"Who?" Kat furrowed her brow and pulled the towel tighter around her body. She watched him warily as he peered under the stall doors. *Please God don't let him find Greyson. Please. Please.*

"Eric! I heard you scream and figured Eric had come back to finish the job," Kevin panted when he was satisfied with his search.

"Oh, that. Yeah. Um, there was a massive sewer cockroach in the shower. Scared the shit out of me." Kat blushed.

The wind whooshed from his chest like he'd been holding his breath the entire time. His eyes shot to the shower door. "Did you want me to kill it for you?"

"Thanks, but I sucked it up and got it with a shoe. Nasty mess it made too..." She faked a shudder.

He smirked. "Our fearless Kat is afraid of cockroaches, who'da guessed?" She watched as his eyes dropped from hers and traveled the length of her soaked, towel-clad body. The concern in his eyes shifted to desire. "Fuck, Kat. No wonder Eric lost it when you broke up with him..."

"Out," Kat demanded.

"Sorry. I didn't mean..."

"Out." Her eyes narrowed as she shoved him through the door.

He caught the door with one hand as she tried to shut it in his face. "Kat, please. I didn't mean it like that."

"I know what you meant Kevin. I just can't fucking deal with this now okay?"

"We cool?" He gave his best impression of a sad puppy dog.

"Yeah, we're cool." She shoved the door closed in his face. The reassuring sound of the lock flipping into place helped slow her frantic heart.

Her heart skipped a beat when a whisper echoed from the farthest bathroom stall.

"All clear?" Greyson peeked his head over the top of the stall door.

Kat nodded. A lump grew in her throat until it threatened to cut off her breathing. She had just had the most amazing orgasm in her life and had practically ruined everything she worked so hard to get in the process.

He opened the door and paced slowly down the row of stalls. The unsure look in his eyes brought fresh tears to her eyes. He was still completely naked, the bright florescent lights illuminating every ridge of muscle. He looked every bit like a glowing archangel.

Greyson pulled her into his arms. "You okay?" The reassuring warmth of his arms around her seeped into her and the light scattering of hair on his hard chest caressed her cheek softly.

She nodded and nuzzled his chest. She could still hear the pounding of her heart in her ears. "I'm sorry."

"It's not your fault. I should have..." His voice vibrating his chest sent tiny shivers through her body.

"We can't let this happen again." Tears burned her eyes at the thought of never feeling his arms around her, his mouth on hers, his body buried deep in hers. Her heart wrenched at the thought of letting him go. But she'd thrown her life into her career and no amount of amazing sex was worth giving that up. Love maybe, but...

"I know." He sighed and clutched her tighter. He buried his face in the damp softness of her hair and inhaled, trying to memorize her scent, the way she smelled like lavender, vanilla and Kat.

She pulled back and looked into his chocolaty eyes. Her heart ached at the way his features were contorted in pain. But this was just sex to him. So it should be easy for him to end this.

"Kat, I..." He lowered his lips to hers. She had made her decision. The second that Kevin pounded on that door he knew that she would have to decide one way or another. And she had chosen her career. She wouldn't be his Kat if she hadn't.

His lips were gentle on hers, tentative almost. She could taste her tears as they mixed with his taste. She sighed and wrapped her arms around his shoulders. If this was the last time, she would savor every second. Who knew when it would be brought crashing to an end?

Greyson groaned when she wrapped her arms around his shoulders and her towel fell from her body. The soft mounds of her breasts pressed hard against his chest. This may be the last time he held her, caressed her, but she was forever burned into his heart.

He spread the towel out with his foot to shield her from the icy floor and slowly lowered her on to it. His heart lurched at the sheen of tears in her eyes. *Could it be possible? Even with the horrors his brother put her through?*

It didn't matter. He'd resolved to do what was best for her, to make her decision easy. She had chosen her career. He respected her for that. Hell, he loved her for that.

He gazed down at her, with her hair fanned out around her head like a dark halo, her stormy blue eyes sparkling with tears. Her damp golden skin shimmered in the light. She reminded him of a dark, heartbroken angel.

He supported his weight on his elbows on either side of her head and gently brushed her lips with his, breathing in her heady scent. Each caress, each taste of her burned into his brain. If he was never to have this again, this last memory would have to last him a lifetime.

She sighed and gently ran her hands up his chest, longing to have this moment last forever. If only things could be this simple. Just the weight of his body on hers, the heat of his skin seeping into hers, the taste of his lips on hers. But life didn't work that way. Eric was still out there, lurking in the shadows. And her career was more important than any amount of no-strings-attached sex. Regardless of how he made her feel deep in her heart, he didn't feel the same way. But for now, right now, she would give herself up to this one last time. One last memory to sustain her.

Her body tensed as the desperation that overwhelmed her. She wanted to remember everything. Every touch. Every taste. Every feeling. She wrapped her arms around his shoulders and clung to him.

"Give me one more memory before we end this..." Kat murmured before drowning his response in a kiss so tender, so desperate, that she couldn't stop the tears that burned her eyes from rolling hot trails down her cheeks. Her tongue darted out and teased his lips, flicking and nudging at his to let her in.

His groan was all the answer she needed. His lips parted and her tongue delved into his mouth, only to have him battle back with his own. He tasted the same as always, the intoxicating flavor of coffee and hazelnuts and chocolate. His taste made her heart clench and her body ache simultaneously. I love you, her mind screamed. But her mouth stayed locked with his. Now was not the time to throw that giant elephant into the room.

He shifted so that he was supporting all his weight on one elbow, while keeping up his assault on her mouth, his hand traced intricate paths along her damp, naked skin. He memorized every curve, every ridge, every hollow of her body. Her hips thrust against him when his palm came in contact with her smooth mound. A tiny moan escaped her lips, but he muffled it with his mouth as it crushed hers. He'd miss the noises she made as he pleasured her. He steeled his jaw against the onslaught of emotions that threatened to overwhelm him. *Tell her you love her. Tell her...*

His fingers parted her and found that tight, sensitive nub. She clenched down on her bottom lip to stifle the cry of pleasure that the contact brought her. Why did his touch bring her to such extreme pleasure like no one in her entire life?

She whimpered when he pulled his lips away from hers and slid down her body, leaving a trail of kisses in his wake. He kissed each sensitive peak of her nipples, the jut of her ribs, the hollow of her stomach, the rise of each hipbone.

"Greyson!" She gasped as he placed a kiss between her legs.

"Shh, love," he murmured and spread her thighs wide, bracing her heels against his shoulder blades.

She lay exposed, her thighs spread wide, his mouth breathing hot puffs of air onto her sensitive lips. Before she could protest further his fingers spread her folds wide and his mouth was on her, his tongue delving into her wetness.

Hot flames of ecstasy overwhelmed her as he devoured her. She chewed her bottom lip so hard to keep from crying out she could taste blood.

The taste of her was so intoxicating that he nearly lost it. She was so sweet, a mixture of cinnamon, honey and ripe peach. She was so wet, her juices flowing as he ran his tongue firmly against her clit. Her body stiffened with each flick of his tongue. He glanced up and found her clenching her bottom lip tightly in her teeth.

"Am I hurting you?" His hot breath puffed against her sensitive skin.

"Noooo," she moaned and writhed against his lips. She opened her eyes and gazed down at him. The sight of his face buried between her legs brought another wave of arousal tightening her abdomen. Her nipples hardened. His eyes locked with hers as he flicked his tongue against her tight nub.

She couldn't contain the moan that escaped her lips. "Fuck, Greyson!" She arched her hips off the towel. His hands caught under her hips and he pushed his mouth harder against her lips. He was obviously intent on getting them caught again with her screams of ecstasy.

"Please, no more." She gazed down at him through the haze of her arousal. Her body shuddered as the first waves of her orgasm washed over her.

With one long lick he released her from his torturous touch. She watched as he shifted to one side, ripped open a little packet and sheathed himself before sliding over her. He lowered his lips to hers in a gentle kiss.

"Mmm."

He leaned back slightly. "What?"

"I can taste myself on your lips..." She buried her hands in his hair and brought him back down to her lips, trailing her tongue across his lips.

He growled and sucked her tongue into his mouth. What the fuck was he doing? She was the most amazing woman he'd ever met. A dedicated firefighter, incredible cook, intense lover, self-sufficient and ambitious. Why couldn't he just say the words? Keep her to himself. Let her transfer to another station. At least he'd get to keep her.

But would he get to keep her? Her determination and dedication to her job at station three was who she was. If she transferred, would she resent him? And what about Eric? She couldn't possibly forget that Eric was his brother. So he'd lose her either way? At least this way, he still got to see her, the same fiery, dedicated, sensual Kat.

He nestled between her thighs, the tip of his manhood resting against her sweet opening. His heart and cock ached at the thought that this would be the last time he would sink into her warmth, last time he would pump his release into her. The last time he would see her eyes darken with desire as she screamed in ecstasy.

He covered her lips with his, stifling her moan as he entered her. God, how he'd miss the way she couldn't control her moans when he was pleasuring her. He loved hearing her lose control. He bit his lip as her muscles clenched around him, sucking him deeper into her warmth. Excruciatingly slowly he pulled back and slid inside again. He wanted to savor the way her body sucked him in with each thrust. The way her heat surrounded him and seeped into him.

But the feeling of being buried deep inside of her, the tremors of her pussy as it clenched him was too much. Each thrust became more frantic, more forceful than the last. Her full breasts bounced with each thrust, her breath coming in pants against his lips.

"I love you," she whispered against his lips as the white-hot explosion of ecstasy overwhelmed her. It was as if sparks flew out from her body in every direction like a roman candle. Her body trembled against his as he shuddered and collapsed on to her. Her breath came in pants. Her eyes slid closed and she held him to her, his shoulders rising and falling rhythmically as he tried to catch his own breath.

Her mind replayed the experience over and over in the minutes that they lay there, spent in each other's arms. Her cheeks tingled with the memory of him tasting her the way he did. How could it be that each orgasm with him could be more intense than the last? And the fact that those words fell from her lips as she came. Her breath caught in her throat.

Holy fucking shit. Those words fell from her lips when she came. Shit. Shit. Shit. Had she really told him she loved him right before she came? What the hell was she thinking? That was the kiss of death. True, they were ending this, but to throw that out there, what the fuck?

Her stomach churned as he rolled off of her and wrapped the towel around her. He helped her to her feet. His gaze was everywhere but on hers. Shit. She really had fucked things up this time.

"I'm sorry, Kat. I shouldn't have let that happen," he murmured and pulled a dry set of clothes from his locker and quickly shrugged into them.

Tears of mortification burned her eyes. If it weren't for the towel, the blush that rushed to her cheeks probably would have spread from head to toe. Not only had he heard her, but he wasn't acknowledging it and was ashamed of what they did. Fucking great.

"Me too," she whispered. She didn't trust her voice not to crack and humiliate her further.

She padded to her locker and pulled out her own set of dry clothes and turned away from him. She rolled her eyes at the lacy black thong in her hand. Could this day get any worse?

She shimmied into the skimpy underwear before quickly sliding into her shorts and t-shirt. Once she was fully clothed, she felt more like herself, more in control of the situation.

She turned to find him standing directly behind her, his hands hanging at his sides clenched into fists, his jaw steeled like he was in pain. His eyes bored into hers.

"I'm gonna miss this," he whispered and pulled her into his arms. His lips crushed hers in a ferocious kiss. Like a man dying of dehydration finally getting drink of water, he drank in her essence, the taste of her on his lips, the feel of her soft body in his arms. His hands trailed over her body as his tongue traced her lips.

She sighed and melted into his arms. In the back of her mind she couldn't squash the glimmer of worry that he heard her proclamation of love as she came. But right now, as he devoured her with his kiss, she couldn't think. She couldn't breathe. She could only be. Tears burned her eyes at the thought of loosing this feeling, this satisfying completeness that she felt in his embrace.

A loud snap from the hall ripped them apart. Her heart leapt into her throat, her cheeks burned with embarrassment. Had someone else come to catch them in the act again?

Greyson tiptoed to the door and silently flipped the lock. He eased the door open, careful to avoid the ear-splitting creak that the hinges sometimes emitted. Thankfully, they remained silent. He poked his head into the darkened hallway and peered in each direction. Empty.

He closed the door and turned to face her. Her cheeks were a delicious shade of pink that was quickly deepening. He wanted to cross the room and kiss that blush from her cheeks, but from the look on her face he knew it was over.

Kat nodded at the question in his eyes. They both knew the time had come. She crossed the room and cupped his cheeks in her hands. She stood on her tiptoes and placed a gentle kiss on his lips. A single tear escaped her eye and fell down her cheek as she disappeared through the door.

Her bare feet padded along the icy cold tile of the hallway. She forgot her boots in the bathroom, but it didn't matter. No one would notice, hopefully. She tiptoed to her bunk, which almost seemed silly amongst the earth-shattering pitch of the chainsaw-snoring symphony. The cool sheets felt like sandpaper against her over sensitized skin as she slid between them. She sighed and her eyes fell closed as the physical and emotional exhaustion overwhelmed her. She fell asleep to the background symphony of the chainsaws.

21

Chapter Twenty-one

Greyson tried, but sleep wouldn't come. He kept replaying the day in his head. His brother hiding somewhere in the darkness. The sightless eyes of charred corpses tied to their beds. Kat begging him to make her forget what she had seen. Kevin interrupting them when her scream of ecstasy woke him. The tenderness of the last time they made love. The tears glistening in her eyes as they said goodbye. His chest felt like someone had reached in with the Jaws of Life and tore his heart from his body.

But he'd do it all over again for her. If only they could have made it work. He could have transferred to a different station. It would be a demotion, but it would be worth it for her. But she never would have allowed it. And he wouldn't allow her to transfer from station three. It was a well known fact that Chief Phillips, back in his front-line firefighting days, had pulled Kat and her twin brother from their burning home moments before the roof collapsed onto their bunk beds. But it was too late for her brother. He succumbed a few days later from inhaling the super-heated gas. They couldn't save him.

He thought of the trauma that Kat had encountered in her life. He admired her persistence. To have a brother claimed by the fire, then vow to become a firefighter and battle the thing she feared the most was incredible. Her dream was to work under Chief Phillips at station three. So how could he possibly think of letting her accept a transfer to another station?

He couldn't. So he had to let her go. To not give her the opportunity to give her dreams up for him. So he'd made it easy on her and made the decision for her.

He flopped onto his side and stared across the room. In the corner Kat was asleep soundly on her bunk, curled into a fetal position on her side. Even in the dim light he could make out her hands flat, palms touching, tucked under one cheek, the tangled dark waves of her hair draped around her head in a messy halo. So innocent, so beautiful. His heart wrenched. Tears burned his eyes. He blinked them away and flopped over onto his back.

He had done the right thing. It was wrong of him to take advantage of the situation like he had after Eric had tried to kill her. But the thought that he had almost lost her again pushed him over the edge.

But things could be fixed. They could go back to the way they were, like nothing had ever changed. At least they still got to work together. She would be happy she didn't have to worry about them being found out, and he could accept the promotion Chief Phillips had proposed to him with a clear conscience. Kevin might be pissed that he was being passed up, again, for the promotion, but he couldn't give a shit about what Kevin wanted. All that mattered to him was Kat.

Eventually his thoughts blurred one into another until they were a blended mess of images. Most were of Kat's naked body. He finally succumbed to sleep with the picture of Kat's innocent form, looking so much like a child at sleep, burned into his brain.

At first the alarm ringing felt like it was inside his head. He pried his crusty eyes open and blinked to clear them. He rolled onto his side and pulled the pillow over his head to dampen the ringing in his brain. He glanced over at Kat's bunk, but it was empty.

He shot up from his bunk, his gaze darting around the room frantically. Every bunk had the covers ripped off of it, like its occupant vacated it in a hurry.

The insistent ringing continued as he darted from his bunk. He skidded around the corner and lunged at the fire pole, wrapping his arms and legs around it as he spiraled into the engine bay.

"Thanks for joining us, sleepy head!" Jake shouted as he climbed into the cab.

He made it into his bunker gear in record time and climbed into the cab as Jake pulled the engine out of the garage. He strapped himself in and glanced into the back.

The withering glare that Kevin shot back at him was enough to melt paint. Had Kevin figured out what had been going on in the shower earlier?

He glanced at Kat, but her gaze stayed glued on the window, watching the streetlamps as they whizzed by. She'd pulled her hair back into a neat ponytail that she had tucked into the collar of her jacket.

His heart lurched at the shadows beneath her eyes. Was it just sleep deprivation from him keeping her up or was there more? Had she been crying? He turned around in his seat and stared out the windshield into the darkness. Every so often an orange streetlamp or a stoplight would blur past.

"What the fuck is up with you three tonight?" Jake asked as he angled the truck in front of the accident to divert traffic.

"Nothing Cap," Greyson murmured.

"Well whatever the fuck is going on, head in the game people," Jake growled as he crammed his helmet on and climbed down from the cab.

"Head in the game," Kevin murmured and slammed his door behind him.

"Kat," Greyson said with a sigh.

"Please don't Greyson. Not here. There's nothing more to say." She didn't look at him. Her eyes locked on the car accident. She opened the door and climbed out, slamming the door behind her.

It was like she had slammed his heart in the door. He quickly unhooked himself and climbed from the cab.

The black Escalade had managed to flip completely onto its roof, successfully crushing half of a small Toyota Prius that had been unlucky enough to be in its path. CPD patrols were already on-scene. They had already pulled three survivors from the Escalade with little more than scratches and concussions. The driver of the Prius wasn't so lucky.

"Let's get the Jaws people," Jake ordered as he surveyed the scene.

Kat nodded and ran back to the truck with Kevin to pull the heavy-duty equipment from the locker where it was safely stored. The entire rear of the Prius was smashed flat under the Escalade, and the frame bent so severely in the impact that the doors were sealed shut.

Kevin's eyes locked with hers as they reached the driver's side door of the Prius. Within minutes, they had popped the hinges on the door and pulled the twisted metal away. Kat peeked in between the bent door-frame and the drivers seat. Her heart leapt into her throat when she saw the bottom of a car seat in the center of what used to be the backseat, which was now squashed under the flattened roof of the Prius.

"Are you alone?" Kat fought to keep her voice calm. She'd seen everything during her career, from the tame to the gory. But the only thing that stuck with her, that haunted her when she closed her eyes, that made her question why she became a firefighter, was the sight of an injured child. Or worse.

"Huh?" The woman glanced around in confusion for a moment.

"The car seat! Are you alone in the car?" Kat asked again, this time her voice laced with anxiety.

"Oh! Yeah. Thank God I decided to leave my son home with my husband! I had to take my mom to the airport." the dazed woman replied.

Kats shoulders relaxed and her heart resumed its regular rhythm. She tried not to picture how the scene might have looked had the woman not left her son at home. Once she had ascertained that the driver had only sustained minor injuries she pulled her from the seat and gently settled her on the ground beside the rig.

"My mom's cat! We're supposed to watch him while she's in Florida! He's still in the car!" the woman gasped.

"I'll get him," Kat murmured and returned to the car.

She found the carrier on the floor of the rear passenger seat. She tugged. The purse-like carrier came out partially, but the strap was caught on something. She tugged harder.

The hair on the back of her neck stood up like soldiers at attention at the sharp screech of tires on asphalt followed by the sickening metallic crunch of a car smashing into another. As if in slow motion, she looked up in time to see the blinding light of a pair of smashed headlights coming at her. The Prius lurched as the car connected with the passenger side door. She flew forward, her breath forced from her body as she connected with driver's seat and then flung backwards into the steering wheel. White light exploded in her vision and searing pain overwhelmed all else. As the blackness descended on her, she heard Greyson screaming her name over the blood pounding in her ears.

**

Greyson's heart leapt from his chest as he watched the Taurus careen towards the mangled Prius with Kat perched inside on her hands and knees. What the hell was she doing in there?

"KAT!" he roared. Her head shot up a second before the Taurus collided with the car, shoving it back against the median.

The inertia caused her body to lurch forward, slamming chest-first into the driver's seat and bounced backwards into the steering wheel. The wheel contorted from the pressure of her slamming into it and her limp body crumpled to the floor.

"KAT!" Greyson screamed and ran for the mangled car. Other voices roared around him, but he was deaf but to the frantic pumping of his heartbeat in his ears. *Oh my God. She's dead.*

The driver of the Taurus staggered out of the vehicle and blocked his path.

"Dude! What the fuck just happened?" he slurred.

"MOVE!" Greyson bellowed and shoved the inebriated man down.

"Kat!" he shouted and slid over the hood of the Taurus and brushed away the crumbled passenger window glass from his way. The orange glow from the sodium lights filtered through the cracked windshield he could make out Kat's crumpled form on the floor of the car. Her head was propped on the seat and a trickle of blood escaped her lips. Seeing her bleeding made his own blood run cold.

"Kat?" he asked tentatively as he climbed into the passenger seat.

A choked moan escaped her lips. She coughed, a pained, rough sound. But she was alive. He released the breath he had been holding since the moment the Taurus shot across his field of vision towards the disabled Prius. She was alive.

"Don't move, love," he murmured and stroked the hair that had been ripped free from her ponytail back from her face. He braced her head with both hands to prevent her from moving and causing herself further injury.

Her thick lashes fluttered and parted to reveal the deep blue depths of her eyes. She squinted to focus on his face.

"Greyson? What..." she croaked.

"Shh, love. Secondary accident."

She coughed again and winced, the blood trickling down her chin anew.

"Broken ribs, punctured lung," she wheezed.

"You don't know that," he murmured. But from her symptoms, that's exactly what she had, at a minimum.

Her chest burned for air. She tried to take a deep breath but sharp stabbing pains stopped her. She tried to move but she was pinned beneath the steering wheel. The chill of panic started to seep into her muscles. She needed to move. Now. A gentle touch stroked her hair back from her face again. Somehow, just his touch was enough to calm her.

"Just relax. We'll get you out of here. I promise. Try not to move, okay?" he soothed.

A metallic crunching like someone going at a piece of sheet metal with a chainsaw filled the tiny space. She wanted to cover her ears with her hands, but they were trapped beneath her body. Please God, don't let anything else be broken.

The roof of the Prius rolled back like a sardine can and revealed the graying sky above, indicating sunrise was eminent. It felt like an omen. Within minutes they hooked a chain around the steering column and again Kat wanted to cover her ears at the intense rumble of the hydraulic generator as they used the Jaws of Life to pull the steering column up and away from her.

As the pressure from the wheel against her back lessened, the intense pain that replaced it was immediate, and tears filled Kat's eyes. She hugged her arms around her chest, relieved that at least they weren't broken. Everything else, however...

Greyson took the neck brace Kevin handed down to him and gingerly wrapped it around her neck and slid the KED back brace into place. Kat watched through tear-filled eyes as he deftly fastened the straps around her. Just the pressure from the straps eased her pain a bit, like they were somehow holding her lungs inside her chest.

He took a deep breath and gently eased her from beneath the steering column. Kevin stood on the hood of the mangled Prius and helped Greyson pull her from the twisted wreckage.

They smoothly transferred her to Eve and Jake as they cleared the wreckage. Eve quickly strapped her onto the gurney and tucked the oxygen tank beside her.

On the way to the ambulance Eve quickly surveyed the damage. She plugged her stethoscope into her ears and listened.

"Breathe deeply, if you can," she murmured.

"I can't," Kat wheezed.

Eve listened for a moment as Kat struggled to breathe. Concern etched her features and Eve's blue eyes met hers.

"Punctured lung, huh," she struggled.

Eve nodded. "We need to transport you, ASAP." With a glance at her partner Chris, she stepped up into the truck. Chris pushed the gurney into the ambulance and the click of the wheels as they folded up and locked beneath her sent her stomach into somersaults. This was the third time she'd been in the back of Eve's rig, and second time being transported away to the hospital. She didn't like the pattern that was beginning to emerge.

"Hold up!" Greyson's voice filtered into the ambulance from far away.

"Greyson, we have to go, now. I'll call you guys and let you know how she's doing," Eve started to close the door.

Greyson grabbed the door, effectively stopping Eve from closing it. "I'm coming with her."

"That's not necessary. I promise I'll take good care of her," Eve's voice was tinged with annoyance.

"I'm still coming," he growled.

"Kat?" Eve asked.

"Okay," Kat wheezed and winced at the pain that the sound coming from her lips caused in her chest.

The ambulance shifted as he climbed inside and sat beside her. His warm hand closed over hers as the doors slammed shut and the sirens blared. The ambulance jerked. Kat winced at the pain the movement caused. Out of the corner of her eye she could see the top of his dark brown hair, his strong eyebrows knit with concern.

"I'm going to put this oxygen mask on you to help you breathe okay, Kat?" Eve asked.

Kat nodded slightly, impeded by the neck brace. The translucent clear-green plastic mask came over her head and covered her mouth and nose. The medicinal smell of oxygen overwhelmed her momentarily, but the spots before her eyes and the headache lessened.

Greyson squeezed her hand reassuringly.

Within a few minutes of being loaded into the ambulance she was unloaded and rushed through the emergency department of Chandler Regional Hospital. Other emergency crews stood out of the way as they rushed her through the hall. Faces she recognized dotted the ceiling tiles occasionally, the look on their faces the same: sadness, concern and anger.

After a brief check by the ER triage doctor, they transferred her to a patient room. Kat's head spun as a flurry of activity happened around her. Greyson's quiet murmuring as various nurses and doctors came and went. The hiss of the oxygen as it pumped into the mask. She was wheeled back and forth for chest X-rays. Her heart became a block of ice when the words "pneumothorax and chest tube" fell from the examining doctor's lips.

When the tube was placed, it was little more than a small tube inserted beneath her breast near her sternum and directly into her lung. After she returned from more chest X-rays, Greyson was finally allowed back into the room. He collapsed into a chair by the head of her bed. Lines etched along his brow, dark shadows circled his worried eyes.

"Thought I lost you," he murmured with a half-smile that didn't reach his eyes.

"You did," she said.

"I know." He leaned forward to bury his head in his hands.

"Why are you here, Greyson?" Tears burned her eyes. She'd practically died tonight. Again. And Greyson had rescued her. Again.

"I had to know you were going to be okay." He clenched his hair with his hands.

"I'll be okay. Thank you for coming with me." Her heart ached at the way he looked like he was being tortured. "You should probably get back to the station. They're probably wondering why you came with me. What are you going to tell them?"

"That you're okay, or will be. And whatever the discharge instructions from the ER doc will be."

"Oh, she's not getting discharged for a few days," Dr. Monty said as he swept into the room. "She's going to be in here for a few days, until I'm sure her lung is capable of supporting itself. Then it's four weeks off work." His dark eyebrows rose over his ebony eyes. His sexy New York accent and demeanor left Kat struggling to find words to argue with him.

"Wow," Greyson said with a gush. "Are you planning on keeping her tied to the bed for that long? Because there's no way she –"

"Shut up, Greyson," Kat growled.

His mouth snapped shut.

"Oh, I don't think I'll have to tie her to the bed, unless she wants me to." Dr. Monty winked at her. "I think she'll be a good patient for me, won't you?" His wide smile lit up his dark, exotic features. Her face flamed. She glanced at Greyson and found his jaw set in a hard line, like he was grinding his teeth.

"I'll be good," Kat promised. Good thing he didn't see her fingers crossed under the blanket. Dr. Monty often used his hotness to persuade his female patients to follow his orders. Were she not in love with Greyson, it probably would have been a very effective technique with her as well.

Greyson clenched the armrests of the chair, his knuckles almost white.

Kat smirked.

"The good news is that there isn't more damage. I'm surprised with the bruises where you connected with the steering wheel that you didn't break your back. Luckily, you only sustained a few broken ribs, some nasty bruises and a punctured lung. It could have been *a lot* worse." Dr. Monty flipped through her chart. "Looks like this Kat's got nine lives," he joked.

She rolled her eyes.

"Well, she's down to four now Doc." The scalding glare Greyson shot the poor doctor would wither a lesser man.

"Well then, let's just make sure she doesn't lose any more. I'll be back to check on you later, Kat. Okay?" Dr. Monty patted her knee. With a smile that lit up his whole face he spun on his heel and walked out of the room.

"Fuck." Greyson slumped back into the chair.

"You can't do that you know," Kat snapped.

"Do what?"

"Act like I'm your property. We ended this, remember?" Had he heard her earlier when she told him she loved him?

"I know." He stared at the linoleum floor. "I'm sorry."

Kat stiffened when her mother's nasally voice shrieked from down the hall. "I'm here to see my daughter. Is she okay? Get out of my way. Where is she? KAT!"

From the flurry of commotion outside of her room it was clear Jake had called her but that she had come to her own conclusions. Kat rolled her eyes and caught Greyson's worried expression.

Kat sighed. "You should get out of here before she lays into you. It's gonna get ugly."

"Why would she?" He raised an eyebrow at her.

"Because you should have seen the car coming with your Spidey sense and gotten me out of the car before it got hit." She exaggerated an eye roll.

"You know, I think I'll stay and see this one out. I'd like to meet your mom anyway." He crossed his arms and leaned back in the chair.

"You're fucking nuts. I'd be out of this bed and down the hall by now if I wasn't attached to all this crap." She waved a hand absently at the IV poles and chest tube.

"Do you want me to go?"

Kat nodded.

A wounded expression crossed his handsome features. "Oh. Okay," he conceded and got up from the chair.

"Please don't take it personally. My mom's ten kinds of crazy and I don't want you to witness it. I'd rather you remember me as I was than to see a picture of what I will someday become," she said with a chuckle. She winced and clutched her rib cage.

His chuckle matched her own. Her eyes fell closed as he leaned over and gently brushed his lips across her forehead.

"As you wish," he whispered.

Her heart skipped a beat. Had they talked about her favorite movies before?

With a rustle of thick fabric and heavy boot steps, he was gone.

"Kitty! Oh my Gawd! I saw the news! Are you alright?" Mildred Hale marched into the room, shrugging out of the grasp of an exasperated nurse.

Kat shot the nurse an apologetic smile. "It's alright. She's my mom."

The nurse nodded and disappeared through the door.

"What happened? What the hell is all this stuff attached to you? Are you dying?" She surveyed the wires and hoses coming out of her daughter.

"Broken ribs and a punctured lung, Mom. Really, it's no big deal. I'll be in the hospital a few days and then some time off work to recoup. You really didn't have to come down here." Talking to her mother was kind-of like talking into a phone with the mute on. You could talk all you wanted, but she didn't hear a thing.

"I called Pastor Miller. He said he'll be here for visiting hours to anoint you." She rifled through her suitcase-sized purse.

Kat rolled her eyes. "Mom, you really didn't have to..."

"Yes, I did. The Lord will watch over you and speed your recovery. I'll be writing up the announcement for the church bulletin as soon as I get home."

"This is nothing that needs to be put in your church bulletin. For God's sake, Mom! I don't even go to your church anymore!" Kat snapped. Her side screamed but it didn't matter. Thank God she didn't know about what happened with Eric. How she managed to miss the headlines about her house fire she'd never know.

"You used to. You used to have faith."

"It wasn't God who pulled us from that fire, was it? And where was God when Jason died? He was seven-fucking-years-old, Mom!" Her blood pounded in her ears. She could feel the tape from the chest tube pulling at her skin. Her blood pressure monitor beeped at a furious pace.

"You should have put your faith in God instead of turning from him when Jason died. That's how I got through..."

"Yeah, well not everyone believes in blind faith. I need proof. And so far *He* hasn't proven himself worthy of my faith." She ground her teeth and glared at her mother.

Mildred's face flushed magenta and her pudgy cheeks puffed out like a blow fish. For a moment Kat considered pushing the nurse call button to get her help. But as she blew the breath she had been holding out slowly, her face returned to its slightly ruddy complexion.

God, how she wished she could have had a normal relationship with her mother. She was a normal, happy mom before Jason died. But shortly after Jason's death, her behavior started changing, she became more withdrawn, depressed even. Eventually she and her dad split up. She always wondered if her mother blamed her for Jason's death. Guilty simply by surviving when Jason hadn't.

The fire had been deemed accidental, and a cigarette butt near the side of the house was deemed the probable cause. No suspects, no charges filed. Simply a tragedy befalling a middle-class family. Eventually her mom put her faith in God and began to climb out of her downward-spiral of depression. But the damage to their relationship was done.

"Okay, Kat. That's your choice. I'm glad you're okay, honey." She leaned over to kiss Kat on the cheek.

"Thanks, Mom," Kat murmured. This whole bipolar thing was really starting to get old.

The blood pressure monitor was still going off, the insistent pinging rattling around in her head. The nurse rushed in and checked the monitor, wrote something down on the chart and caught Kat's eye. A quick eyebrow raise from the nurse, followed by a discrete nod from Kat. The nurse sent a scalding glare at her mother.

"I'm sorry, I'm afraid I'm going to have to ask you to leave. The patient needs her rest."

"Excuse me. I'm her mother and I'll stay as long as I..."

"Mom, please go. I really do need to rest," Kat pleaded. Why did her mother have to be so confrontational about everything? The entire interaction with her mother just reminded her why she limited visits with her to holidays and an occasional Wednesday night dinner with her.

"Okay. Call me first thing in the morning, okay?" She bent over and pressed her puffy lips to Kat's cheek.

"Okay. I'll call you when I can," Kat replied. That way she wasn't lying when she didn't call first thing in the morning.

"Promise!" her mother hissed.

"I promise. Please, let me go to sleep now." Kat closed her eyes. Hopefully her mother would get the not-so-subtle hint.

She didn't realize how exhausted she was until her eyes slid closed in an attempt to get her mother to leave. She didn't hear her mother's quiet footsteps retreat from the room. She didn't hear the nurse come in to check her dressings. And she didn't hear the quiet footsteps as they crept into her room or the rustle of fabric as someone eased into the chair beside her bed.

**

She'd kill him if she knew that he'd been waiting in the hallway the entire time. He could hear the exchange between Kat and her mother. He had no idea that their relationship was so strained. How anyone could treat Kat with anything but respect and love astounded him. Especially her own mother.

He had a long look at Kat's mom as she fought off security and nurses in her search for Kat's room. Her tightly permed salt-and-pepper hair was cut short, resembling a skull-cap of poodle-like curls. Her metallic silver stretch pants and beaded house shoes were paired with an oversized knit sweater made up of glittering silver and gold yarn. Everything about the woman screamed excess. How the strong, independent, beautiful woman lying in that hospital bed was raised by this squawking peacock before him he'd never know. Did her brother's death have anything to do with this spectacle before him?

Guilt washed over him as he gazed down at the plump aging woman standing a few feet away. Exact copies of Kat's stormy blue eyes flashed to him for a moment before she shrugged out of a nurse's hold and dashed into Kat's room. But the resemblance stopped there.

The conversation between Kat and her mother started innocently enough, until it turned to God. He could practically hear Kat's teeth grinding. He smiled. He could picture the stubborn glare she was shooting at her mother. He'd been on the receiving end of that glare more times than he could count.

"Greyson!" Martinez from station two called from down the hall. Greyson waved but apparently Martinez wasn't going to be satisfied with just a congenial hello.

They met in the middle of the hallway, shook hands and did a half-bro hug.

"I heard about the accident, man! How's she doing?" Martinez asked. His hazel eyes followed the hallway to Kat's door.

"Broken ribs, punctured lung. Needed a chest tube. But it could have been a lot worse. Everyone is amazed that she didn't break her back when she hit the steering wheel," Greyson said with a relieved huff.

"Damn, man. I owe her my life y'know? How long she gonna be out for?" Martinez asked.

"Doc Monty said a few weeks, but I think we'll have to tie her down if we want to keep her down that long," Greyson said with a smirk.

"I'll volunteer for that!" Martinez joked.

"Excuse me?" Greyson growled.

"Sorry man. I didn't mean it like that," Martinez backpedaled, holding his hands up defensively.

Greyson nodded and sucked in a shaky breath. What the hell were these possessive, jealous emotions running through his veins? No woman had ever incited a response like this out of him. Even the ones he 'said' he loved.

He patted Greyson on the back. "How's your brother doin'? Haven't seen him at the station in a couple days. Cap won't tell us anything."

Greyson's eyes narrowed at the mention of his brother. "He's alive."

Martinez looked confused for a moment, but quickly composed himself. "Well, let us know if she needs anything," he said and went back to his patient.

Greyson nodded. He turned and started to walk back to Kat's room but paused when Mildred Hale emerged, her plump face drawn, eyes slightly teary. She avoided eye contact with him as she rushed to the exit, blotting her eyes with a Kleenex. What happened while he was distracted? His skin tingled and he forced himself to keep a casual pace as he neared the doorway.

He peeked into the room and found Kat lying with her eyes closed, her chest rising and falling rhythmically. He tiptoed to the chair and collapsed into it. The reassuring beep of her pulse on the monitor and the hiss of oxygen filled the room. He reached up and gently laid his hand on hers on the bed. Exhaustion quickly overtook him.

His eyes popped open to the sound of swift footfalls around him. It took a moment to focus his weary eyes as they wheeled Kat's gurney from the room. The metallic taste of panic filled his mouth.

"Wait, what are you doing with her?" he asked, his speech slightly slurred from sleep.

"Relax lover boy, we're just moving her upstairs," the chubby orderly grumbled.

Greyson stumbled after them.

"Sorry. Family only." The man grunted as he loaded Kat into the elevator. Even with the movement she didn't stir.

"I'm her, uh, boyfriend," Greyson stumbled over the word. Well, at least Kat was asleep for that...

"Well, in that case, come on." He waved a stubby hand to usher Greyson into the elevator.

The doors slid closed and the elevator lurched to life. Greyson gazed down at Kat's sleeping form. The sheets were pulled up to her neck. Tubes emerged from above the sheet and were hooked to an IV pole that was attached to the bed.

"Word is this kitty has nine lives," the orderly joked. His round belly jiggling as he chuckled.

Greyson grunted. The man coughed to cover the chuckle and squinted up at the glowing red numbers as they ticked by.

The elevator dinged and the door slid open. He followed the orderly as he pushed Kat's gurney to the end of the hall and into the room where she would spend the next few days.

22

Chapter Twenty-two

Somewhere in the darkness, a voice called out for Greyson. Kat knew it wasn't her voice, but it was vaguely familiar. She fought against the darkness that held her down, kept her from being able to open her eyes. She could hear fabric rustling in the darkness and wanted to cry out when his heavy boot steps retreated from her side. She struggled to call out to him, beg him not to leave, but her mouth wouldn't move. Panic seared through her and she finally forced her eyes open. She squinted at the wall and its patterned wallpaper wavered like it was underwater. Nausea overwhelmed her as she tried to focus on her surroundings. *Where am I?*

She knew she was lying in a bed and could feel the scratchy sheets against her skin. But everything beyond her tiny circle of vision was blurry and cloaked in shadows. She tried to move, but her body remained immobile. Panic constricted her throat. *What happened to me?*

The sound of a door opening and quiet footsteps drifted over her. A wave of relief surged over her. Greyson was back. He'd be able to tell her what happened and where she was.

The footsteps came around the side of her bed and a blurry figure towered over her. "G—" she tried to say his name, but, like the rest of her body, her lips were numb.

"Shh, babe."

If she weren't already immobile, she would have been paralyzed with fear. Eric reached his hand out and stroked her cheek with the back of his fingers. She struggled to recoil in disgust. But she couldn't move.

Eric leaned down and put his face into her line of vision. "Oh, sweetheart. I'm so sorry you had to go through this." He leaned in and pressed his lips to hers in a brief kiss.

Kat clenched her eyes shut and a tear rolled down her cheek.

He reached out and caught the tear on his fingertip and brought it to his lips. "Don't cry, babe. I'm so sorry, about everything. Especially sorry about what I have to do next..."

Kat's eyes burned. This was it. He was going to finish what he started in her bedroom. How could she ever have been in love with this stranger?

He leaned down and kissed her softly. "I will always love you, Kat."

He reached up and touched something above her head, out of her line of sight.

The walls warped and twisted around her. Then everything went dark.

**

Greyson's eyes popped open when a soft female voice called his name from the hallway. His heart skipped a beat when he glanced at Kat, lying motionless on the bed. Her chest rose and fell softly, the air puffing through the oxygen tube tucked under her nose. The steady beeping of the pulse monitor was a reassuring sound in the tiny room. Tubes snaked around her arms to various IV bags and monitors.

The memory of Kat's accident rushed back to him, churning his stomach and making his pulse race. He clenched her hand. He'd practically lost her. Again.

The familiar voice called to him again from the hall. He tore his gaze from Kat to the source of the voice. A female figure stood backlit in the doorway. "Greyson?" she called softly again.

Her voice registered this time. "Hey, Eve." He gently untangled Kat's fingers from his and got up, crossing the room with gentle steps. He cringed as his bunker gear rustled and his boot steps were way too loud on the tile floor.

"How's she doing?" Eve asked as they stepped out into the hallway.

Greyson shoved a hand through his tangled hair and leaned against the wall outside her door. "She's banged up really bad. But she'll make it through."

Eve nodded. "Hey, can we take a walk? There's something I want to say, but --" she nodded toward the nurses' station.

Greyson's gaze shot back to Kat's door. He really didn't want to leave her alone, even for a second.

Eve ducked into Greyson's line of vision. "She'll be fine. We won't go far." She shot him a million dollar smile. "Besides, the medical care here is second to none. She's in good hands."

He stared at Kat's open door for a moment more, then sighed. "Fine."

Eve grabbed his hand and pulled him away from the wall. "It'll only take a minute."

They made their way down the hall and out into an open-air court-yard. The night was giving way to dawn, setting the courtyard off in tones of blue and gray. The dew-laden air was fresh with the promise of a new day.

Greyson sucked in a deep, refreshing breath. "So what did you want to talk to me about?"

Eve stopped and flopped down on the bench, as if the weight of the world was heavy on her shoulders. "We almost lost her, Greyson."

He nodded. He didn't need her to tell him this. He'd been by her side since the accident. "I know."

"And Eric is still on the loose."

The sound of his brother's name was like a punch in the gut. It brought up waves of guilt and anger that he really didn't need to deal with on top of almost losing Kat. Again. "Eve, please. I need to get back to her."

Eve nodded. "I know. But don't you think that you're putting her in danger being near her?"

Greyson frowned. He'd never even considered the thought. "How so?"

"She was dating Eric. Suddenly he's gone and you step in? If he's still trying to get at her, don't you think it's going to make him even more irrational to see his big brother with his girl?"

The air left his chest in one big breath. "I'm putting her in danger by being near her," he whispered.

Eve nodded. "It didn't occur to me until we were on the way to the hospital with Kat tonight. But it seems like, with Eric's whereabouts unknown, that doing anything else to piss him off might make him even more unpredictable."

"He's already unpredictable. He tried to kill Kat once."

"Which is why we don't want him to try again, right?"

Greyson nodded. A lump grew in his throat. He had to stay away from her. To keep her safe.

**

Kat's eyes fluttered open to the cheery yellow light filtering in from the window. Her head spun as she glanced around the room. Where the hell was she?

She shifted to sit up, but a sharp pain in her side coupled with a mangle of tubes stuck under her skin and extending in all directions stopped her movement. Something was stuck under her nose and the medicinal smell of oxygen and plastic filled her lungs. The room was filled with the hiss of oxygen as it pumped into the tube stuck under her nose, the insistent beeping of a... pulse monitor? beeped in her ears.

Fractured memories of her shift the night before filtered into her thoughts -- the amazing sex with Greyson, ending their tryst with a vow to keep it professional from now on. A little sleep. Pulling a woman from a smashed car. A cat trapped in the car. Memories flooded faster and faster before her eyes. Headlights coming at her. Flying through the air and connecting with the steering wheel. Waking up to Greyson's voice. The chest tube. Her mom in the ER. Greyson telling someone he was her boyfriend. Someone calling Greyson away and Eric saying he would always love her.

She gasped. She attempted to reach for her side to soothe the sharp pain that her sudden movement caused, but her hand was restrained. *They tied me to the bed?* A cold wave of panic washed over her. Her gaze tentatively traveled down her arm, over the IV tube taped along her skin to her hand.

Greyson's big hand encompassed hers, their fingers entwined. Tears sprung to her eyes as she lifted her gaze to his sleeping face next to her hand on the bed. His eyes were ringed with deep shadows, his forehead furrowed like he was thinking really hard. Even in sleep he looked worried.

With a tentative touch she traced the lines across his forehead before gently cupping his cheek with her palm. His beard was longer than she'd ever seen it. When was the last time he'd shaved? He'd been so preoccupied with her lately that she wondered what else he had been putting off.

The worry etched across his sleeping face faded at her touch and he smiled in his sleep. Tears pricked her eyes as she gazed down at him, the worried expression fading and replaced by an almost child-like innocent smile.

"Mmmm," he murmured. His deep brown eyes fluttered open. A satisfied smile crossed his face and he rubbed his cheek against her palm. His eyes widened and his smile fell away. "Oh, um, sorry about that." He straightened in his chair and ran a hand roughly through his mussed hair.

She smiled. For a moment it was as if everything in the world was right. But reality quickly came crashing down on them. Everything in the world wasn't right, but there wasn't anything they could do about it.

He stayed. Eric was just a dream. A horrible, drug-induced dream. "You stayed." A bewildered smile stretched across her face. How much trouble was he in for not returning to finish his shift once she was safely at the hospital? And why the hell had he stayed? He knew she was going to be fine. Her heart fluttered. She wanted nothing more than to tell him that she loved him. But what the hell would that do, but throw another wrench into their already complicated relationship?

"Yeah." He dropped his gaze and studied the linoleum.

"Why?"

His gaze snapped to hers. Something flashed in his eyes for a moment but disappeared. He shrugged. "I just wanted to make sure that you were okay."

"Oh." It was her turn to drop her gaze.

"So, the prognosis was that you'll be in the hospital for a few days and then out of work for a few weeks..."

"I know." She pouted. If she didn't have that stupid chest tube she'd have crossed her arms over her chest in the most immature, child-like fashion.

"Kat..."

"Thanks for staying with me Greyson. It means a lot to me," she interrupted. You have no idea how much it means to me, she thought.

"I should get back to the station. I'll let them know you're okay." He got up, obviously stiff from sleeping in the chair beside her for so many hours. He leaned over and placed a gentle kiss on her forehead.

"Greyson?" she whispered and tilted her head up to look in his eyes.

"Yeah?" He gazed down at her.

"Thank you." She pulled his head down for one long, hard kiss. Had she thought about doing it, she would have talked herself out of it. It definitely wasn't the smartest thing to do, considering they had ended their brief relationship not even twenty-four hours earlier. But she almost died. So maybe he would allow her this one liberty.

He returned her urgent kiss, ignoring the fact that her oxygen tube was squished between them. He kissed her hard and fast, desperation overwhelming any attempts to be gentle. He devoured her, drinking in her essence into his heart.

He reluctantly pulled away. "I should go," he murmured as he straightened.

Kat nodded.

He reached out a hand but paused and pulled it back, clenching it in a fist to his chest.

"Take care," he murmured before he dashed from the room.

As she watched him walk away, it was like someone had grabbed her heart in their hands and was squeezing it, trying to stop it from beating. Her eyes burned with unshed tears. The pulse monitor on the wall accelerated. She gasped for breath, the stitches on her chest tube pulling, her ribs screaming in protest at the exertion.

It was really over.

23

Chapter Twenty-three

The days blurred one into the next. All sense of time outside of her hospital room disappeared. The constant influx of visitors, nurses and doctors left Kat exhausted and sleep deprived. So the day that she was released from the hospital felt like a miracle.

"You ready to go?" Eve asked.

"Yeah. Thanks again for offering to take me to get my truck," Kat murmured.

Eve smiled and hefted Kat's bag off the bed. "No problem! Do the guys know you're coming to get your truck right now?"

Kat nodded. "I just got off the phone with Jake. Told him we'd be there in ten."

Eve's smile wavered for a moment before returning full force. "Surprised you called Jake and not Greyson."

Kat flinched. Was that jealousy in her voice? Did she have a crush on Jake? Kat sighed. Greyson didn't come back to visit her after that first day. Which was to be expected, she guessed. They had ended it. Too much contact outside of work would have left people suspicious. Eve had come to visit her every day, whether out of pity or potential friendship Kat was still unsure. Her mother, on the other hand, called every three hours like clockwork. So, it would be heaven to be out of reach at the hotel.

The chubby orderly pushed Kat in the wheelchair to the valet area where Eve's car was parked. Kat grit her teeth as she was wheeled to the curb. She was fine, the chest tube taken out a few days ago. She had just been kept for observation. She was perfectly able to walk, but hospital policy required a wheelchair ride. Luckily, she didn't pass any of the other CFD firefighters on the way. A woman could only stand so much humiliation.

Kat settled herself into the seat and clicked the seatbelt into place. Eve climbed in and her door shut with a thud.

Both of them jumped at a loud honk from behind them.

Eve swore and flipped the bird to the dirty white Civic behind them. "What an asshole. It's a HOSPITAL PICK UP AREA for God's sake!" Eve shouted the "hospital pick up area" out her window. The car darted around them and Kat's heart lurched. For a moment, the driver looked like Eric. She frantically looked at the license plate on the car, which looked so much like Eric's old Civic. Her galloping heartbeat slowed when she realized didn't recognize the out-of-state license plate.

"So, um..." Eve mumbled as she pulled out of the parking lot.

Adrenaline still hummed through Kat's body, even though what she thought she saw was a mistake. "What?" Kat hated when people beat around the bush. Just lay it on the table. Geez.

"Have you seen Greyson since you were admitted?" she asked sheepishly.

"I saw him the morning they moved me to my room, why?" A tingle of suspicion crept up her spine.

"I just thought you guys were, you know, a thing." Eve glanced back and forth from the road to Kat.

"No, we're not a thing. Why would you think that?" *Shit.*

"The way the two of you look at each other. I don't know how to explain it. There's just something about it."

Kat just shrugged. Probably the less said the better. Since joining the station, she had gotten to know Eve at various scenes and occasionally they'd been to lunch. But it was only since Eve had been visiting her in the hospital that she'd started to consider Eve a friend. But there was still so much she didn't know. She wasn't sure that Eve was quite trustworthy of such a bombshell yet...

"So, um, considering you're not a thing..." Eve worried her perfectly painted pink bottom lip between her bleached teeth.

Please, please, please don't ask me what you're thinking about asking me. Please...

"Okay. I'm just going to say it. We're adults right?"

"Yes," Kat replied, the suspicion clear in her voice.

"I was wondering if it would bug you if I went out with Greyson." Her cheeks turned pink. She hurried to complete her thought. "But I mean, if you want him, I'll keep my hands off. But, you know, if you're not interested in him, I..." she babbled.

A heat wave rushed over Kat, starting with the top of her head and gaining speed as it passed her shredded heart. The blood pounded in her ears. Her ribs screamed as she fought to control her breathing. *He's not mine. He never was. So why should it bug me if she's asking my permission to pursue him? Any other woman wouldn't even ask...*

"Oh, um. I guess if he asks you it doesn't matter to me..." Kat choked out. Each word tasted bitter, like the artificial sourness they put into nail polish remover to keep kids from drinking it.

"You sure? Because I totally don't want to screw up anything you and Greyson..."

"It's fine, Eve," Kat snapped. She wanted to reach over and snap her new friend's head from her body.

But Eve had been there for her when Greyson hadn't. She didn't have any female friends, as being a member of the boy's club generally disqualified you for being the member of any girl's ones. Besides, she'd always gotten along better with guys anyway. They weren't catty, and if they had a beef with you, they'd out and tell you, rather than whispering and plotting behind your back like a girl.

But the thought of Eve in Greyson's arms made Kat's throat burn. If she loved Greyson, she should want him to be happy. Eve was really nice, and from what she had learned of her over the past few days, actually a really good match for him.

But she did love him. Her heart ached with the weight of her love for him. If it were anything but her career on the line, she'd give it up in a heartbeat to be able to belong to Greyson. But it *was* her career. And she had made the decision of her career over her relationship with him. It's only fair that she let him be happy with whomever he chose to be with. It wasn't like she had any claim on him or anything.

It wasn't fair. There were no rules keeping Eve and Greyson from dating. She wasn't ex's with his brother. They could be completely out in the open with their relationship. No one would lose their job. No one could say a word. They could flaunt their relationship all over the table directly in front of Kat and there wasn't a damn thing she could do about it. Except get up and leave. Or transfer to another station.

"Why, did he?" Kat started to ask if he asked her out. But it was none of her business. He wasn't hers. She had no right to know who he asked out.

"No, I wish. I just wanted to clear it with you if he did ask me out. I would like to think of you as a friend, Kat." Eve glanced at her. It was impossible to think any mean thoughts about her. The pure innocence in her face proved that she had no malicious intent. She truly wanted to be her friend.

"I'd love to be friends, Eve. I don't have many girlfriends...Well, any for that matter," she grumbled.

"Well, you hang out with boys all day. Where are you supposed to meet any female friends, anyway?" Eve laughed.

"No shit," Kat laughed.

"You really aren't dating Greyson?"

"No."

Eve beamed like a kid on Christmas morning.

Kat wrapped her arms around her chest as she felt the tear that had been ripped in her heart a week ago after she and Greyson had almost been caught in the shower ripped a little more.

**

Greyson wiped the sweat from his forehead with his t-shirt. Today was one hell of a scorcher. And of course that meant that it was a great day to tune up the rig. He tugged at the wrench, fighting with the massive bolt. What had they done? Spot-welded the fucking bolt on? He tugged again but the stubborn hunk of metal held its ground.

"Fuck!" he growled.

"Hey, look who's back!" Kevin shouted from where he was checking the levels in the emergency air tanks. Thankfully, after Kat's accident, Kevin seemed to get over whatever the hell was up his ass.

He was mid-tug and his sweaty hand slipped off the wrench. It flew up into the air and hit the concrete with a resounding clank. He spun around as the bright yellow VW Jetta pulled into the spot next to Kat's truck.

His heart lurched. He hadn't seen Kat since the morning she woke up in the hospital after her accident. It had been hell to stay away from her. But he'd resolved to make the split as easy as possible. And that meant keeping his distance. Would she be happy to see him? Or pissed?

Jake beat him to the door. He shot Greyson a triumphant look as he bent to grab the door handle.

"Hey, Kat!" Jake said and opened the door for her.

"Thanks, Jake," Kat murmured.

Greyson's breath caught in his throat. Instead of her traditional ponytail, her hair fell in dark, thick waves over her shoulders. Her cheeks flushed pink at Jake's chivalry. She looked as gorgeous, if not more so, than usual.

"C'mere," Jake growled and wrapped Kat in a bear hug.

"Ow! Jake!" Kat complained as he squeezed her.

"Oh, shit, sorry. Forgot about the ribs!" Jake released her. "We were so fuckin' worried about you!"

"I know. Thanks for coming to visit me in the slammer."

"Slammer. Please. It was a vacation. Chandler Regional has great food," he scoffed.

"And nurses coming in every few hours, and doctors, and my mother calling non-stop. Yep. Real vacation." She rolled her eyes.

"Bleh. Okay I concede," Jake said with a laugh. "I gotta get back inside. I'm totally missing a conference call to see you..."

"Go." Kat smiled and nodded towards the station.

"Hey, Kat," Greyson murmured over her shoulder. God, he hated the way her shoulders stiffened when she heard his voice.

She spun around, her hair fanning out in a dark curtain and falling against her shoulders. She glanced up at him and something flashed across her face for a moment before she quickly composed herself. Was it sadness?

"Oh, hey, Greyson. I didn't see you there." Kat looked everywhere but him.

"Glad to see you're okay," he said. *Please look at me.*

She nodded and studied the glittering asphalt at her feet.

"Hey, Greyson!" Eve bounded around the car with Kat's bag.

"Oh, uh. Hi, Eve." Greyson didn't take his eyes off Kat. *Look at me damn it. Look at me.*

Kat's shoulders stiffened and her head shot up as Eve stopped beside her.

"Hey, I bet you two have a lot to talk about." Kat's voice was laced with obvious sarcasm. She snatched the bag out of Eve's hand. "Thanks for everything, Eve. Bye, Greyson." Her eyes finally caught his for a moment before she turned and threw the door to her truck open and climbed inside. *Were those tears in her eyes?*

Eve shot an annoyed look at Kat before turning her attention back to him.

"So what have you been up to lately, Greyson?" Eve batted her eyelashes at him.

He stared at her for a moment in confusion. *What had she just said to him?*

"Huh? Oh, uh. Will you excuse me for a second?" He sidestepped Eve to get to Kat's window.

"Can we talk?" Greyson braced his hand on the doorframe of her truck. Her truck's lift kit raised it up just enough that she had to look down at him.

She shook her head and stared at his hand on her door.

"Please?" His hand clenched the door. He had to make things right with her. This was no way to leave things between them. They still had to work together, for God's sake.

"No. We can't." Her voice caught and she cleared her throat. "Eve's waiting for you. You should get back to her."

"Please, Kat. We need to talk. Please," he pleaded.

"No." Her fiery gaze finally locked with his. She stared at him through a sheen of tears. His heart felt like it was ripping in two. Had he lost her completely?

She threw the truck into reverse and checked her mirror briefly before reeling backwards. Her tires squealed as she threw the truck back into drive and barreled into the road, practically getting t-boned by an oncoming SUV.

"What the hell was that all about?" Eve put a hand on his shoulder.

He turned and found Eve's clear blue eyes staring up at him innocently.

24

Chapter Twenty-four

Tears blurred Kat's vision as she tore out of the parking lot. Seeing Eve's hand on Greyson's shoulder was the final straw. She hadn't handled that very well, but she'd done her best, all things considered.

What the hell did he want from her? Still have sex with her on the down-low, so long as no heartstrings were attached? Was that why he needed to talk to her so bad? To make sure she wasn't going to go running to Chief Phillips to tell him how he had taken advantage of her and seduced her after the terrifying ordeal with Eric? Did he think that it would hurt his chances for the promotion that he was up for?

Of course she wouldn't do that. She had as much to lose as he did if their relationship became public. Chief Phillip's respect. Her position at the station. Her reputation. She wouldn't have to transfer just out of the station, she'd have to transfer to a different city. And her rep of being the station whore would probably precede her there.

What was worse was that her heart was involved. Were it just sex, it would be simple to just leave it at that. But she loved him. Even if he hadn't come to visit her in the hospital. Maybe he had a good reason for that. They had decided to end it after all.

The picture of Eve's hand on Greyson's broad shoulder flashed before her eyes. Her stomach churned violently, her heart throbbed in her chest. How the hell was she supposed to work with him? They were moving on. He was going to sleep with other women. Maybe even fall in love and get married to one. All while she had to watch. All while she kept her love for him under lock and key. Could she do that?

Her tires squealed as she swung around the corner. An annoyed soccer mom in a minivan blared her horn and swerved around her. The hotel was just a few more miles away, but she seriously questioned her ability to drive safely. The light turned red and she slammed on her brakes.

The intersection turned into a blur of color as the tears filled her eyes and spilled down her cheeks. She crossed her arms over her steering wheel and laid her head on her arms and sobbed, her ribs screaming in protest as her heart broke in two.

Over her ragged sobs the angry blaring of horns sounded. She sat up and glared at the green light before her. She accelerated through the light, pulled off to the side of the road and threw the truck into park. She wrapped her arms tightly around her protesting ribs, gasping for breath as she sobbed.

After what seemed like hours, her tears finally ran dry. Her heart ragged, her eyes burning, she sat up and stared out the windshield. She was half a block from the hotel. The sun was setting over South Mountain, sending golden rays filtering through the clouds.

She took a deep breath. She would get through this. Who the hell did Greyson think he was? This was her job. Her life. Her choice. She could be like nothing happened between them. Like she hadn't fallen in love with him. What the fuck had happened to her? She was a strong, determined firefighter. Her goal in life was to make it in the boy's club of firefighting. And she had done it. She wanted to work under Chief Phillips. She'd done that. She'd accomplished everything in her life that she'd set out to do. Being distracted by a guy was never, ever in the plan. Relationships were complicated and stressful. Exhibit A with Eric and exhibit B with Greyson were perfect examples of why she didn't need either of those in her life.

With renewed resolve she shifted the truck back into drive and pulled back onto the road. She drove the half-block to the hotel and pulled into the valet. She sighed as she glanced at herself in the rear-view mirror. Her eyes were red and swollen. Her nose too. Well at least the concierge wouldn't try to make small talk while checking her in.

Kat exchanged her key for a ticket and, with her head down, crossed the marble lobby and approached the concierge.

"Checking in?" the concierge asked, the smile evident in her voice.

Kat nodded.

"Name?"

"Hale." She glanced up at the plump woman. Her bleached hair was fluffed into a bird's wing-like structure perched on her head. Her frosted pink lips pursed as her gaze searched the screen.

"Ah, yes. I have you right here. One adult, non-smoking, top floor if possible. Paid for by your insurance company." She perused the reservation. "I'm sorry for your loss."

"It was just a house. No one died," Kat grumbled.

"Well, still. Losing everything you own in a fire can't be fun. Here let me see about something..." The plump woman's magenta acrylic nails clicked away on the keyboard.

"There. That's more like it. I've upgraded to one of our suites. It's got a kitchen and living room and overlooks the lake behind the hotel. Much more like home, at least until you get things figured out." A motherly smile crossed her face.

"Oh, um, wow. That's really nice of you. But I'm sure I can't afford that. The insurance company will only pay—"

"It's a complimentary upgrade. Your insurance company will only get the bill for the original amount." She stared at Kat, like she was trying to telepathically communicate something to her.

"Oh! Thank you!" Kat was stunned. This woman didn't owe her anything. Heck, she wasn't even the one paying the bill!

The woman nodded. She handed her the room key and a map of the hotel. She rattled off the directions to the room and handed her a huge stack of complimentary breakfast passes.

Kat reiterated her thanks and took off for the elevator. It was either that or have the woman start offering to give her furniture from the lobby, most likely.

Like the lady said, the room was perfect, exactly what she needed to settle down and figure out what the hell to do. She needed to find a new house, or at least one to rent while she looked for a new one. From what the insurance adjuster told her while she was in the hospital, the house had sustained so much damage they determined that the property was a complete loss, and therefore no repair was going to happen. It would have to be a complete tear-down and rebuild. And Kat couldn't afford to pay rent and her mortgage at the same time. So, she needed to buy another house and let the mortgage company take what was left of the property.

The free Wi-Fi at the hotel was an added bonus that Kat was happy to have at her disposal. It would make the house hunting so much easier. She pulled out her MacBook, one of the few things that had managed to escape the fire because she had left it in her bag in her car after work that fateful day. So, luckily, her music, her pictures, all of her electronic documents were safe. But all of her material possessions, including her birth certificate, passport, and such had to be replaced.

She logged into her bank's online system and clicked for her balance. She stared at the screen. Apparently the electronic check from the insurance company for her contents had been deposited. At least she wouldn't have to worry about having to pay for new clothes and furniture. Thank God for her insurance company.

She closed the banking window and opened her email. She sighed as the browser loaded and loaded. It was going to be one hell of a massive pile of emails. One hundred and sixty-five new messages. Ugh.

She spent the next hour and a half deleting and responding to message after message. Friends, family, even acquaintances from elementary school had emailed her to send their well-wishes. She wondered what the news had aired about what had happened. Did they say that the victim had been sexually assaulted? She didn't need that kind of stress right now. As the messages got newer, the concern changed to outrage about her choice of occupation. Nice. The car accident must have hit the news too.

The picture of Greyson's face beside her on the bed the morning she woke up after the accident flashed before her eyes. His eyes were filled with relief, and maybe something else? No. It didn't do any good to think about what could have been. She wanted to end it. She had to end it to protect her job.

Tears filled her eyes as she continued to delete email after email. Interspersed between the junk-emails were fewer and fewer emails of concern. People must have realized after a week of non-response that they probably weren't going to get one. Good. She didn't feel like responding anyway.

She finally got to the newest email in her inbox. Dated an hour ago from some email address titled Hot4you@emails4free.com. The subject of the message was "Enjoy the view from your private suite at the top of a luxury four-star hotel!!" Her finger hovered over the delete button. Stupid junk mail.

She jumped when her phone sang to life in her pocket. Ville Valo's smooth voice singing "Would you die tonight for love?" filled the room. She smirked. *Ironic. Fucking ironic.* She glanced down at the number. It was Eve. *Great.* Just who she wanted to talk to.

She tapped the screen and held the phone to her ear. "Yeah, Eve?" Kat growled. *Please let this be short and not about Greyson.* She couldn't trust herself to control her reaction should she be faced with the thought of Greyson in Eve's arms again.

"Hey, Kat! You okay?" Eve's cheery voice rang through the earpiece.

"Yeah, I'm fine. What's up?" Why the hell did her voice sound so ragged, haggard even, while Eve's sounded so cheery and melodic?

"You peeled out of here so fast. I was worried about you. Are you sure everything's ok?" Eve asked again.

"Everything is fine. I was just, um, in a hurry to get to the hotel. Sorry I ran out without saying goodbye." Her voice felt forced, even to her own ears.

"It's okay. I bet after a week in lock-down at the hospital the feeling of being completely alone again had to feel good."

"Yeah." Where the hell was this conversation going? Over the last few days at the hospital conversation with Eve had been so easy. But once she indicated an interest in Greyson all that went to shit.

"Anyway, I wanted to tell you what happened between me and Greyson after you left!"

"Okay..." The sound of the phrase "me and Greyson" coming from Eve's lips made her stomach churn. Tears burned her eyes. Here we go.

"Well I told him that I was free for dinner tonight, if he didn't have plans," Eve gushed.

"You asked him out?" Kat choked. This wasn't fair to Greyson. She should be fine with this. They'd ended it. And besides, it's not like they had a committed relationship anyway. So what was to stop him from dating other women?

"Yeah. Crashed and burned."

Kat fought to control the smile that came to her face at Eve's confession. "I'm sorry."

"It's okay. He said that he's involved with someone already. He was very nice about it. Whoever this mystery woman is, she's a very lucky woman," Eve said, ending on a wistful sigh. "You should have seen how his eyes sparkled when he said that he was involved with someone else. He didn't say he was in love, but it was obvious in his face, the way he looked right through me like I wasn't even there."

"Oh. Um, I'm sorry. I wonder who it is?" Kat's heart lurched. Could he possibly have been talking about her? Or some other woman that he didn't tell her about? They never discussed his being involved with anyone before. So maybe he *was* involved with someone else and she was just an at work diversion.

"Did you hear what I said?" Eve asked again.

"What? Oh, sorry. No. What did you say?"

"Never mind. It's not important. So what are your plans for tonight? Feel like some girl time?"

"Actually I'd like that. They put me up in a massive suite. And the room service menu does look amazing." It would be nice to have a diversion from thinking about Greyson. And for some reason Eve felt more like one of the guys than one of the girls anyway.

"Great! Because I need some Hagen Daz and some really sappy movies. You up for it?"

"Absolutely. You bring the Hagen Daz. I'll order the movies. You wouldn't believe how big the TV is in this hotel room." The smile that stretched across her face was genuine, her heart warmed at the thought of having a girlfriend.

Two hours later the knock on the door announced Eve's arrival. Kat'd already scoped out the mini bar and finding it lacking, asked Eve to bring a bottle of wine too. Nothing like getting sloshed and giving each other facials and pedicures to round out a girl's night.

"God damn, it's like trying to get into Fort Knox getting into this hotel! Did you see all the security?" Eve asked as she whisked in the room with two pints of Hagen Daz and a bottle of Malbec in one arm. The other carried a massive case containing all the girly essentials.

Kat nodded and helped her unload the contraband. "That's why I chose this place. Made me feel safe. You know, with Eric still on the loose and all."

Eve snorted. "Well, no one is laying a hand on you in this place. Talk about overkill."

Kat shrugged and inspected the ice cream container absently. She really didn't want to talk about the tingle of dread that skirted around the edges of her thoughts. Talking about it would acknowledge it. Acknowledging it would give it power.

Eve nodded to the wine. "You sure you're supposed to have this stuff with the pain meds you're on?"

"I stopped taking that crap the second day in the hospital. I didn't like the way it made me feel. It was like I was constantly on a free-fall, even though I was laying flat on the bed. Gave me horrible dreams, too. Nasty stuff." Kat made a gagging face.

"That's good to hear. The stuff they put you on is pretty addictive."

"Yuck. Who'd want to feel like that 24/7?"

"People who think it feels better than the reality they face I guess. Anyway, dark chocolate Hagen Daz and good wine is a better bane to have anyway!" Eve giggled and set her armload down on the countertop.

"Mmm, dark chocolate..." Kat purred. She rifled through the drawer beneath the microwave and managed to find two spoons. She spun around, wielding them like mighty swords. "Victory!"

They plopped down on the overstuffed microfiber couch with a glass of wine and tub of ice cream in hand. Kat flipped on the massive flat screen. The antics of Reese Whitherspoon in the romantic comedy had them laughing and crying into their ice cream.

"That was fantastic. I totally needed that." Kat rolled her neck and rubbed her eyes as the final credits scrolled over the massive TV screen.

"Me too! Thanks for having me over. It was nice to have some girl time. I don't really have any girlfriends..." Eve stared into her empty Hagen Daz container.

"Me too. It's nice to know that I'm not the only one who doesn't have any girlfriends!" Kat laughed.

"I'd like to be your friend, Kat."

"I'd like that." Maybe they could be friends. Now that she wasn't trying to steal Greyson anymore. But friendships based on mistrust were doomed. "But I've to come clean with you then, if we are really going to be friends..."

"You're seeing Greyson," Eve said matter-of-factly. Her voice was flat, but the smile that spread across her face and warmed her light blue eyes

"Well, I was, sort of..." Just admitting it out loud brought a fresh wave of panic washing over her.

"What happened?"

"We ended it. We didn't want it to jeopardize our jobs. We both have our reasons for wanting to stay at station three. And our desire to not impact our careers made a relationship impossible. Besides, all the shit with Eric..." Somehow, she managed to choke the whole thing out without her voice cracking, even though her throat got tight as she spoke the words.

"When did you end it?"

"A week ago. The morning of the accident that landed me in the hospital."

"Oh!" Eve's eyes shot to Kat's. "And here I go and throw myself at him, even ask your permission! Why the hell didn't you just say "keep away he's mine?""

"Because he's not mine. He never was and never will be." Tears welled up in her eyes. It was as if someone reached their hands into her chest and grabbed her heart with a choke hold, intent on squeezing the last drops of life out of it.

"I'm so sorry, Kat. I wish I had known!" Eve scooted across the couch and gathered Kat into her willowy arms.

Much against her will, hot tears streamed down her cheeks. Just the thought of Greyson brought a fresh bout of tears to her eyes. Damn him.

Eve pulled back to look into Kat's eyes. "Well, I think he is yours, even if you don't want him."

"Why do you say that?" Kat sniffled and wiped her eyes with her t-shirt.

"You should have seen the way he looked as you drove away. It was like he'd been hit in the chest with a sledgehammer. I didn't realize what it was at the time, but now that I know, I'm sure of it." A wide grin crossed Eve's model-like face.

"It doesn't matter. We can't be together. And I'm sure he's not interested in a committed relationship. And then there's the whole work issue. Not to mention that his brother tried to kill me." Kat heaved a heavy sigh.

"That's not how it looked to me. Why would he have turned me down if he wasn't interested in a committed relationship? I mean look at me!" Eve laughed and stood, turning around like a model. "Who wouldn't want to bang this?"

"No shit!" Kat laughed. Jake would definitely bang her. And probably Kevin too for that matter.

"No wonder we have no girlfriends. We're a couple of dudes!" Eve flopped back onto the cough and giggled.

Kat flounced back onto the couch beside her with a chuckle. "A couple of dudes who look like chicks who play in the boy's club."

25

Chapter Twenty-five

The next evening Kat gritted her teeth as she flicked through racks of clothes at the mall a short distance from the hotel. As much as she loathed clothes shopping, the fire had destroyed everything she owned, including her wardrobe. She could only get away with wearing her station shirts and shorts for so long.

She sifted through the frilly, pink and lacy, desperately hoping to find something that didn't make her gag in the racks. So far, no luck. Kat sighed. It was the third store she'd visited, and besides the silky fire engine red cocktail dress she splurged on at Saks, she'd come out empty handed.

Out of nowhere, she got the nagging feeling like someone was watching her. From the corner of her eye, a tall figure in black moved between the racks. She wouldn't have even noticed, but the person's dark wardrobe stood out amongst the ocean of pastels. She turned to get a better look at the person, who seemed as out of place in the girly-girly section as she did. She could see a profile, a strong nose sticking out from behind the hood that had been pulled up to cover the person's head. They started to turn toward her slightly, as if realizing they were now the one being watched.

"Can I help you find something?" a nasally female voice asked from her other side.

Startled, Kat blinked at the middle-aged woman beside her. "Um, no, thanks. Just looking," Kat stammered.

"Well, let me know if I can help you find anything."

Kat nodded and turned back to where the person in black had been. He was gone, but the clothes on the racks still swayed. Kat snatched her Saks bag off the ground and raced to where the person had been. She turned in a circle, trying to figure out where he had gone.

In the throng of people heading toward the store exit, a hooded figure stood out a good six inches above them. Kat took off after the man. Her feet skidded on the shiny linoleum when a woman with a stroller meandered into her way.

She darted around the woman, her eyes locked on the man's dark form as he slipped through the exit doors. She raced into the parking lot and her eyes searched the darkness. He was gone.

Her heart thundered as she fished her keys from her purse and walked to her truck. She scanned the lot around her, constantly searching the darkness for the man in black.

She was almost at her truck when she heard footsteps closing in fast on her. She spun around just in time to see the man in black stop just out of reach of the orange glow from the dim streetlight above her truck.

"Kat..."

Kat gasped when her name fell from his lips. She had prayed that she'd never hear his voice again. Terror seeped through her body as he approached, his ice blue eyes standing out like beacons in the darkness.

"Stay away from me, Eric." Kat warned.

He held his hands up in what was meant to be a reassuring gesture and took another step towards her.

Kat backed up against her truck. There was nowhere to run. "Stop right there."

Surprisingly, he obeyed, stopping a few feet from her.

"I'm so sorry about what happened, but you have to listen to me. You're..."

A bright search light flashed over Kat and she turned toward the blinding light.

"Is everything okay, miss?" the security guard asked from the window of his SUV.

Kat glanced back at Eric. He was gone.

**

The next few weeks were a flurry of activity for Kat. She didn't tell anyone about the Eric sighting at the mall. She was beginning to think she was going crazy, and that the fear that Eric was lurking somewhere waiting to hurt her was making her hallucinate. To get her mind off things, she decided to start looking at houses. A fresh start for a new, Eric-free life. Which was why she was following this over-primped Pomeranian of a real estate agent all around town looking at new houses.

"This four-bedroom has a massive backyard with a diving pool and tons of grass, you know, for the little ones in your life," the real estate broker prattled as she slid the key into the lock and pushed open the heavy oak door. "And it's right in the middle of your price range."

Kat grunted. She stifled the urge to correct the stuffily dressed woman and bit her tongue instead. She was probably used to quaint little housewives with two-point-five kids and a little dog looking for their dream home with the white picket fence. If only she knew just how wrong she was. She honestly couldn't picture little ones fitting into the life path she'd chosen for herself.

Kat's eyes widened as she stepped over the threshold and into the foyer. Shining cherry wood floors stretched out before her, beige walls with white trim reached up to a rounded, almost tower-like entry. Windows high above let the afternoon light filter into the otherwise dark house. While it was excessive for one person, the shiny cherry hardwood floors and cabinets were calling Kat's name. She could almost hear Diesel's nails clattering down the hall towards the door.

God she missed him. Greyson had offered to keep him until she could get a place that would suit him. She wondered how they were getting along?

"And here's the back yard," the broker's nasally voice echoed from far away.

Kat stepped through the French doors off the kitchen and stifled a gasp. The quarter-acre lot sprawled out before her was the resort-like backyard of her dreams. A lagoon shaped pool and whirlpool took up one corner of the massive yard, surrounded by swaying palm trees, complete with a large rock waterfall and slide. The whirlpool could definitely come in handy after a long shift at the station.

The rest of the yard was covered in a thick blanket of lush grass, interspersed with massive fruit trees, which made huge patches of shade on the grass. She could see herself spread out on a blanket under one of the trees reading one of her favorite books.

Her vision of herself sprawled under a tree looked up as a pair of kids streaked past her and splashed into the pool, soaking their father. A deep chuckle filled her ears as Greyson shook the water from his hair and caught a dark-haired, blue eyed kid in each arm.

"Come on Mommy!" the girl squealed at her before he dunked her.

"Do it again Daddy!" the boy laughed before he received the same treatment.

Tears misted in her eyes as the vision dissolved. The annoying drone of the real estate agent buzzed like a bee at the back of her brain.

Of course this house was perfect. Perfect for the family she could have with the only man she could picture spending the rest her life with. The family and future she could never have because of her career.

**

Greyson held out the remote and flipped through the channels, the massive flat screen on the wall in his bedroom flashing from an overly-primped supermodel to a graying news anchor to baseball. Nothing interested him anymore. Not since Kat tore out of the parking lot after she was discharged from the hospital. After she was gone Eve had asked him out, and while he might have been interested before he met Kat, she held no interest for him now.

He sighed as Diesel nosed under his hand and plopped onto the bed next to him. The dog was a constant reminder of her. Every fucking molecule in his condo reminded him of her. The shower. His bedroom. And as weird as it was, he never washed the pillow that she had slept on. It still smelled like her.

He clicked off the TV and buried his face in her pillow, encompassing himself in her scent. His heart ached at the memory of her in his bed. His mind threw around various scenarios of how to make things work with Kat. Every scenario ended tragically. Kat fired and hating him. Kat transferred and hating him. Him transferred and Kat hating him. Both of them staying on at the station, and Kat hating him. Kat quitting her job as a firefighter because she is pregnant with his child, and resenting him for making her give up her career for their family. The thought of Kat's belly growing with his child brought a wave of blood rushing to his cock. Did she even want kids? Knowing Kat, probably not. It would throw a stumbling block in her career goals.

He wanted kids. Someday. But he wanted Kat more. Was he willing to give up the thought of ever having a family because Kat didn't want kids?

The emptiness that filled his heart at the thought of never having kids almost brought tears to his eyes. But the emptiness of his life without Kat made him feel like someone had reached into his chest and ripped his heart out in bleeding shreds. He could deal with the emptiness. But to not have Kat in his life was not an option.

His eyelids grew heavy as he contemplated the emptiness of his life without Kat.

"Greyson?" Kat murmured and slid a hand up his torso under his shirt.

His eyes fluttered open. Kat was lying on the bed beside him in her station-issued t-shirt and shorts, her hand tracing the muscles on his stomach.

"Mmmm." He caught her hand and brought it to his lips. "God, I've missed you." He inhaled deeply as he kissed each finger, savoring the heady wet lavender and vanilla scent of her skin.

She smiled and cupped his face in her palms, leaning up to place a kiss on his lips. The taste of her was enough to push him over the edge. His tongue traced the softness of her lips. She opened them, allowing him entry. His tongue delved into her, battling with hers.

She gasped as he rolled her onto her back and he slid between her legs. His shaft strained painfully against the fabric of his shorts as he rubbed against her. Damn clothes.

He pushed back onto his knees and ripped his t-shirt over his head before leaning down to crush her lips in a kiss so desperate, so hungry, in the back of his mind he worried that he was hurting her.

She moaned and clutched at his bare shoulders, tracing the hard planes of his biceps with firm strokes.

Every touch threatened to send him over the edge. He wanted in her. Now.

He reached down to free himself of his shorts and boxers, but she stilled his movements by grabbing his hand. He freed her lips and pulled back slightly to gaze into her flushed face.

"Kat?" he panted.

She shook her head, a wicked smile spreading across her face.

His brow furrowed in confusion as her hands slid up his shoulders. She shoved, effectively pushing him off balance. He flopped back onto the bed with an oomph.

"What?" he choked as she straddled his hips. He strained painfully against the fabric of his shorts. The heat from her wet cleft radiated through both of their clothes, bringing another rush of blood to his already swollen cock.

Her stormy blue eyes darkened with desire as they locked with his, an unreadable expression on her beautiful face. She leaned down and pressed her lips to his, tracing her tongue across his playfully. He gasped and nipped at her tongue, trying to suck it into his mouth for another taste.

A chuckle rumbled in her throat as she pulled away.

"Please Kat," he groaned.

Another mischievous smile crossed her face as she shook her head. She kissed a trail down his shoulder, down the hard plane of his pectoral to his nipple. She smiled wickedly and sucked it into her mouth.

He gasped as she bit down gently. "Fuck!"

She held a finger to her lips and traced the ridges of his stomach with her other hand.

His breath caught as her fingers slipped beneath the waistband of his shorts, gently caressing the hard ridge of muscle on his hip, following it down, pushing the fabric as she eagerly explored his body.

Her hands worshiped his hips, tracing the deep V that led down. The cloth stopped at the base of his shaft, hooked by the curving length of him. She gasped with pleasure and glanced up at him, her mouth open slightly in a half-smile. His heart accelerated at the erotic picture of her sweet lips so close to him. What would that mouth feel like on him?

He bit his lip to stifle a groan, his eyes half-closed as he watched his manhood bob proudly as she freed it. The head of his shaft throbbed when her tongue snaked out to wet her lips.

Her eyes locked with his. God she was beautiful. He wanted to grab her and hold on to her forever, never let her out of his sight. But she wasn't his.

A hiss escaped his throat when her hand wrapped around his length. He couldn't handle this. He was already about to explode. Any more torture like this and he'd lose it.

"Fuck! Kat!" he cried out as her lips closed over the pulsing head of his cock. She smiled, the head of his penis still in her mouth, her eyebrows raised defiantly.

"Shit." He closed his eyes and buried his hands in the softness of her hair as she slowly slid her mouth up and down his length. Her tongue circled the tip and teased the sensitive skin underneath. His fingers clenched her silky hair as the pleasure intensified exponentially.

He chewed his lip, fighting the building pressure as the wetness of her mouth and the suction threatened to pull him over the edge. His balls tightened and the hot rush of ecstasy rushed up his shaft like magma shooting from a volcano.

His arms flew out and hit the bed on either side of him as Diesel's frantic barking woke him from the best dream he'd had, ever. His cock throbbed painfully, straining against the restricting fabric of his shorts. He slid out of bed and hobbled to where Diesel was frantically clawing at the door. He shifted his equipment in his shorts in an attempt to ease the ache, to no avail.

"What the hell, Diesel?"

The boxer whined pitifully at him. He glanced at the clock. Had he really been asleep for two hours? The poor dog danced pathetically by the door, a low-whine punctuating his dance.

He cracked open the door and Diesel tore through the opening, racing down the stairs and over to a bush. Greyson watched from the door as Diesel watered every unsuspecting bush and two neighbor's tires before calling him. Those people were inconsiderate jerks anyway, slamming their doors and leaving their TV's on way too loud during the day while certain night-shift working people were trying to sleep.

Diesel made it up to the third step, sniffing all the way. He growled at the scent on the stairs and spun, following his nose down the sidewalk until he was standing before a dingy older model white Civic.

"Diesel! Come!" Greyson called from his perch at the door. He really didn't want to have to chase the dog in his boxers with a raging hard-on through the complex.

The dog froze, his hair standing on end, a growl rumbling through his body. Greyson couldn't see anyone in the car, since its windows were tinted within an inch of their life, probably five shades darker than street legal.

Like a twig had snapped in Diesel's brain, he dove at the car door, barking and scratching at the old paint.

"DIESEL!" Greyson bellowed.

The dog froze and whined, as if begging permission to continue the attack on the vehicle.

"Diesel, come!"

The stubborn boxer hung his head as he moped towards the condo. Greyson took one last glance at the car Diesel attacked. It seemed vaguely familiar, but the number of late model Civics in this town probably outnumbered the number of drive thru coffee joints.

26

Chapter Twenty-six

The wet slap of mop against floor echoed across the empty locker room as Kat scrubbed the checkerboard tiles until they gleamed. Her stomach clenched and an ache flared between her legs as she stared at the gleaming wet tiles before her. She could almost feel their coolness at her back as her memory of Greyson pressed her against the floor.

Kat closed her eyes and sucked in two deep breaths. It didn't do anyone any good reminiscing about things that can never be. She'd barely been back a week and she'd done everything in her power to avoid Greyson. She didn't need any more complications. Things were already screwed up enough as it was. Harping over the one guy she couldn't have was just an exercise in masochism.

The door behind her closed with a quiet click.

"Hey, Kat."

Greyson's deep voice caressed her and she clenched the mop handle with a death grip to stop the shiver that raced over her skin. She shot a cursory glance over her shoulder. "Hey."

He sucked in a shaky breath. "Listen," he began, but was interrupted when the door behind him flung open again and heavy footsteps stomped into the room. Kat spun around to find a flushed Jake standing before them. He opened his mouth as if to say something, paused, and snapped it shut. His gaze shot to Greyson, as if he could find the words he needed to say in his face.

Jake heaved a heavy sigh and marched to his locker, spun the lock and flung it open with more force than necessary. She stood in silence and watched as he rifled in his bag for something. He pulled out a bottle of Tylenol, shaking out way more than the recommended dosage into his palm before tossing the pills into his mouth and chasing it with a huge gulp of water.

He sucked in another breath and turned to face them. "Chief Phillips wants to see you and Greyson in the conference room. Now," Jake snapped and slammed the door to his locker.

"Sir," Greyson murmured and shot Kat a worried glance.

A lump built in her throat as she stared after Jake's retreating form. This was it. It was all over.

The walk down the shiny tile hallway felt like a death march. She glanced over at Greyson, who walked silently beside her.

"What are we going to tell them?" Her voice sounded more frantic than she had hoped.

"The truth. Lying will just make things worse," he murmured.

Her heart fell at the sorrow obvious in his voice. "They're going to fire at least one of us."

He nodded. "I know." He grabbed the door handle and hesitated. "For what it's worth, I'm sorry, you know, for everything." His gaze met hers.

She winced at the sting of his words. The words meant to ease the pain of what was about to happen had the opposite effect. She never regretted one second of the time that they'd been together. But apparently, he had.

"Don't be. I am a grown woman capable of making my own decisions. I knew the consequences of my actions. Come on, let's get this over with." She nodded to the door.

"Kat, please." He released the door handle and reached for her hand.

"Don't, Greyson, just don't." She shrugged away from his grasp and yanked the door open and disappeared through it. The door slammed shut behind her as she stepped into the conference room. The clank echoed through the room like a judge's gavel. A chill raced over her skin at the sound.

"Please have a seat, Kat." Chief Phillips' baritone voice echoed through the room. He sat on the far side of the table next to Jake, his chocolate brown eyes watching her carefully from under his bushy dark eyebrows.

With determined strides Kat crossed the room and sat in the seat before him.

The door behind her opened and Greyson strode into the room. The chief's eyes narrowed. "Thanks for joining us, Greyson. Please have a seat."

"Sir." Greyson nodded and slid into the seat next to Kat.

"Let's get this over with." The chief slid a packet across the table to Kat. "I received a packet of disturbing pictures on my desk yesterday. Unfortunately, along with the other complaints I've received lately I can't let this slide."

The nape of Kat's neck tingled as her fingers closed around the familiar manila envelope with blood-red lettering on the front. She already knew what the package contained. They were pictures taken from outside Greyson's condo the day of the fire. The first time she and Greyson had slept together.

"Open it," Chief Phillips commanded.

"I don't need to. I already know what they are," Kat murmured.

Jake's sea-foam green eyes shot a confused glance at her. She slid the packet of photos across the table to him.

"Then you know why you both are here." Chief Phillips' chocolate eyes locked with hers, the disapproving fatherly look he was giving her enough to melt any child into tears and confessions.

She nodded.

Greyson's hand brushed her thigh under the table.

"As you know, it's frowned upon to have a relationship with a fellow firefighter on the same shift. While things are sometimes overlooked, if something happens while on-duty, standard procedure is to terminate both offenders."

Kat swallowed, trying to dislodge the lump that stuck in her throat the moment Jake told her Chief Phillips wanted to see them and had grown to almost choking proportions as he spoke. "Yes, Sir."

Greyson's voice filled the room. "Please, Sir. I take full responsibility for the events that have unfolded since Kat signed onto our shift. It was not her fault. She tried to stop me because she did not want to jeopardize her job. This was solely my fault."

Kat shot a surprised glance at him. *What the hell was he doing?*

"So, you're saying you raped her?" Chief Phillips asked incredulously. The disbelief on his face was obvious.

"From the look on her face in these pictures, she doesn't look like she's being raped," Jake laughed as he flipped through the pictures.

Chief Phillips shot a murderous glare at him.

Jake coughed to cover his laugh.

"No sir, he didn't rape me." Her cheeks flamed as she caught Jake's gaze.

"I appreciate you trying to protect Kat, but hear me out before you throw yourself under the bus." Chief Phillip's ice-cold stare warmed slightly. "I don't want to fire either one of you. You are both incredible firefighters and with the exception of this incident, are the most dedicated, professional firefighters I have on my force. But I can't let this go unpunished." The fatherly look that Kat had come to love returned, and his gaze warmed as his eyes fell on her.

Kat stared at him, waiting for the guillotine to drop.

"Now comes the really hard part. I'm putting you both on administrative leave until one of you transfers to another station. I will let you two make that decision."

"I'll do it," Kat blurted, not even allowing Chief Phillips to finish his thought.

"No!" Greyson growled. "I'll take the transfer sir."

"No you won't. This is what I want." Kat's locked with Greyson's for a second before she turned her attention back to Chief Phillips. "I'll have my locker cleaned out before I leave, Sir." She shoved back from the table and stood up. She reached across the table to shake Chief Phillip's hand. "Thank you, Sir, for giving me the opportunity to work with you at station three. It has been a dream come true. I hope you'll provide a letter of recommendation for my transfer."

"Absolutely, Hale. It's been a pleasure to work with you. I'm sad to be losing you." His dark eyebrows knitted together over his sad eyes.

"Thank you," she murmured and left the room. The second the door closed behind her she took off at a dead run for the locker room. Hopefully she'd make it there before the tears that burned her eyes made a break for it.

The conference room door slammed behind her as she turned the corner. Heavy footsteps pounded after her. The tears welled in her eyes. *Just a little further.*

"Kat, wait!" Greyson called from close behind her. His big, strong hand closed around her arm and she skidded to a stop.

"Please don't make this any harder than it has to be." She kept her eyes locked on the locker room door. She slowly took deep breaths and tried to keep the tears from escaping.

"Kat, please, you don't have to do this," Greyson pleaded. He caught her chin and turned her to face him. "Please."

She shook her head. A single tear escaped and slipped down her cheek. She raised her eyes to meet his. "I'm sorry. This is just the way it has to be, Greyson. We both always knew it would end this way. There never was any hope for us."

"But I can transfer. We can still be together now."

"I'll always resent you for not letting me take the transfer. And you'll always resent me if I let you. Let's just end this now. No resentment. No one's fault. It just didn't work out, okay?"

"But I love you, Kat." His gaze searched hers.

Kat's heart lurched and tears burned her eyes. "Well, you shouldn't. I'm not good for you. Obviously. Look at the fucking mess that I've gotten us both into. And I've still got Eric after me remember? Nothing is ever going to be right unless I leave. Please, just let me leave."

"I can't," he growled and pulled her into his arms, his lips melding with hers.

Tears fell unchecked from her eyes, but her hands slid up and buried in the hair at the nape of his neck. The desperation in his kiss left her feeling raw, physically and emotionally. She couldn't allow him to be hurt by her ever again. She allowed herself one more second of bliss before pushing against his chest and tearing her lips from his. "Please let me go," she whispered.

He let out a shuddering sigh and stepped back.

She slipped into the locker room and closed the door behind her. Her back pressed against the door as she slid to the floor and wrapped her arms around her knees. The tears fell unchecked down her cheeks and her shoulders shook as she sobbed into her arms. The echoes of Greyson's retreating footsteps were like nails in her coffin, each one effectively sealing her off from him forever.

A few minutes later a soft knock came from the other side of the door.

"Kat?" Jake's voice echoed through the door.

She sobered up at the sound of her ex-captain's voice. She scrubbed her eyes with the heels of her palms as she hauled herself off the floor and cracked open the door.

Somehow, he managed to squeeze his massive shoulders through the door without opening it all the way. He slid the lock back into place.

"Before you jump off the nearest roof, we have a different proposition for you..." Jake whispered and held out a small envelope out to her. A crooked smile spread across his handsome face and his eyes twinkled mischievously.

27

Chapter Twenty-seven

The days blurred one into the next. The weeks into months. Every second without Kat was like an eternity. He hadn't seen her since the night the shit hit the fan, after she'd offered to take the transfer. The night she came to pick up Diesel. That was almost as hard as Kat leaving herself. He'd grown damned fond of that dumb dog.

He lifted his mug of hazelnut coffee to his lips and tried to focus on the paper in his hands. Arson had been investigating the fires in their jurisdiction, and they all had the same M.O. But in the months since Kat had left, the fires had died off. He was sure it was his brother. It had to be. The little cocksucker. If he managed to run into him ever again...

"Damn it, Greyson. It's been two fucking months. Get over her already!" Kevin grumbled from the recliner across the room.

"I know how long it's been, Kevin. Thanks for reminding me," Greyson growled.

"Listen. It's a hard fucking time when you break up. But move on. She's not coming back. If she wanted you back she would have called or emailed or some shit," Kevin said enthusiastically.

"Maybe she's been busy, Greyson." Jake didn't look up from behind the screen of his laptop.

Greyson lowered the folder that he was using as a shield and stared across the room at Jake. "What do you mean?"

"Well maybe she's busy. She's training, making new friends, you know, whatever. You remember how hard it is being the new kid."

"Busy..." His heart leapt. Maybe she was just busy. Maybe she did want him. But the way they had left it hadn't given him much hope.

"Okay, that's it. We are going out tonight. The four of us. Get Greyson some tail, or at least really hammered," Jake said with a laugh and nodded to Dustin "the rookie", a.k.a. Kat's replacement, who was fumbling around in the kitchen.

"I don't want any tail. I want Kat," Greyson snapped and glanced up to find three sets of eyes staring at him incredulously. He sighed. "Fine."

"I've got plans already. Sorry guys," Kevin said.

"So cancel 'em," Jake snapped.

"Can't. Sorry," Kevin growled.

Jake frowned. "Whatever. You used to be so much fun. What the fuck happened to you Kev?"

"Maybe I fucking grew up. Try it sometime asshole." Kevin slammed the remote down on the coffee table and stomped out.

"What the hell is his problem?" Jake said. "I know Kat's absence has affected each of us in different ways. But come on. It's been two months. Let it go. Get over it," Jake said.

Greyson nodded and took another sip of coffee. Kevin had been PM-Sing since Kat left. Maybe he was rooting for him to leave than Kat. Hell, that's what he wanted too. But stubborn Kat had to do it her way. Better for everyone my ass, Greyson thought. She's the only one that doesn't seem to be hurting from the separation. Hell. She probably had another guy already. Someone safe. Someone who treated her right. Someone she could hold hands with in public. Someone she could love. Someone she could fuck that didn't remind her of her almost-rape.

The thought of another man's hands on Kat's sleek form sent cold shivers of fury through his veins and made his stomach churn. "Fuck," Greyson growled and tossed the arson investigation notes on the table.

"What?" Jake asked.

He sighed. "Nothing."

"She's better off, you know." Jake crossed the room and clapped Greyson on the back.

"I know." He didn't want to talk about it. Not with Jake. Not with anyone.

"So you're in for tonight?"

"Yeah. I'm in." Maybe he could find someone to divert his attention off of Kat. Off of thinking of some other guy's grubby mitts on her.

"Nice! There's a waitress at Kono's that I've been dying to bang. With my wingman I can't miss that target!" Jake mimicked fucking someone from behind, punctuating his 'uh's' with smacking their ass. He leaned back and shouted into the kitchen "Hey rookie, you in?"

Dustin stood so quickly that his head knocked the pans that were hanging above the counter. They crashed onto the counter loudly. "Huh?"

Jake smirked. "Nevermind."

Greyson rolled his eyes. At least a guy's night out would help him take his mind off of Kat.

**

The scene at the club was just like he remembered. The pounding music, the smell of alcohol mixed with sweat and cheap perfume, the stuffy, steamy air surrounding the sea of grinding, oversexed bodies.

"Just like old times right man?" Jake shouted above the thumping bass. He made his sexy face at the waitress when she handed him the beers.

"Yeah." Greyson took his beer and leaned against the bar. His eyes scanned the dance floor. "Exactly like old times." He hadn't been back since Kat started at the station. It was as if his subconscious already knew that Kat was the one. The one he'd love. The one who'd break his heart. Maybe that's why he stopped clubbing with the guys after she started. Or maybe he'd just grown out of it. Who the hell knew.

"Seriously, Greyson. She'd want you to move on. To be happy," Jake shouted into Greyson's ear.

"Can we please stop talking about her? I'm fine."

Jake held up his hands in defeat with his beer balanced in two fingers. "What fucking ever, man. You can wallow in pity by yourself. I'm going to go find someone a little more fun to hang out with. I'll catch up with you later." He sauntered away from the bar and quickly zeroed in on a statuesque chick with dark curls and huge boobs. She giggled at whatever dumb shit he whispered to her – which Greyson was sure she couldn't even hear – and put her hand on his bicep, her fingers stroking circles across his arm.

Greyson grunted. He wouldn't catch up with him later. Jake would be catching up with some club slut and bang her in his truck. Or, if he was lucky, make it back to one of their places before getting it on.

From the looks of Jake's progress, Greyson would have to guess that they wouldn't make it further than the backseat. If they managed to make it out of the club first. He fought a sneer as the curly-haired boob girl flung herself into Jake's arms and sucked at his face. Now there's a classy chick.

His eyes scanned the darkened club. Why the hell had he let Jake talk him into this? He took another swig from his beer and leaned back against the bar, watching the mass of drunken people sway in time to the music.

"Hey there," a sultry voice shouted into his ear over the bass.

He glanced over at the owner of the almost, but not quite, Kat voice. Her long, sandy blonde hair tumbled in waves over her too-big breasts. This girl's were perfectly shaped as they spilled out of her deep v-neck shirt. They were probably implants. While most guys would be rock hard staring at those, they paled in comparison to Kat's natural, gorgeous curves.

His eyes traveled up her neck to her wide hazel eyes, fringed with dark, thick lashes coated in way too many coats of mascara. Beneath all the makeup, he could see some potential. But this girl obviously had one thing on her mind dressing like that.

Greyson simply nodded at her. Best not to lead the poor thing on. Wouldn't want to waste her time.

"I know you right?" she shouted.

"Huh? Um, no, I don't think so?" He furrowed his brow and studied her features. Nothing triggered any memories.

"'Scuse me." The waitress shoved behind the girl and pushed her off balance.

She glared at the waitress and scooted out of the way, closer to him. "I'm Shana. You're a firefighter right?" Her giant boobs pressed against his arm.

"Um, yeah. Shana?" He racked his brain. The picture of the checker at the Randall's down by the station, her sandy blonde hair piled in a bun on top of her head, sprays of hair falling around her freshly washed face, her hazel eyes flashing at him. "Wait, Randall's right?" He smiled at her. What the hell was that innocent girl doing here, looking like that? And how the hell did she hide those underneath the Randall's uniform? And wait, wasn't she like eighteen?

"Right! I can't believe you remember me!" she giggled, making those cream-colored globes bounce up and down provocatively.

"Of course I do. You're our favorite checker!" Ugh. What the hell am I doing? He thought.

"And you're my favorite fireman..." She leaned in, and he could swear he felt her nipples harden against his arm.

The thought of Kat's nipples hardening against him flashed through his mind, and his cock strained at his zipper. He wondered if her body responded to other guys like it had to him. He ground his teeth at the thought. Well if Kat was fucking other guys, why couldn't he fuck other girls? It wasn't like she had spoken to him in the two months that they had been apart. Not even a fucking email.

"Oh really," he said and leaned in slightly to her.

"Really." She licked her lips. The color reminded him of a freshly picked apple.

The picture of her fresh-faced at the Randall's flashed through his mind. "How old are you?"

"Twenty one," she purred and ran a finger over his chest seductively.

She's trying too damn hard. Something a teenager would do…"Are you lying?"

She looked shocked. "Maybe," she pouted.

"I'll ask again. How old are you?"

She leaned into him and stood on her tiptoes to shout into his ear. "Nineteen." She pulled back and her hazel eyes held his. This time it was the truth.

"Still legal then?"

She nodded, and a sexy smile crossed her face.

"Good enough for me." She wasn't *that* much younger than him. What, six years? He put his beer down on the bar and grabbed her hand. "Do you want to get out of here?"

"Yeah," she shouted.

Greyson caught Jake's eye across the dance floor where he was grinding against the curly haired girl with the giant tits. While they were fully clothed, it was almost like they were having sex right in the middle of the dance floor. Her face was flushed and sweat glistened on her olive skin. Were she not already shit-faced, she might have actually been pretty.

Greyson shot him a 'don't be a dick' look. Jake shot him a thumbs up and turned back to the drunk girl.

The second they got to the parking lot Shana grabbed him by the shirt and shoved him against the truck. The dim lights from the lot didn't reach them.

"Slow down," Greyson murmured as her lips smashed against his. She kissed him so hard his teeth hurt. This was definitely not the gentle, yet frantic, way Kat kissed.

She pulled away and ran her hands down to the waistband of his jeans. "I want you. Now." She punctuated between kisses.

"Here?" Greyson choked out. Fucking in a car in the club parking lot wasn't his style.

"Now." Her fingers undid the button and worked to slide the zipper down. Kat's face flashed before him. It felt like aliens were pawing at his body.

He caught her roving fingers. "Slow down."

She sighed and pulled away. "Fine."

He gently pushed her away, unlocked the passenger door and opened it for her. Was he really going to do this?

She half-smiled and her pink tongue darted out to moisten her cherry red lips. "My place." She grabbed the handle and climbed into the truck.

His groin tightened when she bent over, causing her miniskirt to lift up just enough to give him a view of her tight, round ass. She wasn't wearing underwear.

He climbed into the truck. The engine roared to life. The cab filled with the smell of Shana's perfume, something strong and musky, like walking by the Evecrombie and Mitch store in the mall. His nose burned.

His stomach clenched when he thought about the last woman he'd had in his truck. Rather than the overpowering scent of barely-legal trying too hard, the cab had been filled with the sultry scent of vanilla and lavender and Kat.

Back to reality Greyson. She's gone. And probably fucking other guys. It's been two months. Are you never going to have sex again, just because some chick dumped you?

Greyson shook his head to clear it and followed Shana's directions to her apartment, which ironically was just across the street from the Randall's. He wondered if she even owned a car.

He followed her up the stairs, watching her hips sway as she precariously climbed the stairs in her stripper platform heels. Occasionally she'd waver like she'd had one (or twelve) too many.

"My roommate's out of town. So, it's just us." She sent him a 'come hither' look and pulled him into the darkened apartment.

It was exactly as he pictured any nineteen-year-old's first apartment. A threadbare couch, and a wide screen TV in the living room. A little vase of daisies decorated an ugly folding table in the dining area with two folding chairs.

"My room's this way." She didn't look back as she kicked off her heels into the corner and sauntered down the hallway, catching herself on the doorway as she lost her balance.

She flicked on the light in her bedroom and the pink was overwhelming. Pink curtains, pink duvet, pink throw carpet.

"Pink?" He raised an eyebrow.

She turned and grabbed his hand, leading him to the bed. "I like pink. I bet you do too. Would you like to see what else I have that's pink?" She shoved him down on the bed.

"Um."

"I've always wanted to know how it feels to fuck a firefighter." She quickly stripped her shirt off, revealing a lacy pink bra barely containing her fake breasts.

His groin tightened. He was a man after all, and the sight of her firm breasts straining at the lace of her bra would give a celibate priest a boner.

She knelt before him. "Hmm. I think you'd like to fuck me too." She cupped him through the fabric of his pants.

A hiss escaped his gritted teeth.

She pushed him back to lie on the bed and climbed on top, straddling him. He could feel the heat radiating from between her legs on his cock, still safely contained in his jeans. She crushed his lips again with hers in a sloppy, drunk college girl kind of way.

She pulled back and unhooked her bra, letting it fall onto his chest. "You want me, don't you firefighter boy?" Her tight, pink nipples stood at attention in the glaring light from the fluorescent floor lamp. She leaned back into him and kissed him, softer this time, more tentatively. Her nipples pressed against his chest as she sucked his lip into her mouth.

The image of Kat's face, flushed with desire, her golden breasts heaving as she rode him flashed before his eyes, like it was her, not this drunk bar girl straddling him. Her thick hair fell in dark waves over her shoulders and chest. Her eyes were the same vibrant blue, like a stormy sea, her lips swollen from his kiss. But rather the desire in her eyes, he saw sadness. Her lips moved, but it wasn't Kat's voice. "Don't you want me firefighter boy?"

He blinked. Kat's image faded and was replaced by the disheveled, topless blonde stranger straddling him.

He cleared his throat and rolled her off of him. "I'm sorry, I can't do this." He handed her shirt to her and shoved off the bed.

"Did I do something wrong?" Tears filled her eyes.

"No. I did." He raked a hand through his hair. "I'm sorry. I have to go."

He couldn't escape the barren apartment fast enough.

28

Chapter Twenty-eight

Antonio peered over his wine glass at Kat, his brown eyes twinkling in the candlelight. "So how did you get into arson investigations?" He rolled his r's seductively with his Spanish accent.

"I was a firefighter and then this opportunity fell in my lap. Luckily my boxer, Diesel, turned out to be the perfect arson dog." Kat poked at her filet mignon with her fork. He'd insisted that she order the most expensive cut of meat on the menu. Probably so she'd feel obligated to let him in her pants.

"A boxer, now that's a dumb dog," he sneered.

Dear God. Can this just be over now? She was going to kill Eve when she saw her. This had to be the worst blind date she'd set her up on so far. She'd let Eve set her up on a couple of blind dates since she'd gotten back from training in D.C. two weeks ago. While he was gorgeous, with his tall, lean frame and dark features, his ego was so big she was surprised he could fit it through the restaurant's door.

"Actually, boxers are very intelligent. It's all about the training. We trained for two months with a group of other trainers and dogs, and he was at the top of the class." Kat tried to keep the annoyance from her voice.

"Huh," he grunted. "Do you want more wine?" Without waiting for an answer, he started pouring.

"No, thanks. I'm done." Boy, was she done. Done with this date. Done with this night. The only thing she wanted to do was go back to her new house, the one that had been sitting empty and neglected since she had left abruptly to go to Washington, D.C. for the arson dog training. Diesel probably was tearing up the cherry wood floors waiting to go outside. Maybe she'd stop by the home improvement warehouse on the way home and pick up a doggy door to install for him.

The waitress put the bill on the table in front of Antonio, but Kat snatched it up before he could even consider paying for her meal. There was no way she'd owe this macho, egotistical jerk anything.

"Please, let me," he purred in what she was sure was supposed to be a seductive growl meant to make her go weak in the knees.

Instead, it made her go weak in the stomach. The expensive dinner that she was about to shell over forty bucks for her half of the bill rose in her throat. She shoved two twenties into the sleeve and slid the bill over to him.

"That should cover my portion of the bill and tip. Thanks for the company. It was nice meeting you." She shoved away from the table and marched from the restaurant, as fast as her stilettos could take her. She didn't dare glance back at the shocked look on his handsome face.

**

Kat shoved the florescent orange cart before her as she wandered the aisles at the home improvement store, her eyes glued on the racks of nails. She could feel the eyes of every sweaty, dirty man in the place on her. She knew what they saw: an overdressed girl in stiletto lace-up heels and a black cocktail dress at the local home improvement store after dark.

She stood on one foot to reach the nails on the shelf above her head. Her fingers brushed the box, but didn't make purchase around it.

"Ugh!" Kat grumbled. Now she'd have to find an associate, and look like the helpless, clueless girl in stilettos in the home improvement store. She was *so* not that girl.

"Kat?" Chills raced over her skin as his familiar voice caressed her name.

"Greyson!" Kat spun around. It'd been months. He'd let his hair grow out until it just brushed his collar in sexy, tousled waves. But the intense look in his caramel eyes sent shivers through her, like usual.

His arms encircled her, and he pulled her to his chest. It felt so right in his arms. Her eyes closed and she inhaled deeply, savoring the scent that she'd dreamt about for so many months. It was one hundred times more intense, and she felt dizzy from it. Too soon she was released from the heaven of his arms.

His eyes trailed over her hungrily. Her skin tingled in the wake of his gaze. "You look great. How've you been?"

She'd never forgotten the way his eyes reminded her of melted chocolate.

"I've been good." Kat dropped her gaze to stare at the doggie door in her cart. "How've you been?"

"Miserable," his voice rumbled low in his chest.

Her eyes shot to his, which smoldered as he gazed at her. Her breath caught. It took everything in her to let the word "Why?" whisper from her lips.

He took a step closer, his body heating the air between their bodies. Her skin tingled at the memory of how his touch sent electric currents racing across her skin.

He reached out, his hand held in mid-air for a moment before dropping it to his side. His Adam's apple bobbed as he swallowed hard. "I miss you, Kat."

Her jaw dropped. "I..."

The crash of two shopping carts colliding shook Kat from her stupor. She glared with annoyance at the girl, with her messy brunette hair pulled back into one of those messy buns under a bejeweled hat, and huge dark sunglasses. Her skin held that oompa-loompa orange fake tan glow. She mumbled an apology in Spanish and shuffled past. There was something vaguely familiar about her voice.

A chill coursed over her skin as the stranger turned the corner. She blinked and glanced at Greyson, who still stared at her intently. She sighed. "I, uh, I have to go."

Greyson nodded and stepped back, his face fell with defeat. "It was really good seeing you."

Kat smiled weakly, feeling a rock land in the pit of her stomach. "You too." She dug into her purse and pulled out a card and handed it to him. "Call me sometime and we can get together for coffee, or something."

His eyes lit up as he took the card from her and flipped it over. His fingers traced over the red embossed letters spelling out Chandler Fire Department. Her name, followed by the title of K-9 Arson investigator. His gaze shot to hers. "Arson?"

Her cheeks flamed as she nodded. "K-9 arson investigations."

His eyes widened in shock. "Diesel!?" Her poor dog's name was more of a gasp than an actual word.

Kat giggled. "He's a really smart dog, top of his class in fact."

"Wow. I knew that dog had something special in him. Just didn't think it was arson investigations!"

The topic of Diesel brought her attention back to the cart, which was why she had braved the home improvement store in stilettos and a cocktail dress in the first place. "Speaking of Diesel, he's probably tearing up my new wood floors right now. Call me, okay?" She swallowed the lump in her throat. Would they really see each other again?

"See ya around, Kat." Greyson stepped aside as Kat pushed her cart away. She could feel his eyes on her and turned to catch his gaze once before she turned the corner.

Luckily, there managed to only be the rude girl who smashed her cart into hers on the nail aisle in front of her at the checkout line. She kept her gaze averted as she piled her items on the conveyor belt. Rope, butane, duct tape, paint thinner, paintbrushes and one can of white exterior house paint.

She watched her frizzy hair peeking out from under her stupid hat in annoyance as she fished out a stack of bills from her oversized purse. Who the hell paid with cash anymore?

Finally, the cashier counted back her change and handed her the plastic bag and receipt.

Kat hauled the doggie door onto the conveyor belt.

"Looks like you've got a hot date for a Friday night." The checker said as he scanned the box. He had to be sixteen, just barely, with acne marking his otherwise potentially handsome face. Once his face cleared up, he'd be a total lady killer.

"Yep," Kat murmured and swiped her debit card.

"Lucky dog," the kid muttered under his breath as he put the doggie door back into her cart and handed her the receipt.

Kat rolled her eyes and took the receipt from him.

The sliding doors whooshed open before her, revealing what had been threatening in the sky all evening. While she was inside, it was as if someone had ripped the clouds open. Rain sheeted down before her.

She marched across the darkened parking lot, the rickety wheels of the cart rattling across the wet, uneven asphalt as she hurried towards her truck. The raindrops splashed off the pavement and up onto her legs as she navigated the slippery surface in her stilettos.

The alarm beeped and she flung the door open, tossing her bag in before turning to maneuver the huge doggie door box into the back seat. She had just slid it across the floor and was about to step up on to the side bars when through the wet air she heard a male voice calling her name.

She spun, her damp hair slapping her face as she turned. A dark figure dashed from the entrance of the store towards her.

"Kat! Wait!" Greyson's voice drifted towards her through the patter of raindrops as they hit the asphalt. His long strides ate up the distance between them in seconds. By the time he got skidded to a stop before her, his dark hair was plastered against his head. The water ran in rivulets down his chiseled face and disappeared into his soaked Chandler Fire t-shirt that clung to his body like a second skin. His chest heaved as he fought to catch his breath. His melted chocolate eyes smoldered as he stared at her, the rain pouring down between them.

"Greyson?" Kat asked as the rain pelted her.

He took the two steps left to close the distance between them. "Kat, I..." His arms were around her and his lips were on hers before he could finish his sentence. They were as soft as she remembered them, but there was something different about the way he kissed her. Like he was afraid she'd disappear.

She'd dreamed about this since the day she took the transfer. The day she removed herself from Greyson's life forever. But she couldn't remove him from her heart. She ran her tongue across his lips and smiled when he trembled in against her. Her fingers wound in his hair on their own accord.

Her blood sang as it raced through her body, her heart pounding to the beat of the rain pouring down on them. The scent of wet desert overwhelmed her senses and mixed with his heady taste. His hands traced over her back, her hips, like he was memorizing the way they felt under his fingers.

She fought a moan of disappointment when he pulled back.

"I'm sorry. I know we agreed to end it. But I just..." He cleared his throat, his cheeks reddening a bit.

Her gaze dropped to the wet asphalt. She studied the ricocheting droplets like they had the answers she was looking for. "I missed you too, Greyson."

Over the background noise of the rain pouring down on them, the sound of his breath catching in his throat made her stomach clench. His wet boots came into her field of vision. His hand caught her chin and tilted her head up. The cool droplets of rain bounced off her face and rolled down her neck. But it wasn't the water's trails down her body that made her shiver. It was the intensity in his gaze that made chills race over her skin.

His stormy gaze searched hers for a moment. "I love you, Kat."

Her gasp was covered by his lips. She wanted to freeze time, to stay forever in that moment. The words she always craved but never imagined hearing again from him fell from his lips. And from the look in his eyes when he uttered the words, he meant it.

Her skin tingled as he ran his hands over her and devoured her with his lips. She caught his hand when it reached her breast. Reluctantly she tore her lips away and whispered a throaty "Wait..."

The pained look that crossed his face almost brought tears to her eyes. "We can't do this. Not here." She glanced around the almost deserted parking lot, the streetlights lighting up the raindrops in an orange haze.

"I know." He glanced towards his truck, parked a few rows over in a darkened portion of the lot. "I have to get to the station. But I'm off tomorrow."

Kat smiled and stood on her tiptoes. "Then we'll have our first real date tomorrow." She smiled and pressed her lips to his.

He pulled the door open and Kat climbed in. "Tomorrow."

Kat smiled and nodded. She reached one hand out and cupped his face, leaning over to plant one more kiss on his lips. "Tomorrow."

**

Greyson watched as the red glow of her truck's taillights disappeared around the corner before running across the waterlogged lot to his truck. He pulled out his keys and the lights flashed as he deactivated the alarm. He was soaked to the bone. And his heart was overflowing the confines of his chest. He'd finally get to take Kat out. On a real date. With no fear of being found out. They could date like any other couple. He'd even told her he loved her.

His skin warmed at the thought. He told her he loved her. And her reaction had been to kiss him with every fiber of her being. But she hadn't said she loved him back. She...

A sharp pain at the back of his neck dislodged any thought beyond the blinding pain. Lights flashed before his eyes before he blacked out.

29

Chapter Twenty-nine

Kat cringed at the sound of Diesel's nails as he dug at the door from the garage to the house. She hefted the doggie door out of the back seat and unlocked the door. He practically bowled her over in his effort to get into the garage between her legs. He lunged at the garage door as it rattled shut, digging at it and barking ferociously.

"Diesel! Chill!" She kicked the door open and stumbled into the darkened kitchen. She dumped the heavy box onto the island and flicked on the lights. The recessed can lights flickered to life, setting the cherry cabinets off in a gentle glow. She yanked open the stainless-steel door on the fridge and pulled out a bottle of water and nudged it shut with her hip.

She leaned against the counter and stared across the house, which was still mostly empty. The house was way too big for just her, but when the real estate agent showed it to her, she couldn't picture herself living anywhere else. Sadly, she hadn't had time to buy furniture before she left for Washington D.C. after the fire. And since she got back, she'd picked up just a few necessities. The butter-soft beige suede couch and her California king bed were the first major pieces of furniture she had bought since she got back. But other than that, her sprawling three-thousand square foot house was empty.

Which is why she bought the doggie door. It was vital to keep busy during the time she wasn't working. Otherwise, the loneliness and fear would start creeping in. She mentally made the note to go furniture shopping with her insurance check. Living like this was kind-of pathetic.

But what use was a bunch of expensive furniture in an empty house when Eric was still out there somewhere? He hadn't shown up in months, not since she went to Washington, D.C. In fact, according to Chief Phillips, even the arson fires stopped once she was gone.

Kat's skin tightened at the thought of Eric. She snatched the scissors off the counter and went to work prying open the doggie door box. Nothing like a midnight hammering project from the newest resident to piss off the HOA.

Diesel's nails clattered across the hardwood as he raced back into the house and tore down the hallway towards the front door. The sounds of him lunging and digging at the front door had her teeth grinding against each other.

Kat tossed the scissors onto the pile of shredded cardboard on the counter and threw open the French doors to the backyard. "Diesel! Out!" He dug at the floor mat for another second before spinning and dashing out the back door. She shook her head and went back to the kitchen island to get to work on installing the doggie door.

Before she made it to the counter, something poking beneath the front door caught her eye. Her stomach soured at the memory of the envelope that was stuffed under Greyson's door after the fire.

No fear. He doesn't deserve your fear. She marched to the door and picked up the envelope, flipped it over and caught the smeared yet familiar HOA logo on the upper left corner. Her breath gushed from her chest in one huge, relieved sigh as she walked back into the kitchen and dropped the heavy envelope on the counter.

She rifled through the shredded box, sifting through numerous bags of hardware as she searched for the instructions. She spotted the corner peeking up from beneath a pile of Styrofoam. Of course they'd hide the instructions. If she a guy, she totally wouldn't have used them.

She reached for the paper and gasped when a sharp piece of cardboard sliced into her skin. A huge drop of blood pooled on the tip of her finger. She flicked on the faucet and ran water over the half-inch long wound on her finger. Stupid paper cuts.

The water ran red into the granite sink. She shut the water off and was wrapping a towel around her finger when her cell phone rattled on the counter beside the offending box.

She didn't recognize the long-distance number.

"Hello?"

"Miss Hale?" A deep male voice asked.

"Speaking."

"I'm Sergeant Brown with the arson investigation team here in D.C. I have a few questions for you if you have the time."

She pressed the towel to her finger to stop the bleeding and leaned against the counter. "Sure. What's this about?"

"Well, Miss Hale, it's in regard to some arson fires that you worked in Chandler, Arizona before you came to D.C. for arson training."

Her brow furrowed. Why would an arson investigation unit in D.C. be calling her for this info? "Have you spoken to the arson investigation teams for CFD? They know a heck of a lot more than I do. I was just a first responder."

"Actually, Miss Hale, it's related to you personally."

"How do you mean?"

"We had an increase in arson fires in Washington D.C. shortly after you arrived for training. And from what your arson investigators tell us, the fires in Chandler with the same M.O. as these stopped completely. And the fact that you were almost a victim of the arsonist, gives us reason to believe the suspect followed you to Washington DC."

He followed me. The phone slipped from her hand and clattered on the counter. Kat's eyes shot to the waterlogged envelope on her counter. It couldn't be. That envelope had her HOA's logo.

"Hello? Miss Hale?" Sergeant Brown's voice echoed up through the phone.

Her blood ran cold as she picked up the heavy envelope and ripped it open.

It was a stack of photos, rubber banded with a hand-written letter on faded parchment in blood red type. It felt like ice cubes in her hands as she pulled the letter off the pile and read it to the sound of Sergeant Brown's frantic "Hello?" in the background.

Kat,

So glad to have you home. I wish I could say I missed you, but I really did enjoy watching you and that idiot dog of yours training in Washington. And it was nice to taste what Washington had to offer for a few months.

Yes, I followed you.

I planned on sneaking into that huge house of yours and killing you, but when I ran into you and your boyfriend at the Home Warehouse, I knew I had to do this right.

You never deserved him. So, I'm taking care of that. As you can see by the enclosed pictures.

If you want to see your boyfriend alive one more time, meet me at the abandoned microchip factory off Chandler Blvd at midnight. COME ALONE. There will only be his ashes left to say goodbye to if you don't.

See you soon.

E

The letter fell from her hand as she snatched the photos off the counter and rifled through them. Greyson unconscious (she hoped) gagged and tied to a radiator. A pile of combustible material beside him. A lit butane torch near Greyson's face. A close-up of blood trailing from a corner of Greyson's gagged mouth.

The photos tumbled like falling leaves from her hands as she snatched her phone off the counter.

"Hello? Sergeant Brown?" Her voice was tinged with hysteria.

"Miss Hale. What happened?"

"I'll be in touch shortly." Her stomach churned as she hit 'end call' on her phone and laid it on the counter.

**

The scent of butane filtered into the blackness surrounding Greyson. With some effort he managed to open his eyes. The run-down room tilted and shifted beneath him. His head pounded, centering on a throbbing ache on the back of his skull. The last thing he remembered was kissing Kat in the parking lot of that home improvement store. Scheduled a real first date with her. And something hit him as he was getting into his truck.

Shit. He shifted on the dusty wood floor. He tried to lift his hand to brace his head against the sensation of the ground tilting and shifting beneath him, but the rope cinched around his wrists prevented it. He coughed to clear the cottony feeling in his mouth, which only made it worse. The rag crammed in his mouth and tied around his head held fast. Oh God. What the hell was going on?

"Sleeping Beauty awakens." A vaguely familiar yet garbled voice filtered in from somewhere beyond his blurry circle of vision. All he could see were dusty floorboards scattered with yellowed papers. Everything beyond that was oddly blurry.

"You know, she doesn't love you. She would have said so if she did. And she doesn't." A pair of boots came into view, but their owner's face and torso was blurry.

The gag prevented him from responding with anything other than a frustrated grunt.

A maniacal cackle ripped from the person's lips. "You weren't in the plans. It was just supposed to be Eric's ex-girlfriends. And any future ones that aren't me."

The voice rose an octave, and Greyson realized who the owner was. She stepped into the range of his vision as her name crossed his mind. Eve.

"Your brother is a *very* fickle boy, you know that?"

Another muffled grunt.

"All he had to do was to pick me. But the idiot couldn't even do that, could he?"

Greyson grit his teeth against the gag. If only he wasn't tied up...

"I don't really want to hurt you. But Eric just doesn't seem to respond to anything but violence. So, I'm taking everything he loves until he agrees to love me."

His eyes widened when Eve pulled out a butane torch. "And, if he doesn't agree, he and your girlfriend will watch you burn. So hopefully Kat's getting the little package I left on her front doorstep soon so we can get this show on the road." Eve struck the lighter before the torch, which ignited and glowed blue-white as she knelt before Greyson.

The heat from the torch was unbearable. Even without the flame touching him, he could feel his skin crackling from the intense heat. He couldn't fight the scream that ripped from his chest. But the gag muffled it to little more than a gurgling growl.

Greyson let out a pained sigh of relief when Eve extinguished the torch. Until she swung the bottle towards his face. The world plunged again into darkness.

30

Chapter Thirty

"Stay," Kat commanded and climbed out of her truck in the empty parking lot. The rain had stopped, leaving huge muddy puddles in the potholes that peppered the lot. The microchip factory hadn't been used in many years, and the jagged asphalt parking lot showed the neglect.

Diesel's pained whine followed her as she crossed in front of the truck and leaned into the open window. "If I am not back in a half hour, send in the troops." She scrubbed his ears and kissed him on the head, like she was saying good-bye for the last time.

The double doors to the main building were closed, but the chipped paint and slightly warped frame showed signs of someone prying them open with a crowbar. Her hand trembled slightly as it closed on the cool metal of the handle. A gentle tug and the door swung open, groaning in protest on rusted hinges. The stale air embraced her. Something mixed with the mold and stagnant building smell. Gasoline.

Eric was here.

She flicked on her flashlight and tentatively walked down the hall. She winced as each step echoed down the empty hallway and amplified, almost as if there were two sets of footsteps echoing through the building. Each open door she passed made her heart accelerate. Eric could be hiding behind any of these doors, just waiting to grab her.

She ducked her head into each room, checking for the bastard. Nothing but a pile of newspapers and cardboard boxes, stacked almost to the ceiling. In every room it was almost the same scene. Like someone had planted the garbage there in a particular pattern. Eric.

A thump and scuffle overhead made Kat's heart skip a beat. He was upstairs.

The beam from her flashlight darted down the hallway as she looked for a sign of a stairway. At the far end of the hall a bent sign indicated "Stairs". Her footsteps rattled down the hallway as she ran towards them.

Old papers and trash littered the stairs. And every so often were the unmistakable trails of rat droppings. Kat shuddered and climbed the stairs, avoiding the raisin-shaped turds. Nothing like contracting Hanta virus while battling a deranged serial killer.

A few more precarious steps. Her final step onto the landing on to a crumpled piece of newspaper resulted in a pained squeak from beneath it. She stifled a scream and jumped back. Her hand nearly missed the rusty rail as she careened backwards in her effort to avoid the mangy-looking rat that darted between her legs down the staircase.

Another thump and scuffle sounded from a doorway down the hall. Kat carefully avoided the clutter and tiptoed towards the noise. Just before she reached the door, she pressed her back against the wood paneling and listened.

Breathing. Pained breathing.

She peeked her head into the door and glanced around the window-less room. What was meant to be a quick peek and plaster back to the wall was stalled when she saw Greyson slumped against a radiator. A rag had been tied around his mouth, a thick rope tied around his hands and feet. Angry welts peeked out from beneath the rope, like the rope burns she'd experienced as a result of Eric's handy work. She couldn't contain her gasp as his name came to her lips. Any thought other than getting Greyson out of there dissolved as she stared at his battered face.

Greyson's eyes popped open and almost bugged out of his head when he saw her in the doorway. He writhed at his bonds and screamed against his gag.

Kat took two steps towards him before her breath was knocked from her chest as someone tackled her from behind. Her chin scrapped the floor as she went skidding across it on her stomach. The weight on her back made it impossible to suck in anything deeper than a shallow breath.

"Hello, Kitty Kat," Eve whispered into her ear.

Had she been able to breathe, she would have gasped. Shock and confusion stole what little breath Kat had. Eve was Eric's *accomplice*?

"So glad you got my note."

"Why are you doing this?" What was supposed to be a growl came out more like a pained squeak from her compressed chest.

"Because you didn't deserve him. You don't deserve either of them. But they both chose you." Eve flipped her on to her back and straddled her chest.

Kat stared up into the eyes of the woman she thought was her friend. "But Eric..."

"You're as dumb as you look, you know that? How you ever got through the fire academy is anybody's guess," Eve snarled.

Kat glared at her, rage simmering.

Eve sighed. "I have to spell it out for you, don't I?"

Kat's gaze narrowed, yet she didn't respond.

"I set the fires, you idiot. This whole time you were blaming Eric. It was me. Every woman who felt Eric's touch got to feel the kiss from the flames. Except you. But that'll soon be remedied." Eve shook out her long, blonde hair and smiled. "I'm a horribly jealous person, you see. Ever since college, I've had my sights set on him. We were supposed to live happily ever after. But he was deceived by sluts and whores who made him think that they were better than me. That he wanted them and not me. So, I've been cleaning up after him, disposing of his leftovers, waiting for the right moment to remind him why he should love me over all of you. Because I love him more than any of you ever did."

Kat frowned. The psycho bitch was obsessed. "Greyson?" Kat squeaked. Her vision was starting to get spotty from Eve's full weight compressing her lungs.

Eve shrugged. "Greyson's just an innocent bystander who got caught in the crossfire. It was *you* I was after. In all honesty, I should have ended you in DC when I had the chance. But I wanted Eric to see the lengths at which I would go for his love."

Her blue eyes flicked towards Greyson for a moment, out of the corner of her eye, Kat could him straining at his bonds. The chafed skin had broken open and was soaking the rope with blood.

"Maybe your boyfriend would enjoy a little show? I wonder, would he enjoy seeing you burn?" She reached into her pocket and pulled out a miniature butane torch. A smirk screwed up her face. She ignited the torch and leaned towards Kat's face.

Kat cringed and turned her head, unable to dislodge Eve from her chest. Her tear-filled gaze caught Greyson's, which were narrowed and bloodshot with fury. *Don't give up.* She could practically hear him saying the words. She twisted and bucked against Eve to dislodge her weight from her chest.

Her skin prickled at the intense heat. Kat gritted her teeth and tried not to cry out as the heat intensified. She wouldn't give Eve the pleasure of hearing her pain. She clenched her eyes closed and tried to take measured breaths into her constricted chest.

A pained grunt filled the air and suddenly the weight disappeared from Kat's chest. Her eyes popped open in time to watch Eve fly across the room with a dark figure wrapped around her. Kat scrambled back as the pair wrestled for the torch in the corner beside the stacks of delivery pallets and loose papers.

Kat dashed for Greyson and pulled his gag from his mouth, keeping one eye on Eve and her rescuer. "Are you okay?" She searched him for other injuries. But besides the bloodied lip, raw wounds on his wrists and ripening black eye, he seemed to be intact. Her gaze darted between the wrestling duo and Greyson's battered face.

"Are you?" He asked, his caramel eyes searched hers.

Kat nodded. That was a good question. "I'm fine. Let's get out of here."

"She's got the place rigged."

Kat's breath caught in her throat. She was really going to kill Greyson. "Psycho bitch."

"Understatement. I saw her stash a knife behind those crates over there." He nodded towards one of the smaller campfire-looking stacks of crates. "Careful, she's got it all rigged to ignite if anything gets moved."

Kat glanced at the fighters in the corner and cringed when her savior reached back and let a punch fly into Eve's model-like face. She groaned and crumpled to the floor. Kat dashed to the stack and snatched up the six-inch hunting knife.

The man turned and Kat's heart lurched when she found Eric staring down at her with his ice-blue eyes.

"Eric?" Kat raised the knife before her defensively. Tears filled her eyes and months of repressed fear and heartbreak bubbled to the surface. "How could you be involved in all this? I trusted you! I loved you!"

"I wasn't!"

"You tried to burn me to death!"

Eric frowned and gazed at her with a confused look on his face. All the color drained from his face as he studied her. "The house fire? That was my fault?"

Kat nodded. "You knocked the candle into the trashcan. Greyson barely got me out in time!"

Eric shook his head and took a step closer. Kat raised the knife up defensively. "Oh, Kat. I'm so sorry! I had no idea. Please, believe me when I say it wasn't intentional! I'd never do anything to hurt you, Kat."

"You tried to rape me."

He crammed a hand through his hair. "I was drunk, Kat. Oh God, I'm so sorry."

"If you didn't do it intentionally, why'd you go into hiding?"

Eric sighed. "I found out that Eve was responsible for all those murders. When I learned why, I had to keep you safe. And I couldn't do that if I was behind bars for attempted rape." He lifted his hands up in a helpless gesture. "This is all my fault. I made her go off the deep end. One night after you and I had a fight, I went to the bar and got piss-ass drunk. Eve showed up and somehow, we ended up back at my place. I knew she was obsessed with me, but I was so drunk, and I wanted to hurt you. When I woke up next to her in the morning, I realized what a horrible mistake I'd made. I told her so, but she wouldn't accept that. She locked herself in the bathroom and refused to come out until I confessed my love for her. I literally had to break down the door and throw her out of my apartment."

"The address book?"

"She must've found it when she locked herself in my bathroom and realized the crossed-out names were my ex's."

Tears brimmed her eyes and rolled down her cheeks. She could see the truth in his eyes. An overwhelming sense of relief crashed over her and she sunk to her knees under the weight of her relief. The knife clattered to the floor beside her.

Eric sunk to his knees before her and pulled her into his arms. "I'm so sorry," he chanted.

"It's too late," Kat murmured. "I'm sorry, Eric."

A muffled groan in the direction where Eric had left Eve brought their attention to the present. Eric nodded and pulled her to her feet, snatching the knife off the floor as he stood. He handed it back to her and nodded towards Greyson. "Go help him."

Kat knelt beside Greyson and made quick work of relieving him of his bonds. She flung one of his arms over her shoulder and stumbled to the door. The faint smell of smoke drifted to her nose and the hair on her arms stood on end. Eric was beside them in a second, shoving a shoulder under Greyson's other arm.

The flicker in the corner of the room stopped them dead in their tracks. Flames licked up the stack of crates in the corner. Eve slowly regained consciousness at the base of the stack.

Eric and Kat's eyes met for a moment. "We can't leave her," Eric sighed and handed Greyson's weight back off to Kat.

He raced to Eve and scooped her up into his arms and raced back for the door. They opened it and encountered a smoke-filled hallway. They circled back, aiming for the door on the other side of the room. Eve's disoriented chuckle brought the hair on the back of Kat's neck up.

"Too late," Eve sneered.

Kat shot a death-glare at Eve. "What did you do?" Kat growled.

"If I can't have him, no one can." She wriggled free of Eric's grasp and snatched the discarded knife off the floor and pointed it at them. "No one is going anywhere."

Eric held his hands up. "Listen to me, Eve. We are all going to burn to death if we don't get out of here. Now."

Eve scowled and swiped the air with the knife. "Why couldn't you just choose me? I loved you, Eric! More than any of those other whores. Why couldn't you have just chosen me?"

Eric shook his head. "I'm sorry, Eve. I really am. I'm an idiot. Give me the knife and we can talk about it, okay?"

Eve shook her head. "You don't love me. You love *her*." She inclined her head toward Kat. "You've always loved her. Even when she didn't want you. I want that kind of love." Tears rolled down her bruised cheeks.

"You can have that, Eve." Eric took another step towards her.

"No, I can't! She took that away from me!" Eve screamed and lunged at him.

Kat couldn't stifle the scream tore from her lips as she watched Eve lunge at Eric with the knife. A sickening gurgle bubbled up through Eric's chest as the knife found its home in his stomach.

Eve reeled back in horror, clasping her bloodied hands to her mouth. The knife clattered to the ground. "Oh my God, what have I done? Eric!"

Eric stumbled towards Kat and Greyson. "Go!" He clenched his hands against his abdomen in an attempt to stop the bleeding.

"Eric!" Kat gasped. There was blood. So much blood.

"Greyson! Get her the fuck out of here!" Eric pleaded.

Greyson shifted off Kat's shoulder and grabbed her by the hand and dragged her down the back stairwell with Eric following close behind.

"Eric!" Eve's frantic voice shrieked from the top of the stairway.

"Go!" Eric growled and pushed them out of the way as Eve lunged down the stairs after them, her knife flashing in the firelight.

A rumble shook the building and flaming rafters crashed down onto the stairs between them and onto Eve.

"Eric!" Kat and Greyson screamed simultaneously. There was no way of getting across to him.

"Take her and get out!" Eric braced against the wall with one hand, the other still pressed against the wound in his abdomen. He slumped to his knees on the stairs, the bloodstain quickly spreading on his shirt. "I love you both, more than life itself." The smoke choked him and he coughed hard. "Take care of each other."

She couldn't tear her gaze away from him as he slumped down the wall, leaving a bloody smear on the blackening plaster.

"No..." Kat coughed. The smoke billowing in the room seared her lungs. A strangled sob erupted from Greyson's throat as he pulled her down the stairs.

Kat struggled at his hold, but he held firm. "Come on! There's nothing we can do!" Greyson shouted and hauled her down the shuddering staircase.

Their feet pounded the concrete and flaming rafters and debris fell around them as they raced for the doors, which were flung open to the clear night air. So close.

The sound of a freight train hitting the building drowned out all else. The sweet heaven of freedom was only a few feet away when the ceiling collapsed on top of them.

31

Chapter Thirty-one

Rats scratched at her brain and an elephant sat on her chest. Kat tried to take a deep breath, but the most she could manage was a tiny squeak of air into her lungs. Her eyes fluttered open to blackness. Heat licked at her face.

Greyson's hand was in hers. She squeezed it, but he didn't respond.

She tried to move her legs, but the rubble encasing her only shifted and filled in the tiny void her movements had made.

The scratching intensified over her head, and Kat's skin crawled with the thought of the millions of rats that must be running over her head as they escaped the burning building. Her blood froze in her veins as the heat pricked at her skin. They were still inside the building, trapped under the collapsed ceiling.

"Greyson," Kat squeaked.

His limp hand slipped from hers.

If she had enough breath, she would have screamed out his name. But she could barely breathe as it was. Instead, tears fell unchecked down her cheeks as she struggled to breathe in the smoke-filled confined space. Lights flashed before her eyes. She tried slowing her breathing, but the minimal oxygen in the small space gave out and blackness descended on her.

The elephant finally got up off her chest and Kat sucked in a deep breath of wet, soot-filled air.

Her eyes fluttered open to the darting beams of flashlights over her head. Something wet lapped at her face and snuffled in her ear. She gingerly turned her head to Diesel's frantic sniffing and licking and raised a shaky hand to scratch him.

"Take it easy, Kat," Jake's concerned voice sounded from somewhere over her head.

"Greyson?" Kat whispered.

"We've got him. He's already outside. Pretty banged up." He punctuated the word 'up' with a grunt as he heaved another piece of ceiling off her.

She tentatively stretched her limbs, waiting for the sharp pain from broken bones. But nothing seemed to be broken. "I'm good." She sat up and the rubble shifted around her.

"How'd you find us?" Kat asked as Jake helped her out of the rubble and they quickly exited the smoldering building.

Jake pulled his mask off. "Sargeant Brown called me when you hung up on him. I went by your place. You left your garage door wide open. I found the letter and photos and came straight here. Luckily, Super Dog here knew something was up and led me straight to you."

Kat smiled and scratched Diesel's ears. "Good boy."

Diesel responded by furiously licking her face.

Jake held Diesel's collar as they walked towards the ambulance where Chris was pressing blood-soaked gauze to a puncture wound in Greyson's abdomen.

His eyes fluttered open as she approached and he squinted up at her. "Kat." He tried to reach out towards her, but a sharp hiss of pain forced him to stop mid-reach.

"We've got to transport him now. He's got a ruptured spleen and is bleeding profusely." Chris caught Kat's eye as he loaded him into the ambulance.

Kat glanced at Jake for a moment, who was loading Diesel into her truck. He nodded and climbed in after the dog.

"I'm coming." Kat climbed into the back of the ambulance and sat down on the little bench beside Greyson's gurney.

The memory of riding in Eve's rig to the hospital after the accident that almost killed her rushed through her head. It was odd to see the inside of the ambulance from this perspective. The last three times she'd been the one on the gurney. And for once Eve wasn't by her side. And Eric...

A choked sob threatened to escape her. She bit it back and focused on the man before her. She'd have time to grieve later.

Kat's heart squeezed as she watched the man she loved strapped to the gurney. Every inch of his body was banged up. The only thing that was the same was his chocolate eyes, which watched her intently.

She didn't say a word as they raced through the dark, nearly deserted streets towards Chandler Regional. Within a few minutes, they pulled up to the ambulance entrance, unloaded Greyson and raced through the halls. A nurse put a restraining hand on Kat's shoulder when she tried to follow his gurney into a patient room.

"Sorry, family only," the nurse said.

Without hesitation, Kat responded with the same excuse Greyson used when she was in there. "I'm his girlfriend."

"Okay." The nurse let go of her shoulder and let her into the room.

There was a flurry of activity around Greyson as nurses and doctors worked on him, checking vital signs, putting pressure on his bleeding wounds, examining his internal organs for damage.

And before she could say a word to him, he was rushed into the operating room. Kat plopped into the chair in his now-empty patient room and waited. While she had no external injuries, her heart bled for Greyson. Her hands trembled as she pulled her knees to her chest, wrapped her arms around her knees, and cried into her folded arms.

**

Greyson's eyes fluttered open to the bright morning light filtering in through the open blinds in the hospital room. His head spun with déjà vu as he stared at the intricate paisley wallpaper. What felt like a lifetime ago he'd woken up to see this wallpaper. But not from this vantage point.

He tried to sit up, but a sharp pain in his abdomen stopped him from moving more than an inch. A warm, feminine hand held his. His eyes followed the soft skin, up a perfectly shaped arm, to a tangled mass of mahogany waves. Unable to restrain himself, he sucked in a deep breath of her vanilla and lavender scent.

Greyson winced at the shooting pain from his abdomen that the deep breath caused, but it was worth the pain. Her scent filled him with a warmth he had been missing for so long. It was like her scent jump-started his frozen heart.

With some effort and more than one pained grunt, he reached his unrestrained hand over to stroke her hair. "My love." The pungent scent of charred wood wafted up from her hair.

Kat shot upright, releasing her grip on his hand to shove her wild mass of tangled waves back from her face. "You're awake." Her blush traveled over her soot-streaked face down her neck to her cleavage, which strained at the streaked and torn t-shirt.

While the sight of her chest was enough to bring him to his knees, her appearance was concerning. His memory of how he got to the hospital was a black hole in his consciousness. Tiny flashes of torture, flames and the horrible feeling of not being in control plagued his sleep. But that was just an anesthesia-induced dream, right? But Kat's appearance begged to differ with that theory. "What happened?"

Confusion crossed her face for a moment. "You had a punctured spleen, among other things."

His eyes caught hers, could see the fear behind her eyes. "I mean how."

Kat sighed. "It was Eve. Not Eric. She grabbed you, took you to the abandoned microchip factory and beat the crap out of you, then used you as bait to lure me there." She gritted her teeth and swallowed, as if trying to swallow down the urge to throw up. "Eve was about to kill us when Eric tackled her. She was the one setting the fires. He didn't turn himself in because he found out I was her next target. He was trying to protect me. He saved our lives." She paused, as if she hadn't completely come to terms with it. "Eve stabbed him in the stomach. He died in the stairwell trying to get us out of the building." Tears filled her eyes. "He's dead and it's all because of me."

Greyson shifted to sitting, despite the protest from his banged-up body and the sharp pain of tissue pulling at fresh stiches and gathered her into his arms. His memory returned as she spoke, each scene in vivid clarity. He stroked her hair and murmured into her ear. "Shh, it's over now."

She shuddered and her words choked out between the sobs that overtook her. "We almost made it to the door before the roof collapsed on us. Diesel led Jake to us."

He kissed the top of her head and his hand ran soothing circles over her back as she cried. "So, Eric rescued you, you rescued me, and Super Dog rescued us." He pulled back and smiled into her tear-streaked face.

She wiped her eyes with the back of one hand. "He's stronger and smarter than you give him credit for."

His eyes locked with hers. "I could say that about you too."
**

The mournful wail of bagpipes drifted on the warm breeze over the sea of firefighters. Each deep thump of the bass drum mimicked the pained pounding of Greyson's heart. He swallowed hard at the lump lodged in his throat.

"Forward, march!"

Like a zombie, he lurched forward, matching the strides of the firefighters around him. He snuck a glance at Kat, who marched silently beside him. She kept her gaze straight ahead, her delicate features standing out against the fading afternoon light. Tears trailed down her cheeks, but she didn't look weak from it. She was strong. After everything she had been through, she had to be.

Greyson's shiny dress boots pounded the pavement in time with the others, but it was as if his feet were blocks of ice. The empty helmet felt like a ton of bricks in his hands. It was all he could do to not look back at E-288 behind him. It was the last time his brother would ever ride on the rig. The last call he'd ever go on.

The picture of the flag-enshrouded casket on the back of E-288 was burned into his brain. His brother was gone. And he never really got to make things right with him.

The bagpipes wailed on as Greyson's heart cried in silence. At least justice had been served. Eve was dead. Greyson grit his teeth as her name crossed his mind. So many deaths because of her. Dave, Eric, so many others. But it was finally over.

They followed the procession of bagpipes and drums towards the church past a motionless ocean of somber firefighters. There were thousands, all in their Class-A dress uniforms, lining the streets at attention.

Greyson looked up at the familiar sight of the church that suddenly loomed before him. He'd give his right arm to never have to see this church again. They marched up the steps and filed into the first row of pews. Greyson's chest burned as the six firefighters carried the flag-covered coffin to the stand at the front of the church. His entire body was numb as he stepped forward and set Eric's helmet on the casket.

He laid a gloved hand on the casket, his words barely a whisper through numb lips. "I'm sorry I couldn't save you, brother." Tears fell unchecked from his cheeks as he returned to his place beside Kat.

**

Kat smoothed the silky red dress down her body. She felt a little overdressed, but she'd had the dress for months and had yet to wear it. It was a shame to let it rot in the back of her closet just because she couldn't bring herself to go out since Eric's funeral. Besides, Chief Phillips had been like a father to her. That made it the perfect occasion.

Her stomach fluttered as she applied her lipstick and slipped her black Louboutin glitter stilettos on her feet. She was NOT dressing up to see Greyson, she reassured herself. She was dressing up for herself. Besides, there was no guarantee he'd even be at the party.

Kat sighed. After Eric's funeral, she'd thrown herself into her work, and otherwise avoided all contact with Greyson. In all fairness, it had nothing to do with him. It was the guilt that plagued her over her suspicion of his brother. If she'd just called Eric out on it before their breakup, maybe none of this would have happened. Eric would still be alive. Tears burned her eyes. Their relationship hadn't been perfect. It had been far from it, and she'd thought of leaving him more than once. They likely would have broken up anyway, but it wouldn't have resulted in his death. Greyson would still have his brother. Now Greyson had nothing.

It had been a few weeks since they had seen each other. Too many times, Kat had reached for her cell phone to call him, only to hit end instead of send. Maybe it was best that they went their separate ways. Greyson hadn't made an effort to contact her either, so maybe he was having a hard time dealing with his brother's death too.

She glanced at the clock on her night stand. Six fifty eight. Kat cringed. She was always one for being on time. But tonight, she'd be lucky if she was fashionably late. One last glance in the mirror to rearrange the long, loose curls she'd spent so long on before she snatched up her purse and raced for the door.

The hotel banquet hall was filled to the brim with people by the time Kat squeezed her way in the door. On the stage, Chief Phillips sat beside his wife. CFD Chief Adams was at the podium relating some story of heroism from Chief Phillips' career. Kat weaved through the people until she found an empty seat in the back corner of the room.

Her skin tightened on the back of her neck when she realized the story Chief Adam's was relating. Chief Phillips, early in his career, pulled twins from a house fire. The boy, sadly, succumbed to smoke inhalation. The girl became a firefighter and worked under Chief Phillips for a while before moving to arson. Kat's breath caught in her throat. Please, don't, Kat silently begged.

"And, thanks to Battalion Chief Phillip's rescue so many years ago, she was able to solve the string of arson fires his battalion had been plagued with."

Kat frowned. She hadn't solved the case. Eric had put two and two together and was protecting her from the arsonist. Kat was just the victim, who played right into Eve's hands. Eric was the true hero.

The applause grew in volume and Chief Phillips nodded his thanks. His eyes scanned the crowd and caught Kat's eye from across the room. He nodded, the warm, fatherly smile stretching across his face. His smile told her that he knew exactly what she was thinking. Her heart warmed and she returned his smile.

It was sad to see him retire, but he'd had a long successful career. He'd narrowly escaped death more times than she could remember. Kat's gaze traveled to Abby, his wife. The relief that her husband was finally safe from his dangerous job was evident on her face. Kat studied her as if she was seeing her for the first time. This woman exuded strength, even more so than her burly firefighter husband. Every day, for almost thirty years, she sent her husband off to work, praying for the best but with the constant niggling fear that that could be the last time she ever saw her husband alive. She wasn't weaker for being the one to stay home with the kids, to nurture and watch them grow. She was the strong one, willing to support and stand by her husband while he pursued the career he loved.

Kat's heart ached at the thought of that kind of love. The kind where you not only were allowed to be the person you wanted to be, but the kind of love that made you a better, stronger person because of their love.

Was there such thing? The evidence in front of her said there was. Kat's eyes scanned the room, over the sea of semi-familiar and familiar faces. Her body reacted before her brain did when her gaze locked with Greyson's. Her chest constricted and her heart raced. But she couldn't tear her gaze from his. Even when the band began to play and the people around her began to rise, she couldn't look away.

He flashed his sexy half-grin at her as he crossed the room towards her. She sat, frozen in her seat and watched his approach.

"Kat." The deep timbre of his voice caressed her name. She closed her eyes to savor the feeling of hearing her name on his lips.

Eric's face flashed before her eyes, and guilt crept around the edges of her heart. His final words to her whispered through her head: "I love you both more than life itself. Take care of each other."

Kat's eyes drifted open to find Greyson studying her intently. "Greyson." His name came out on a sigh. A sigh of relief, of forgiveness, of redemption.

He held out a hand to her. "Want to dance?"

She smiled and nodded, taking his hand. The warmth from it seeped into her very essence.

He turned to watch her as he led her to the dance floor. "You look beautiful."

A blush crept onto her cheeks. "Thank you."

The up-tempo song slowed to something slow and melancholy. Greyson gently pulled her into his arms and began to sway. Kat sighed and laid her head on his chest, the familiar sound of his heart beating against her ear was like water to a man dying of thirst.

"I'm sorry." Greyson's voice rumbled in his chest.

Startled, Kat leaned back to look at him. "Why?"

"Because I just can't get you out of my head. Or my heart. And I feel so guilty about it."

Her breath caught in her throat. She felt the same way. She laced her fingers through his. "Me too."

His eyes darkened as he studied her.

"He wanted us to be happy." A tear slipped down Kat's cheek and she blinked away the rest.

He cleared his throat, like he too was fighting the tears that threatened when the thought of Eric crossed his mind. "I'm not happy without you."

"I'm not happy without you either. And I think Eric knew that."

Greyson's caramel gaze locked with hers. Kat's stomach flip-flopped at the intensity in his gaze. His hand traced up her back, over her shoulder until he cupped her face with his palm.

"I love you, Kat."

She barely had time to whisper "I love you, too" before his lips silenced her.

**

The engine bay was silent save the ticking of the clock on the wall. The click of Kat's stilettos echoed off the concrete walls as she led him between the trucks. With her other hand, she trailed her fingertips along L-281's paint. Greyson's gaze traced her bare arm, over her shoulder, down the curve of her back to where her silky red dress swished with each sway of her hips.

It took everything in him not to push her up against the truck and have his way with her right then.

He cleared his throat quietly and whispered "What are we doing?"

His groin tightened when she turned, flipped her mahogany curls over one shoulder and smiled seductively. "Trust me."

The promise in that smile almost brought him to his knees.

When they reached the front of L-281 she gently pushed on his shoulders until he sat on the bumper. He shifted, trying to lessen the pressure that built between his legs, but just seeing Kat in that dress at Chief Phillip's retirement party gave him a perma-boner.

"Don't go anywhere," Kat murmured and disappeared back around the side of the truck.

"Kat!" Greyson hissed. But he stayed where she put him.

A minute later she was back -- in his bunker gear. And he thought he was hard from watching her hips sway in that sexy dress...

She paused and studied his face. "What?" She blinked innocently. "You don't like it?"

He swallowed hard and finally found his voice. "Like it? You're killing me here."

"And I haven't even gotten to the good part, yet." She bit her lip and watched him through heavy lidded eyes as she sauntered towards the fire pole.

Her hips swayed as she maneuvered around the pole, his bunker gear leaving everything to the imagination. In her days at the station, he'd fantasized about her in this exact position, never dreaming that it would ever become a reality.

His breath caught in his throat when she reached for the first buckle and unhooked it. Excruciatingly slowly, she undid each hook, revealing a little sliver of golden skin in its path. When the coat was completely unhooked, she turned and slipped it from her shoulders, letting it pool at her feet.

His eyes shot from his heavy bunker coat on the floor to her eyes, where she watched him over her shoulder through the curtain of her hair. His gaze traveled down her cascade of espresso hair to her bare waist, to the curve of her naked ass, which was barely covered by his oversized bunker pants.

"Fuck," he growled and shoved a hand roughly through his hair.

The corner of her mouth quirked as she watched him. She grabbed the pole and kicked his discarded jacket out of the way and twirled around the pole again. When she turned, his mouth fell open. Each movement made her breasts sway, the heavenly globes hidden just barely beneath his reflective red suspenders.

She lifted a delicately arched eyebrow at him and continued her path around the pole. As she circled, she hooked one thumb under the suspender strap, sliding it down to where she held it against her breasts. She followed suit with the other suspender.

He shifted slightly, a vain effort to relive the pressure building in his body. But the sight of Kat's supple body, naked in his bunker gear had him straining hard at the cotton of his dress pants.

When she let the suspenders drop to hang from her waist, it took everything in him to remain where he was. Her nipples beaded in the cool air, begging for him to suck them into his mouth.

She continued her torturous dance, her hands slowly sliding across her hips and stomach until they rested on the hook on his bunker pants. Her fingers deftly freed it from the loop, and she pulled the Velcro apart with excruciating detail. The soft skin of her lower abdomen peeked through the gaping pants.

One more round about the pole, and she slid the pants from her hips, so the only thing she had on was her stiletto pumps.

And that was all he could take. He was off the bumper and in front of her before he could even breathe her name. He grabbed his bunker coat off the ground and wrapped her in it before scooping her into his arms and carrying her toward the truck.

"Oh, God, Kat," he murmured reverently between kisses. She wrapped her legs around his hips as he carried her.

"Greyson," she whispered against his lips.

He pushed her against the side of the rig, his mouth never leaving hers as they devoured each other. He could feel her wet heat radiating through his pants onto him.

He fumbled with the door but managed to open it without letting go of her. He'd never let go of her, ever again. He set her on the floor of the cab and climbed in before returning to kissing her senseless. She helped him unbutton his shirt, and her eyes darkened as she slid the material from his shoulders. Her fingertips trailed over his chest and abdomen slowly, lovingly, like she had done to the paint on L-281.

His hand stalled on the button to his trousers. "Are you sure you want to do this here, Kat?"

She nodded.

That was all the answer he needed. He quickly shed his pants and settled over her, his thighs pressing hers apart. Her wet heat licked at his cock. He kissed her long and slow, savoring her taste and the feel of her warm naked body against his. He pulled back and stared into her deep blue eyes. "I love you, Kat."

She smiled and pulled him back to her lips. "I love you too, Greyson."

With their love fresh on his lips, he sunk into her warmth.

As they exploded in each other's arms, the ringing of the station alarms didn't even register. All they could hear was each other's heartbeat, which was in perfect synch with their own.

Acknowledgements

First off, I would like to thank all of the men and women who have dedicated their lives to protecting and serving the public. Your selfless acts of heroism are what inspired this book. Thank you for all that you do, and the risks you take every day to help others.

I would also like to thank firefighters Mark Chiaradonna of Chelsea, MA Fire Department, Greg Conlan from Rescue 2, Boston, MA Fire Department, Mark Sicuso of Norwich, CT Fire Department. This book would not have been possible without your deep knowledge and love of firefighting, and your willingness to put up with my never-ending questions. Thank you.

I would also like to thank the Chandler Fire Department for not having me arrested for stalking and for giving me the inspiration to write this book in the first place. It was all for the research. I promise!

About The Author

Shelley Watters grew up in Tucson, Arizona and currently resides Chandler, Arizona. She graduated from Arizona State University with a Bachelor's in Sociology with a focus on Women's Health Issues and continued on to get a Master's certificate in Public Health Epidemiology and added an MBA just for the fun of it. While her days are spent in the corporate world and her evenings driving her equestrian to the stables, she fills every other spare moment filled devoted to slinging words across the page. Her novels sizzle with the heat and passion that only growing up in the southwest can bring.

Visit her website at www.shelley-watters.com

Follow her on Instagram @ShelleyWatters_author

Made in the USA
Monee, IL
14 April 2025

15608417R00163